J

# THE PENDERWICKS AT LAST

# THE
# PENDERWICKS
# AT LAST

JEANNE BIRDSALL

Alfred A. Knopf
New York

THIS IS A BORZOI BOOK PUBLISHED BY ALFRED A. KNOPF

Visit us on the Web! rhcbooks.com

Educators and librarians, for a variety of teaching tools, visit us at RHTeachersLibrarians.com

Library of Congress Cataloging-in-Publication Data is available upon request.
ISBN 978-0-385-75566-5 (trade) — ISBN 978-0-385-75567-2 (lib. bdg.) — ISBN 978-0-385-75568-9 (ebook)

The text of this book is set in 13-point Goudy.

Printed in the United States of America
May 2018
10 9 8 7 6 5 4 3

First Edition

*For Michelle F. and Barbara S.K.*

# CONTENTS

# CHAPTER ONE
## Dancing at the Bus Stop

Lʏᴅɪᴀ ʙᴇʟɪᴇᴠᴇᴅ ɪɴ ᴅᴀɴᴄɪɴɢ wherever she could—on sidewalks, in supermarket aisles, libraries, swimming pools, parking lots. Today her stage was a bench at the bus stop. It was a challenge dancing on something so narrow, but Lydia took measures to keep from falling—small steps, no leaps, and heavy reliance on upper-body motion.

"Music, Maestro!" she said. "*What tempo, Miss Penderwick?* I believe I'm in the mood for something snappy, Maestro. *Snappy it is, then.*"

Lydia's singing wasn't up to her dancing, and her inner maestro's humming was rarely on key, but the rhythm! Lydia and rhythm were as one while she bopped back and forth, being what her father called the Embodiment of Music. He'd come up with that when Lydia was too young to know what "embodiment" meant. She was now in fifth grade, though, and knew just about any words her father could come up with, as long as they were in English. (Sometimes he spoke in Latin.) Being the embodiment meant that she brought the spirit of music to life in her dancing.

One last spin, and Lydia bowed, waiting for applause that wouldn't come. There were no other people at the bus stop, and the Penderwick dogs weren't paying attention. The older of the two, Sonata, was asleep under the bench. Sonata was often asleep—Lydia's mother called her Zen Dog. The other dog, Feldspar, was Sonata's son, with the same goofy bug eyes, but he was no Zen Dog. He considered life an opportunity for excitement, especially these two parts of life: Lydia's older sister Batty and whatever he'd most recently found to carry around. Today it was a plastic clothes hanger.

"Remember not to chew it up and swallow the pieces," Lydia told him.

Feldspar eyed her with disdain. He knew better than to do such a silly thing. Somewhere deep in his mixed-breed DNA was a bit of retriever, and retrievers never ate the spoils of the hunt, especially when the spoils were plastic and didn't taste good. Just because he'd happened to accidentally eat one of Lydia's headbands didn't mean that his instincts were dead.

Lydia checked the road for incoming buses. She and the dogs were waiting for the one that would deliver Batty, who studied music in Boston. In Lydia's opinion, Batty didn't come home often enough, and left too soon when she did—this time, she'd be gone at the end of the weekend. Of all the Penderwick siblings, Batty was the one who best understood Lydia and her dancing. Probably because Batty was a musician, a singer—they were both expressing music, but in different ways.

With Batty away at college, only Lydia and her brother, Ben, were left at home with their parents. Ben was sixteen and cared primarily about watching and making movies with his best friend, Rafael. Sometimes they put Lydia in their movies. So far, she'd been a child genius murdered by her country's enemies, a chess champion killed by her insane rival, and Joan of Arc burnt at the stake; in the current project, she was a sentient apple that would be eaten at the end of the film. Weary of dying for her brother's art, Lydia wished he would find a new theme.

There were three other sisters in the family, grownups in their twenties. Two of them, Rosalind and Jane, lived in apartments not too far from home and were always popping in and out. The third, Skye, was in California, working on her doctorate in astrophysics. She'd been out west since she'd first left for college—when Lydia was only four—and could get back home to Massachusetts only a few times a year. Lydia missed her greatly. Family lore had it that she'd been the first tiny baby Skye was drawn to. Skye denied it, saying that she hadn't bothered much with Lydia until she was three and could speak some sense, but Lydia didn't believe that. She was certain she could remember being swaddled, safe and warm, gazing up into Skye's blue eyes.

No bus yet, so time for another dance. For this one, Lydia chose to express great longing and beauty with languid gestures. She'd have to imagine the great longing, as she hadn't experienced much of that, but beauty was all around her, in the daffodils abloom in the Ayvazians' yard, across from the bus stop, and—Lydia thought, privately—in her very own hair. She had no pretensions to beauty, but she did have good hair: red, with just the right amount of curliness. It was her mother's hair, and Ben's. None of the other siblings had this hair, because they'd had a different mother, who'd died long before Lydia was born.

As she brought her dance to an end, Feldspar began making the weird noise that his family politely called barking, though it was more a combination of whining and throat clearing. Anything else was impossible with your mouth full of a hanger. But he and Sonata had worked out a system—whenever Feldspar made that noise, Sonata chimed in with actual barking, so that together they made enough noise to accomplish whatever Feldspar had set out to do.

That's what happened now. Sonata woke up and raised her voice high, and Lydia jumped off the bench and took a firm hold on the dogs' leashes. She'd learned long ago that they could sense Batty's approach from afar. If they were clamoring, that meant Batty's bus was about to come into view. And there it was, cresting the hill, steadily approaching with its precious cargo.

When Batty got off the bus, beaming, as pleased to be home as her family would be to have her there, Lydia held back, knowing that the dogs were always greeted first. The dogs knew it, too, pressing against Batty, quivering with joy while she murmured her love to them and gently stroked them head to toe, reassuring herself that they were as happy and healthy as when she'd last seen them. Ben had once dubbed Batty the Saint Francis of Cameron—Cameron was the town where the Penderwicks lived—and no one had disputed him, except for Batty herself, who believed that it should be normal, not saintly, to have limitless love for animals.

Only when this ritual was complete did Batty turn her attention to Lydia, checking her height, having her turn around to be seen from different angles, and gazing intently into her eyes.

"You've grown since I was home last," Batty said.

"An eighth of an inch." Lydia was proud of that eighth of an inch.

"And school's okay?"

"We're learning boring state capitals."

5

"We did, too, and the only one I can still remember is Harrisburg, Pennsylvania, because Henry kept getting in trouble for calling it Harrisburger. And Boston, of course."

Lydia reverted to what she was most interested in. "Sing for me? I'm trying out the flamenco."

Batty rifled through her vast inner library of songs. "I'll go with a standard—'Oye Como Va.'"

She sang, and Lydia danced, just as they'd been doing for most of Lydia's life. Some of her earliest memories were of prancing around the living room while Batty played the piano and sang. Lydia's sisters liked to say that she could dance before she walked, but when Lydia tried to reason this out, it didn't make sense. Today her flamenco was less than fiery—it needed several more years of practice, and shoes that weren't sneakers would have been a big help—but it was awfully fun to do, and Batty even joined in for a few stomps and claps.

"*Excelente*," said Batty when they were done. "It's good to be home."

They had to rouse Sonata—she'd dozed off in the middle of "Oye Como Va"—and headed up Gardam Street, slowly, giving the dogs the time they needed to revisit their favorite scents, and refresh them as needed.

"Wesley's talking again about dropping out of school to go west," said Batty.

"Oh, Batty, no!"

Wesley was an art student Batty had met her first week at college, and had often brought home with her for visits. Lydia liked him more than any of Batty's boyfriends from high school. Indeed, he was among her top four or five picks of all of her sisters' boyfriends put together. She didn't think it was just because he'd sketched her dancing, and that the sketch was now framed and hanging in the living room. No, there was also Wesley's air of quiet mystery. Ben liked that about him, too, enough to suggest making a film with him as a secret agent. Lydia had advised Wesley not to accept, as the secret agent would be sure to die at the end of the film, but Wesley hadn't needed her guidance. He wasn't one for being watched—by a camera or a person—preferring instead to be the watcher.

And then there was Wesley's dog, Hitch, the three-legged Great Dane. When Lydia first fell under Hitch's spell, she worried she was being unfaithful to Feldspar and Sonata. She asked her father if this was so, and he'd said that faithfulness had nothing to do with it—often we simply like people and animals better when they're far away. He even gave her some Latin for it, but it was a particularly long phrase, and she could only remember a single word: *absentes*.

"This is the third—no, fourth—time Wesley's talked about dropping out of school," said Batty. "And I understand. He's got only a year left and says he's not learning anything in his classes."

This Lydia believed. Wesley had told her about

one project, to build an imaginary sculpture and live with it for a semester. She thought that would be more fun than state capitals, for example, but Wesley had been bored almost into a coma. He preferred making real things, with his hands.

Batty added, "But this part about heading west is new. And he asked me if I'd go with him."

Lydia grabbed her sister's arm, ready to keep her in Massachusetts by brute force if necessary. There was already a Penderwick sister on the West Coast. Two would be dreadful. "But you won't, will you?"

"No. I'm not leaving school for a boy, even if he *is* Wesley."

Lydia was pleased that Batty could resist Wesley, but wondered if it was as easy to resist Hitch. With that thought came the usual guilt about Lydia's own dogs. "*Absentes,*" she whispered to herself, "*absentes,*" and tried not to notice that Feldspar was banging his hanger on a neighbor's fence and that Sonata was yawning furiously at him, as though that would do any good.

"Maybe Wesley will just keep talking about going west," she said, "and never really go."

"No, I think he'll go," said Batty, "and I'm determined to protect my heart for when he does."

The sisters were almost to their house when a scruffy old car pulled up, one that should have fallen apart long ago. This was Jane's—she didn't have enough money for a nice car and didn't care, anyway. She cared only about becoming a great novelist. Everything else was secondary, including love and romance. Those she'd sworn off after a few heartbreaks had used up too much of her writing time. In solidarity, Lydia and her friend Tzina had also sworn off love, though to no real effect, as neither had experienced love nor expected to. But the ceremony had been fun, with candles, dancing, and chanting. "Staaay away, love, stay, stay away. Staaay away, love, stay, stay away."

Another proof of Jane's dedication to writing was her waitressing job. It was hard work, and Jane wasn't particularly good at it, but it gave her money for rent and food, and enough time to work on her novel. Lydia was impressed with her sister's single-minded pursuit of her craft and had great faith in her eventual success. Lydia also hoped to show up in one of Jane's books someday. There had been no Lydia in her first two full-length books, abandoned when Jane decided they weren't good enough. And so far, there wasn't one in her current work-in-progress. Jane was probably waiting for a character fabulous enough to be named Lydia, who danced well enough to be an Embodiment of Music.

Whenever Jane came directly from work, Feldspar and Sonata looked for spilled food on her clothes, and almost always found some. They thought she did it for their benefit, but the truth was that if a good idea for her novel popped up while she was serving food, the food tended to slide off its plate. Today the dogs were in luck, as they discovered when she got out of the car. Hummus, a big patch of it, on her skirt.

"Another spill?" asked Batty.

"Yes, but it was worth it. I realized I need to swap two chapters—the plot will work better that way." Jane directed Sonata to a spot of spaghetti sauce on her sock. "This is nothing compared to the whipped-cream disaster when I figured out my art forger's motivation. I looked like I'd just barely survived a snowstorm."

"But she still hasn't dumped any food on the customers," Lydia told Batty. "Only on herself."

"Knock on wood." Jane couldn't find any wood, so she knocked on Lydia's head. "Hey, dogs, take a break while I hug Batty."

The dogs backed off during the hug but barged in again as soon as it was over, determined to get every last bit of food off Jane. They stopped only when Sonata found the peanut butter on the sole of her right shoe, and then there was nowhere else to look.

"Rosalind's still coming for dinner?" Batty asked Jane. "Do we know what her news is yet?"

"What news?" Lydia had heard nothing of any of this.

"We don't know," said Jane. "We just know that Rosy has something to tell the family."

"But we have suspicions," said Batty. "It might be the fruition of—you know."

"I *don't* know!" said Lydia. The chain of communication from older Penderwicks to youngest often failed. "Is it about her wedding?"

Rosalind was getting married this summer to Tommy Geiger, whom she'd been with forever. He'd grown up across the street and been a part of Lydia's life for as long as she could remember. No one had been surprised when they decided to get married—the surprise would have been if they hadn't.

"We think so, but we're not positive," said Batty. "If we're right, it's not bad news. You don't have to worry."

"No, not bad news, but it is interesting," added Jane. "Lyds, go find Ben and tell him Batty's home, okay?"

While Lydia knew she was being gotten rid of so that her sisters could talk about Rosalind, she also knew that refusing to leave wouldn't make them talk in front of her. Maybe Ben had more information. She went upstairs and knocked on his bedroom door. There was no answer, but she knew he was in there, because the door was locked. He always kept it locked when in residence, a habit he'd formed when Lydia was little and constantly trying to bust into his room. Or so he said. Lydia didn't know why she would have been seeking out his company, even without knowing that when he was older, he would keep killing her in movies.

"Ben, stop pretending you're not in there. I won't

go away until you answer." She knocked again. "Batty's home and Jane's here and Rosalind's coming to dinner and has news. Did you know that?"

"What kind of news?"

"I don't know."

He opened the door. "Is it good news or bad?"

"Batty says it's not bad, but she and Jane aren't a hundred percent sure, and they won't tell me."

"Hold on." Ben went down the hall to the bathroom and came back with a sopping wet washcloth. "We'll make it look like you're crying because you're worried about the news, and they'll feel guilty and tell all."

"They won't believe—" But Lydia was cut off by the wet washcloth dripping water down her face.

"Stop laughing. Think of this as a role you're playing." He stepped back to survey his work. "That's good, but you have to look upset."

Lydia forced her mouth to turn down. "Like that?"

"Better. By the way, I'm working on a new script for you about an alien."

"I don't want to be an alien."

"It's going to be a good part, better than the sentient apple—though, unfortunately, the alien will also die at the end," he said. "There! That's the expression I want. Hold that emotion."

# CHAPTER TWO
## *Rosalind's News*

NEITHER JANE NOR BATTY believed in Lydia's tears. Undaunted, Ben re-drenched Lydia when Rosalind arrived, certain he could fool his most softhearted sister. He was wrong—she figured out that the tears were a trick and refused to give even a tiny hint about the news. But she did make him a sandwich to tide him over until dinner.

Lydia saw nothing in Rosalind's demeanor to indicate that the news would be bad. She looked calm and happy, if not quite clean—she helped run an urban farm in a city near Cameron, and sometimes running it meant digging in the dirt, especially now, in the spring, when the planting had begun.

"We're putting in fruit trees." Rosalind flexed her biceps. "Look at these muscles."

"Strong Penderwick women." Jane flexed hers, too. "See? From carrying trays."

Lydia saw no point in flexing her biceps—it wouldn't be impressive. Anyway, she was more interested in Rosalind's news and thought she might learn something if she could be more subtle than weeping fake tears.

"Rosy, please pick a category for your news. A for the farm, B for the wedding, C . . . umm, for a deadly disease—"

"A multiple choice, Lyds! Good try, but I'm not going to answer anything until after dinner. People are more reasonable when their stomachs are full."

Ben was the only one in the family who got unreasonable when he'd gone too long without food, and their mom said it was only because he was going through a growth spurt. Lydia hoped so, because that meant he'd get better one of these days. "Do you mean Ben?"

"She might mean Dad," whispered Jane.

"Shush, Jane," said Rosalind. "After dinner."

Rosalind held firm, and it wasn't until the parents had come home, dinner had been eaten, and Ben and Lydia's mom—Iantha, as the older girls called her— was pouring out coffee that they gave in.

"All right, Rosy, we've waited long enough," said Iantha.

"Yes, please," said their father.

"We just need to call Skye and put her on speaker-

14

phone," said Rosalind. "I told her to be ready at six-thirty, and it's just about that now."

Skye, too? This was indeed big news, thought Lydia. She also thought she should try to stay quiet, hoping that Skye would forget to ask her about math. Lydia enjoyed the math she was taught in school, but not the extra math Skye wanted her to do.

"I'm getting nervous," said Mr. Penderwick.

Lydia smiled to show him solidarity. He smiled back, and also gave her the rest of his ice cream—salted caramel, her favorite.

Jane was talking on her phone. "Skye, we're all here. . . . I'm not sure, but yes, I think that's what it's about. I'm putting you on speakerphone, so be nice."

"I'm always nice," said the phone.

Ben leaned toward the phone. "Skye, tell Dušek I've been researching those sea creatures he told me about, and the giant isopod is amazing. If we could make a costume like that for this alien I'm writing about—"

Lydia forgot she'd meant to be quiet. "I am not dressing up like a giant isopod, whatever that is."

Dušek was from the Czech Republic. He'd come to the United States to study marine biology and found Skye studying the stars, and they'd been together ever since. The Penderwicks liked Dušek very much, but Lydia did wish he wouldn't encourage the outer regions of Ben's film fantasies. A giant isopod was sure to be hideous.

"Hey, Lyds," said the phone. "How's your math going?"

"All right." Lydia knew she should have stayed quiet.

"Have you been working in binary like I suggested?"

Feldspar, who'd been trying to figure out where Skye's voice was coming from, located the phone and, in a frenzy of greeting, knocked it off the table with his hanger. The interruption was a relief for Lydia, who knew only that binary was a number system with zeroes and ones and nothing else, which she didn't think were enough digits to work with. By the time they got the phone back on the table and Feldspar stuffed under Batty's chair, Skye had moved on to base twelve, which seemed to have too *many* digits.

"It's really cool. You use A and B for the extra—"

"Not now, Skye," said Rosalind.

"Thank you," Lydia whispered across the table to her oldest sister.

"I heard that," said Skye.

"All right, everyone—ready?" asked Rosalind. "I called this meeting to discuss the wedding. Tommy and I have a decision to make, and we can't make it on our own. Tommy's talking to his parents, and I'm talking to you. We're thinking of not getting married in the backyard this summer."

"Rosy, this is great news," said Mr. Penderwick. "Yes, you'll marry Tommy eventually, but you're still young— Iantha, why are you shushing me?"

16

"She didn't say they're canceling the wedding, Martin."

"No? Because if she wants to, it would be fine—"

"Poor Dad," said Skye, cutting him off. "But you're going to have to get used to weddings at some point. You may as well get it over with now."

The family went into shock at this mention of weddings in the plural. Skye and Dušek had been together for several years, but she'd never mentioned marrying him. The one time she'd discussed marriage with Lydia, she'd said that marriage wasn't for everyone, and especially not for impatient people. (Skye was impatient.) She'd also said something about marriage being socially outdated—no, that wasn't what she'd said. Lydia would have to ask her again.

Her father seemed to be taking it the hardest. This would normally be an occasion for him to burst into Latin—stress often brought it on. But he seemed unable to say anything in any language. The recent glut of change had been getting to him: Rosalind's upcoming marriage, Batty's first year of college, Lydia's inexorable march toward middle school, Ben's growth spurt. He'd been counting on Jane and Skye not to do anything dramatic for another few years.

Although Lydia's mother wasn't less startled, she could still speak. "What do you mean by *weddings*, Skye, as in, more than one? Are you saying that you and Dušek—?"

"No—not now, anyway."

"You mean you might someday?" asked Jane. "But you always say that marriage is an outmoded social construct."

Aha! That was it, thought Lydia—*outmoded social construct*. She didn't know exactly what it meant, only that it didn't seem to be in favor of marriage.

"But I've never said marriage can't be useful," said the phone, "and Dušek seems to like the idea."

Rosalind eagerly addressed the phone. "Let's make it a double wedding, Skye. Dušek's family is already coming over from Europe for mine—why make them travel twice? We'll do all the organizing at this end, and you and Dušek can just show up and get married. You know you'd hate the organizing part."

"Yes, I would. But that doesn't mean I should get married."

"Why not?"

"Please don't push her, Rosy," said their father, finding his voice. "You're all growing up too quickly as it is."

Rosalind wanted to reassure him. "Ben and Lydia are still children—"

Ben interrupted. "I'm not."

"But you're not getting married soon, are you?"

Lydia risked speaking again, hoping Skye had forgotten about base twelve math. "And Batty won't get married for years and years and years, and Jane keeps saying she might never get married."

"Or not until I'm a successful writer, and then only

18

if I find someone who's a vegetarian," said Jane. "If he likes to cook, that would be great, since I don't."

"He should like to clean, too," added Skye. "You don't do much of that, either."

"Back on topic, please," said Rosalind, stopping Jane and Skye from diving into their favorite argument. "Of course I'm still getting married. This is just a discussion about where it will happen."

It had long been settled that the wedding would take place at the Penderwicks' home, with the reception spilling across Gardam Street to Tommy's parents' home. Years ago, when Lydia was only six, Tommy's older brother, Nick, had been married the same way but opposite, with the wedding at the Geigers', and the reception spilling over to the Penderwicks'. Lydia remembered it as one of the best days of her life. She'd been the flower girl, with a swirly dress and a crown of daisies.

"You've changed your mind about having the ceremony here?" asked Iantha.

"But where, then, Rosy?" added Mr. Penderwick.

"Arundel."

Arundel was a grand estate in the Berkshires where the Penderwicks had vacationed long ago—fifteen years—back when the family was only Mr. Penderwick, the four older sisters, and Hound, their much-loved first dog. Iantha and Ben hadn't yet become Penderwicks, and Lydia hadn't even been thought of.

It was there they'd first met Jeffrey Tifton, the lonely boy living in the estate mansion. The four sisters swept him into their lives and kept him there, permanently. These days they didn't see him often enough—for the last five years, he'd lived in Germany, working as a pianist in jazz clubs. But that made him no less an honorary member of the family, and whenever he came back to the States, he visited them.

While Jeffrey had been the best part of that long-ago vacation—the grand prize that kept getting better—the worst part had been his mother, arrogant Mrs. Tifton. She'd loathed the Penderwicks on first sight and had shown no sign of ever changing her mind. And they cheerfully loathed her back, certain she deserved it. Mostly because she never seemed to appreciate Jeffrey as much as she should, which for a parent was unacceptable. She was the reason the Penderwicks had never gone back to Arundel, and had assumed they never would.

For Lydia, hearing that Rosy might get married at Arundel was like hearing she might get married in Oz or Narnia, other places that existed just in stories. The Arundel stories! She thought she must have heard all of them by now, from her three oldest sisters—Batty had been too young to remember much—from Jeffrey, from her dad, even. The turreted mansion, with its treasure-filled attic, the large luscious gardens, with statues, fountains, a Greek pavilion, and endless possibilities for adventure. Plus, the little yellow cottage where the Penderwicks had stayed, tucked into one corner of the estate. Was all this still there, she wondered, and was she really going to visit it?

While Lydia dreamt, the rest of the family hashed out details. According to Rosalind, Mrs. Tifton had fled Arundel for New York City, leaving behind the memories of a string of bad marriages now associated with her old home. Determined never to go back, she'd signed the estate over to Jeffrey and washed her hands of it. So now this paradise belonged to Jeffrey, and he wanted Rosalind, his honorary sister from his favorite family, to get married there.

"And I want to get married there," she said, "and so does Tommy, but not unless all of you agree."

"Jeffrey is absolutely certain his mother won't show up?" asked Jane. "Because I, for one, am still scared of her."

"I, for two," said Batty, "and I can't even remember her."

"I'm not scared of her," said Skye.

"Fibber," Jane told the phone.

"I would like to meet this Mrs. Tifton," said Ben.

"No, you wouldn't," said Rosalind. "Honest. Even Lydia wouldn't find anything to like about her."

This referred to what Lydia called a family myth—that she liked everyone she'd ever met. There had definitely been one person she'd actively disliked. She

21

didn't remember him, but her sisters had told her the story, and Lydia held on to it like a drowning person clinging to a life raft.

"*Even* Lydia!" she protested. "Rosalind, you make me sound like a marshmallow. Please remember that I disliked that Oliver guy enough to stab him with a quesadilla."

"A highly deserved stab," said Rosalind. Oliver had been her boyfriend during the quesadilla incident, though not for much longer.

"Lyds, that was when you were two years old," said Ben. "You've liked everyone since then."

"I can't help it."

"You don't have to help it," said Iantha. "Liking people isn't being a marshmallow. It's a good quality."

"And even a marshmallow would dislike Mrs. Tifton," said Jane.

"Yes, that's the point I was trying to make," said Rosalind. "If Lydia met Mrs. Tifton, she would despise her as much as we all do. But Lydia won't have to meet her, since Mrs. T. has sworn never to return to Arundel. Would she be the only objection to having the wedding there? Dad and Iantha, would you be disappointed if Tommy and I didn't get married here?"

"You should have your wedding wherever you like, and, no, I won't be disappointed," said Iantha. "After all, if you don't get married here, we won't have to clean the house top to bottom. Lydia and Ben, that was going to be your summer job."

"Arundel!" said Ben. "Definitely get married at Arundel."

"Please." Even if Lydia hadn't always yearned to visit Arundel, she had better plans for her summer than cleaning the house.

"Dad?" asked Rosalind.

"I agree with Iantha," he said. *In pace et celebratione Arundel redeamus.*"

"'Let us return to Arundel in peace and celebration,'" Rosalind said, smiling. "Thank you, Dad; I love you. What about the rest of you? All in favor?"

Everyone was in favor, even the dogs—Batty voted for them—and it was settled. Rosalind's wedding would be at Arundel that summer, and so would Lydia.

# CHAPTER THREE
## *Arundel*

In the months leading up to Arundel, Lydia experienced three life-changing events. The first happened when Ben and Rafael convinced her to be the alien in their new movie, an alien wearing a two-foot-long stuffed plush giant isopod that fell off her head every time she tried to move. The combination of the falling giant isopod and a weak script shut down production halfway through, mortifying Ben enough that he promised Lydia he'd never again ask her to wear a stuffed animal on her head, or even to die. Lydia considered this a personal victory but was wise enough not to rub it in.

Then came Lydia's dancing lessons. She'd taken plenty of dance lessons over the years—ballet, hip-hop, tap, modern, jazz. Each time, she'd set out with enthusiasm, and if she'd ever found a teacher who would let her dance the way she wanted, she would have stayed in class forever. But none did. And while her parents tried to explain that teachers are *supposed* to tell you what steps to do, that doing so is the very essence of teaching, Lydia always decided to quit. She could learn what she needed from watching movies and videos with dancing in them—and even had a brother who could steer her to the best ones.

But for her birthday that year, the Penderwicks' favorite relative, Aunt Claire, offered to give her one last shot at lessons, for any style of dance Lydia chose. She chose ballroom—she'd been watching ancient Fred Astaire movies, and Mr. Astaire danced too quickly to be easily imitated. Unfortunately, Lydia hadn't taken into account that ballroom dancing is done in pairs. Now not only did she have a teacher telling her what to do, she was tied to a partner who either pushed her around the room or resisted being pushed. Once again, she quit and decided never, ever, ever to try dance lessons again. A great burden was lifted, and her dancing was suddenly better than ever. This was her second life-changing event.

The third also had to do with the ballroom lessons. And a girl named Deborah, whom Lydia had never met before, and to whom she took an instant and illogical dislike. With that had come the urge to do something dramatic about her dislike—shout it to the world or kick Deborah in the shins. Lydia managed not to give in to those urges, but her dancing partner told her that she looked fierce and a little scary, which she considered a compliment and repeated to everyone at home, emphasizing that she could no longer be accused of liking everyone except Quesadilla Oliver.

All of this newfound knowledge and strength made Lydia even more excited to go to Arundel. And more excited still when it turned out that she and Batty—and Feldspar and Sonata—would be the first to go. Originally, Jane and Ben were to go with them, but Jane had been asked to work an extra day at the restaurant, and Ben wasn't packed yet. Lydia and Batty would be on their own at Arundel for an entire twenty-four hours, with no parents or older sisters. The possibilities for adventure were endless.

And now it was early morning on departure day, and Lydia and Batty were preparing to leave. Jane was there to say good-bye, and to lend them her car, which Lydia hoped would get them to the Berkshires without falling apart, but if it didn't, that would be a different kind of adventure. Lydia's parents were also there to say good-bye, as was the family cat, Asimov, riding unwillingly in Iantha's arms.

"Lydia, are you certain you want to go with Batty?" she asked. "Your dad and I won't be there for another week and a half."

"We've discussed this, Mom." Lydia put her suitcase into the trunk of the car.

"But remember dance camp, and how homesick and miserable you were."

Two summers earlier, Lydia had gone to a sleepover dance camp—this was before she'd realized how desperately she loathed being told what to do. The head counselor, suffering from a thwarted dream of being a Rockette, compensated by trying to teach the campers to dance in a straight line and do high kicks with utmost precision, everyone exactly the same. On the third day, Lydia had stopped kicking and gone home.

"That wasn't homesickness," she said. "That was the Rockettes."

"There won't be any Rockettes at Arundel," said Batty. "Lyds will be fine, won't you?"

"I will. Don't worry, Mom."

"And, Batty, you'll be fine, too?" asked their father.

"Sure, she will," said Jane. "Wesley is adorable, that is, easily adored, but Batty has successfully resisted heartbreak."

"Don't make me sound cold and unfeeling," said Batty. "I was a mess for a few days."

Those few days had been a week ago. Wesley had made up his mind, for real this time, to drop out of school and head west. He'd offered to wait until after Rosalind's wedding, but Batty had told him no. If she had to lose him—and Hitch—she wanted it to be

27

abruptly and completely, not a painful drawn-out process. She said good-bye to them, hid in her bedroom for forty-eight hours, then came out singing. True, at first it was mostly sad songs, but Batty seemed to be past that now, and at breakfast had been singing about sunshine, lollipops, and rainbows.

While Lydia was glad that Batty had survived the loss of her love, she herself was harboring a secret regret, that she hadn't said good-bye to Wesley and Hitch. Mostly, Hitch. It didn't feel right to be cut off from them forever, without one last kiss on the nose. Hitch's, that is. Lydia had no desire to kiss Wesley's nose.

"But you've gotten over him, Batty," said Jane. "That's the point. Remember how pathetically long it took me to get over Patrick, the guy who wanted me to— Never mind."

Her father groaned.

"It's all right, Martin," said Iantha. "I know the story, and it's not that bad."

"I don't know the story," said Lydia.

"When you're older," said Jane.

Batty was shoving dogs into the backseat of the car. Not that they needed much encouragement. A car plus Batty meant adventure to them, too. Sonata looked wide awake—for now—and Feldspar enthusiastically shook his latest conquest, an old feather duster he'd rescued from the trash.

"Remember that the car vibrates if you push it past

28

fifty-five miles an hour," said Jane. "And, Batty, speak nicely to it—that helps."

"I'm no good at talking to cars. Jane, are you sure I shouldn't just take the van? You can drive your own car and say whatever you want to it."

"No, no, I need the van tomorrow to carry all my stuff—"

"Books," said Lydia. Jane never went anywhere without lots of books.

"And food," said Iantha.

"And Ben and his camera equipment, and my sewing machine." Jane was making Rosalind's wedding gown and the four bridesmaid dresses, one for each sister. All were still in progress—thus the sewing machine.

"I'll talk to your car, Jane." Lydia had ridden with Jane often enough to know what the car liked to hear.

"I love you, sweet Lyds," said her mom, hugging her. "If you get homesick, I'll come get you."

"I won't get homesick. Sorry, Asimov."

The cat had grumpily ended up in the middle of the hug, and while he was too polite to scratch or bite, the noise he made was explicit. Lydia let go and patted him to make up for the discomfort. Now came her father with another hug, but no cat, so it was easier.

"*Infans mea,*" he said.

"Daddy, I know what that means." It meant "my baby," and he wasn't supposed to say it anymore.

"Can't help it," he said.

The two sisters got into the car, buckled up, and waved good-bye. They were off to Arundel.

The trip took longer than it should have. Jane's car seemed to know it didn't have Jane behind the wheel and acted accordingly, snorting and rattling. At a rest stop, it went so far as to pretend to be dead. Lydia tried to talk like Jane, praising the car for its strength of character, et cetera, but it wasn't fooled. Finally, out of desperation, Batty resorted to singing about cars that *liked* to move, hoping this one would be inspired to imitate them. She led off with "Greased Lightnin'," from the musical *Grease*—and it worked. Jane's car started up again, enthusiastically and without rattling. Now, afraid to stop singing, Batty kept going with every car song she could think of while Lydia danced in her seat and chimed in whenever she knew the lyrics. They were on the last song in Batty's repertoire—Tracy Chapman's "Fast Car"—when they spotted the stone pillars that marked the entrance to Arundel.

"Thank goodness. If the car stops now, we can walk the rest of the way," said Batty.

Lydia barely listened, too intent on soaking up the scene. The stone pillars were just as her sisters had described—NUMBER ELEVEN was carved into one, and ARUNDEL into the other. With a little shock, Lydia realized that up until now she hadn't completely believed in Arundel.

"It's an actual place," she said.

"Seems to be."

Batty turned the car off the road, through the pillars, and onto the lane that led to the mansion. But before they could go any farther, the glove compartment started playing Beethoven's *Eroica* Symphony. Feldspar, who by now should have been used to Batty's ringtone, leapt from the backseat to attack it with his feather duster, defending Batty and Lydia against the tiny people playing instruments in the glove compartment. Batty stopped the car and shoved Feldspar back to where he belonged, while Lydia retrieved the phone and handed it over.

"It's Iantha," Batty told her. "Hi . . . Yes, Lydia and I are fine. We just arrived. . . . Lydia, are you homesick yet?"

"Good grief. Tell her I'm not going to get homesick."

Lydia leaned out the window to better survey this storied world, that both was and wasn't the Arundel her sisters had described. The lane was the same, including the double rows of poplars marching alongside. And the mansion was invisible from here—Lydia had expected that. But the broad velvet lawns had disappeared, taken over by waving meadows of tall grasses and wildflowers, white, purple, yellow. Like Sleeping

31

Beauty's castle, she thought, except with grass and flowers instead of vines and brambles, so nothing like Sleeping Beauty, for goodness' sake, get a grip on yourself, Lydia.

She'd imagined herself dancing across those green lawns, waltzing, as befit the elegant setting. But for these meadows, she'd need a less formal dance, one closer to nature. Flitting and floating, tossed by the breezes, along the mown paths. Yes, that would be just right.

Here was something else that hadn't changed from the first Penderwick visit—even at the very beginning of the lane, Arundel felt private, removed. Jane had said that the stone pillars were a magical boundary that kept out the real world. The other sisters had scoffed, but now that Lydia was here, she understood what Jane had meant. Looking back through the pillars, all she saw was in shadow. If cars had driven past, she hadn't seen or heard them. The only sounds were coming from the meadows: the industrious *tap-tap-tap* of a nearby woodpecker, the rise and fall of a cicada's song, and, farther off, a trilling, ecstatic burble from a bird Lydia couldn't identify. High above, a hawk was gliding on the wind. She waved hello—I've arrived, Hawk, and already I love it here.

After Batty told Iantha good-bye, Lydia pulled back into the car, in time to see her sister trying desperately not to sneeze, which made sense, as Feldspar was now vigorously shaking his feather duster in her face.

"Stop, Feldspar, please." Batty gave up the battle with her itchy nose and sneezed lustily. "Iantha called to say that a box arrived from Wesley after we left. I told her to open it—he sent me a mobile he made."

"The one you showed me pictures of? With tiny Hitches dangling from wires?"

"Yes. And a note that said he wanted me to have it so I wouldn't forget Hitch."

"No one could ever forget Hitch." Lydia certainly wouldn't.

"I know. I miss him, too." Batty sneezed again. "Lyds, I swear I'll never again fall for a man who believes his destiny is in Oregon."

Lydia hadn't heard the destiny part of Wesley's story before and wasn't sure what it meant to have a destiny as opposed to simply having a future. "Do you know what your destiny is?"

Batty shook her head. "All I know is that it isn't with Wesley."

When Lydia was six years old, she'd believed she was someone's future, if not his absolute destiny. Her cousin Enam—twin of Marty and son of favorite relative Aunt Claire and almost as favorite relative Uncle Turron—had vowed to marry her when they grew up. Lydia had considered it a binding promise and was proud to be the only Wildwood Elementary first grader engaged to be married. Over time, though, Enam seemed to have forgotten his pledge, and Lydia's hopes had gradually faded away. Then, last year at a family gathering, Lydia had discovered that Enam was not only playing the double bass, he was also hanging around a girl named Imani who looked like a young Beyoncé. Since double basses are among the coolest instruments in the world, and Beyoncé one of the most beautiful women, Lydia decided that Enam was out of her league. She wasn't awfully upset, but was also comforted when Aunt Claire told her that boys—even her own sons—can be dopes when it comes to love, and then took Lydia out for ice cream and a movie. Life had seemed much better afterward.

"I wonder if I'll ever have a destiny," she said.

"If destiny is an actual thing, you already do." Batty sneezed and pushed away Feldspar and his feather duster. "Let's keep going before Jane's car decides to die again."

The meadows went on and on, giving up none of their wildness, until they'd come to an abrupt end, and here was the beginning of civilization—the slender remains of the formerly vast green lawn. One more turn of the lane, and statues appeared, and fountains, and then the mansion, Arundel Hall. Lydia saw the massive pile of gray stone, bathing in the bright morning sun, the glistening windows—so many windows!— and the deep blue shadows cast by the turrets, towers, and terraces. All this she'd expected from the stories.

But she hadn't expected this air of loneliness. Did homes mourn when their people left? Even when the people were mostly mean Mrs. Tifton? And if it did miss Mrs. Tifton, how would it feel about the Penderwicks taking over? Lydia shivered—she wasn't sure she wanted to sleep in a building that might have feelings.

Batty had again stopped the car, and was drinking in Arundel Hall just as avidly as Lydia.

"Does it look familiar?" Lydia asked. "Do you remember anything now?"

Batty shook her head. "I thought I might, but no, and it's hard to separate actual memories from the stories. Like, do I remember Mrs. Tifton being mean to poor old Hound? I think I do, but maybe not. Just like I think I remember Rosalind cutting gum out of my hair before Jeffrey's birthday party, but maybe I just remember being told about it."

Lydia had seen a photo of her sisters ready to go to that party. They were wearing dresses that had been secretly made for them by Mrs. Tifton's housekeeper, Churchie, whom they'd all adored. Skye looked restless and Jane excited, Rosalind was fussing with Batty's hair, Batty was trying to get Rosalind to stop fussing with her hair, and Hound was on guard, as always, in case a monster appeared out of nowhere to snatch up Batty. The best part, Lydia had always thought, was Batty's goofy butterfly wings. According to the old stories, she'd worn them everywhere that summer, taking them off only for baths and bed, and sometimes not even for bed.

"How did you get gum in your hair, anyway? I never heard that part."

"Who knows? I can't remember!" Batty started the car again. "Let's go pick up the mansion key."

# CHAPTER FOUR
## *A Sheep Called Big Papi (or Blossom)*

CHURCHIE, THE BELOVED HOUSEKEEPER, was long gone from Arundel. She'd moved to Hawaii to be near her grandchildren. But there was a person from the old stories still living on the estate—Cagney. Back then, he'd been a young gardener working for Mrs. Tifton. Now he worked for Jeffrey, overseeing the abandoned estate, keeping it from decaying into ruin. And he was the one who had the key to the mansion.

Here's what Lydia knew about the young Cagney: he'd worn a Red Sox baseball cap, lived in the carriage house behind Arundel Hall, dreamt of becoming a history teacher, and had pet rabbits named Yaz and Carla. These rabbits had been involved in one particular Penderwick mishap. Batty had let Yaz escape the carriage house, and he would surely have been lost forever in the gardens if faithful Hound hadn't found and rescued him. But Cagney had forgiven Batty, which Rosalind always said was typical of how nice he was.

In the last few months, Lydia had learned a few things about Cagney in the present. He had a last name, Pelletier—her sisters had always just called him Cagney. His dream of becoming a history teacher had come true. He now lived in the cottage where the Penderwicks had stayed, along with his wife, Natalie, an art teacher whom Jane had talked with on the phone and liked already. And—this was the most interesting part for Lydia—there were two Pelletier children, Jack and Alice, both near in age to Lydia. Lydia would just miss meeting Jack—he'd left this very morning to visit his cousins in Canada. But Alice was going to be here, and Lydia hoped they would become friends. As long as Alice isn't another Deborah, she thought, and thus instantly dislikeable. Lydia knew that the possibility of her finding another person to loathe so soon after Deborah was small. After all, almost nine years had elapsed between Quesadilla Oliver and Deborah, but still, she considered it wise to be cautious.

On the drive to the cottage, stories, memories, imaginings, and reality continued to play tag through Lydia's mind. The Greek pavilion was larger than she'd thought it would be, and the sunken garden wasn't as full of flowers as she'd pictured— Wait, were those tomato plants? And *corn*? Cagney and his family had obviously been making changes to the estate. The meadows, and now tomatoes and corn. Good changes, Lydia thought. She approved.

The tall hedge that surrounded the cottage grounds looked just as it was supposed to. And now here was the cottage. Lydia recognized its porch and climbing roses, but not its color. What had once been a buttery yellow was now a soft blue-gray.

"What about here?" she asked Batty. "Does this feel familiar?"

"Nope. I wonder if I was really here the last time. Maybe I was switched out with a different Batty at some point."

"Or maybe the trauma of almost killing Yaz erased your memories," said Lydia.

"More likely, the trauma of Mrs. Tifton, who apparently thought I was deranged."

Lydia noticed someone who hadn't been there a moment ago, a girl peering out the front door. That had to be Alice. She was too far away to be judged by Deborah standards—Lydia's instant dislikes seemed to happen closer up—and then the girl who was probably Alice disappeared altogether, melting back into the shadows. This didn't bode well for friendship, thought Lydia.

Here came a man who was definitely Cagney, wearing a Red Sox cap so worn and faded it could have been the same one from fifteen years ago. He'd appeared from behind the cottage, and with him came five red chickens, pecking madly at the insects stirred by his passage. No one had told Lydia about the chickens—she thought them an even better surprise than the meadows, tomatoes, and corn, and wondered if she could befriend them even if Alice didn't work out.

Unfortunately, Feldspar and Sonata were also interested in the chickens, loudly proclaiming their enthusiasm—five feather dusters, alive and clucking!

Batty panicked. The last thing she wanted was another disaster with Cagney's animals. "Get out, Lyds, now!"

As Lydia leapt from the car, Batty put it into reverse to flee Cagney and his flock and didn't stop until the dogs had settled down. This put her a hundred or so yards away from where she'd started, far enough to make Lydia feel a bit shy, here alone with Cagney and his chickens. But he seemed unperturbed by Batty's precipitous retreat, and the chickens were too busy to bother with Lydia—four of them because they were insect hunting, and the fifth because she was determined to climb onto Cagney's foot. He kept gently shaking her off, only to have her try again.

"It's Lydia, right?" he asked. "I'm Cagney. Welcome to Arundel."

"Thank you." Lydia thought she should explain about Batty driving away backward. "My sister was worried our dogs would upset your chickens."

"That was probably best." Cagney again dislodged the chicken, and again she climbed back on. "They're easy to upset, not being heavy on brainpower."

Lydia crouched down to get a better view. "Do they have names?"

"Hatshepsut is on my foot. Then Cleopatra I, Nefertiti, Cleopatra VII—I was teaching ancient Egypt when we first got them—and this one my daughter named Batgirl. I wonder where Alice is. She should be out here saying hello."

Lydia didn't think it her job to tell Cagney that Alice had already seen Lydia and found her wanting, but anyway, he'd turned away and started to whistle. This seemed peculiar—her sisters had told her nothing about Cagney and whistling—and it became more so when she realized he was whistling the same two notes, the second lower than the first, over and over again. This was the call of a black-capped chickadee. She knew that because Ben had once considered making a film about a dying (of course) black-capped chickadee, and had tried to get Lydia to whistle like one. She'd never learned how, and was impressed with Cagney's skill, though she wished she knew why he was doing it.

Now he stopped whistling and yelled.

"Alice!" He drew out the first syllable—*Aaa*-lice—and Lydia realized that all along he'd been whistling Alice's name. She was even more impressed than before. Not that it worked. No Alice showed herself.

"It doesn't matter," said Lydia. "Please, if she doesn't want to."

"She's just a little upset right now. A few hours ago, her brother left to visit his cousin in Canada, and she's going to miss him. Let's put away the chickens, and I'll go find her."

Lydia followed him behind the cottage to where the chickens lived in a pen that had lots of space for them to move around, plus a little house of their own with two separate rooms, one for being social and one for laying eggs. Cagney told them to be good girls, then went into the cottage to hunt down the elusive Alice, who, contrarily, was already on the porch when Lydia returned to the front of the cottage. Like her dad, Alice was wearing a cap, but this one was black and yellow with a big *D* on the insignia. If the cap was meant to hide Alice's red, puffy eyes, it wasn't working. Lydia could tell she'd been crying.

"I'm Alice," she said. "I guess you're Lydia."

"I don't want to bother you if, you know . . ." Lydia trailed off, not wanting to mention Alice's tears.

"If I'm crying? I've stopped." Alice lifted her cap to prove it, and it was true that no new tears were forthcoming. "Anyway, my parents think we might be friends while you're here."

Lydia didn't mention that she'd hoped the same thing, not wanting to foist herself on anyone. But at least she hadn't loathed Alice on sight. This was a positive first step. "We don't have to be friends. I'm okay on my own."

"Thank you." Alice pulled down her cap again. "I've heard a lot about you. Your sister Jane told my mother that you like everybody."

"That's not true! Jane should know better."

Alice perked up a little. "Maybe you won't like me."

"I'd already know if I wasn't going to."

Cagney came through the door behind them. "There you are, Alice. I've been looking for you."

"Dad, Jane was wrong. Lydia doesn't like everyone."

"I really don't. I wish my sisters would believe me," said Lydia. "There's this girl, Deborah, I just couldn't stand."

"We'll be sure not to invite Deborah to Arundel," said Cagney.

Alice had something else she wanted to clear up. "My parents said that our family owes the Penderwicks a debt of gratitude, because Mrs. Tifton hated having you here so much that she never rented out our cottage again. Which is how Dad and Mom could move into it when they got married, and why we still live here."

"That wasn't me, though," said Lydia. "I wasn't even born when my family was here last time. You don't owe me anything."

Alice perked up even more. "Dad, did you hear that?"

"You're missing the point, Alice," he said.

"But she truly doesn't owe me anything," said Lydia. If they were to become friends, she didn't want it to be by coercion.

"All right, I'll let you two work it out while I take the key to Batty." He held up a boringly normal old key, not what Lydia had expected—something large, ornate, and made at least of silver, maybe even gold.

As he strode off, Alice sank back into gloomy silence, and Lydia was left staring out at the trees, wondering what to say to this sad person. Eventually, she came up with a question.

"Do you know Mrs. Tifton well?"

It turned out to be a good question. Alice launched enthusiastically into her longest speech so far.

"Sure, I do. When she lived here, she came over almost every day to boss around my dad and tell my mom her problems, like about when her last husband stole everything stored in the attic, sold it, and kept the money, and some of it was really valuable, so he got thousands of dollars. That's when Mrs. Tifton said she was done with husbands, and moved to New York City. No one believes that she's done with husbands— not even her lawyer, which is why he told her to give Arundel to Jeffrey. And Jack, my brother, says she probably moved to New York because husbands are

44

easier to find there. I said she managed to find plenty while living here, and he said that proves that she's run out by now."

This was all interesting, but Lydia's attention had caught on the attic. The attic and the treasures it held—old clothes, furniture, toys, bows and arrows, anything that could be dreamt of—had come up often in her sisters' stories.

"That husband sold everything that was in the attic? There's nothing left?"

"Nothing. And he stole other stuff, too. He was a real winner. The one before that did illegal things on Wall Street and went to prison for a while."

Lydia was disappointed that the attic was now empty. It was going to be one of her first adventures. She also found herself feeling sympathy for Mrs. Tifton. No one deserved such bad husbands.

"My sisters don't like her much," she said.

"Do you want to see how she looks when she's mad?" Alice made a face like she'd bit into a sour pickle. "I kind of miss her. It's more exciting with her around. Or when Jeffrey's home from Germany, though that's a nicer excitement. In March, he brought me this Dynamo Dresden hat because of the *D*, for my middle name, Delaney. He couldn't find any hats in Germany with *A* for Alice."

She took off her cap and showed it to Lydia, who was impressed. Jeffrey had always brought her ballet

45

skirts, fancy ones with embroidery and layers upon layers of tulle. She was outgrowing a few of the earlier ones, and secretly hoped he'd bring her another when he came home for the wedding. But a real sports hat from Germany was also nice. Unlike ballet skirts, hats can't be grown out of.

Alice's long speech must have used up her available words, because conversation now ground to a halt. It was a relief when Batty and Cagney returned in Jane's car.

"We have two dogs, if you want to see them," Lydia told Alice.

Clearly more enthusiastic about dogs than people, Alice ran to the car and peered into the backseat. Feldspar excitedly presented his feather duster. Sonata yawned.

"Batty, this is my daughter, Alice," said Cagney. "Alice, say hello to Batty."

"Hello, Batty. Dad said you wore butterfly wings and were odd."

Cagney groaned. "I apologize for my daughter, Batty. I did not tell her that you were odd. I believe I said 'quiet and very shy.'"

"I *was* a little odd," said Batty. "And they tell me I wore wings, but I don't remember."

"Odd isn't always bad," said Alice graciously. "My brother sometimes calls me that. Can I get into the car with the dogs?"

While Alice rolled around in the backseat with Feldspar and Sonata, Batty conferred quietly with Lydia. Cagney had offered to show them around the mansion, discussing necessities like kitchens and bathrooms, sheets and towels. Did Lydia want to come along or stay with Alice? Lydia had little interest in sheets and towels, but she also didn't want to be with Alice unless Alice wanted her there.

"Should I ask her, or do you want to?" Batty whispered.

"You, please."

Batty reached into the backseat to pull Feldspar's feather duster out of Alice's face.

"Would you like Lydia to stay with you, or should she go with me and your dad to the mansion?"

Alice stared out the car window, apparently considering her options.

"Alice," said Cagney. "Please."

"I'm thinking!" She glanced at Lydia. "Do you like sheep?"

Who doesn't like sheep? There turned out to be an entire flock of them living in a field next to Arundel. When Lydia's sisters had first visited, this field was home to a bull who didn't appreciate Batty crawling under the locked gate and taking over his favorite grazing spot, and who appreciated even less Jeffrey and Skye showing up to rescue her. Lydia had wondered

47

if the bull would still be around, and was a little disappointed to find that she wouldn't get to meet him in real life.

But unlike bulls, sheep don't attempt to murder people who visit their field. This meant that the gate that had once been thick wood was now only wire mesh and wasn't even locked. Alice shoved it open, and in they went. The sheep—Lydia counted seventeen—were gathered in a far corner near their barn, busily chomping on grass. They raised their heads to make sure the new arrivals weren't wolves or coyotes, then went back to their meal.

Except for the one sheep slowly but deliberately making her way toward the girls.

"That's Big Papi." Alice pulled a handful of oats out of her pocket. When Big Papi arrived, she ate the oats right off Alice's hand. "You can pet her if you want."

Lydia started off tentatively patting the sheep's broad back but was soon comfortable enough to bury her hands in the thick wool that smelt like sun, sweaters, and grass. Big Papi ignored her, wanting only oats, and bleated at Alice when she didn't immediately produce more.

"Why does this sheep come to you and the others don't?" asked Lydia, who wanted a sheep to come to her.

"When she was born, her mother couldn't take care of her, so Dad and Mom let her live in our house, and we fed her with a bottle until she was big enough to go back to the other sheep. And she remembers, don't you?" Alice kissed Big Papi's nose. "I wanted to name her Blossom, but Jack named her Big Papi, and she likes that better. Watch: Blossom. Big Papi. Blossom. Big Papi."

Lydia looked carefully into Blossom's eyes—one at a time, because like all sheep's eyes, they were facing in different directions.

"Say both names again."

"Blossom. Big Papi. Blossom. Big Papi."

"I really can't see any diff— Oh, Alice, you're crying again. Is it about Jack? Your dad says you miss him."

"I do not miss him." Alice angrily scrubbed away her tears. "It's just that he gets everything he wants, even naming Big Papi."

"*Blossom!*" Lydia addressed the sheep with emphasis and an extra pat on the head. "I think she responded this time."

"No, she didn't." Alice shook her head, sniffing. "I wanted to visit our cousin in Canada, too, but I wasn't allowed because I'm not old enough yet—I'm ten, and Jack's only twelve, and ten isn't that much younger than twelve, and so what if he has to ride on a train by himself—my mom is dropping him off now, and I could do that, too—and so what if he's going to hockey camp with our cousin Marcel and I don't play hockey. Plus, my parents gave Jack a phone so that

49

he can keep in touch from Canada, but I don't have a phone so I can't keep in touch with anybody, not Marcel or anybody. And Marcel has a Newfoundland puppy named Slapshot."

This Lydia understood. Two summers ago, Ben had gone to Connecticut to visit their cousins Enam and Marty—and Lydia had been devastated that she wasn't allowed to go with him. And back then, Enam and Marty didn't have their dog, Blakey. Lydia couldn't imagine how bad it would have been if she'd had to miss a new puppy on top of everything else.

"That's not fair," she told Alice.

"I know."

Lydia tried to come up with something comforting. "Maybe Jack won't like Canada."

"He'll like it. It's Canada!" Alice got more oats out of her pocket for Big Papi, or Blossom. "And, also, it isn't just that Blossom prefers to be called Big Papi. She even likes Jack best. He's always telling her stories about Jumping Jack Flash and Jack Kennedy the president and these two guys named Jack White and Jack Black that he says are real, but I'm not sure."

"President Kennedy definitely was."

"Yeah, a long time ago." Alice tipped her head, listening, and then Lydia heard it—the two-note call of the black-capped chickadee. "I have to go. I'll show you a shortcut back to the mansion."

After the girls said good-bye to Big Papi (or

Blossom), Alice led Lydia not toward the driveway and lane, but to the hedge that separated the cottage and the estate. When they got close enough, Lydia noticed a clump of tall wildflowers growing up right next to the hedge, and then she knew where she was.

"These flowers block Jeffrey's tunnel," she told Alice, "where he and Skye met. They banged into each other, and she knocked him out."

"The tunnel's mine and Jack's now. Though, actually, with Jack away, it's just mine, isn't it?" At that happy thought, Alice smiled, for the first time since Lydia had met her. It was a crooked smile, a little higher on the left than on the right, and transformed Alice into a funny elf of a girl, with just the right amount of wicked. "Uh-oh, there's my dad whistling again."

Without saying good-bye, Alice whirled around and dashed away.

"Thanks for introducing me to Blossom!" shouted Lydia in her wake.

The only answer was another birdcall.

*Aaa*-lice.

# CHAPTER FIVE
## A Piano and a Bunch of Spiders

LYDIA EMERGED FROM THE tunnel behind a statue of a man wearing a toga and holding a thunderbolt. On the first visit, her sisters had called him the marble thunderbolt man, not realizing until they were older that he was supposed to be Zeus, king of the gods. Lydia circled around to see his face—no wonder they hadn't recognized him as Zeus. He looked less like a king and more like a normal guy who was confused. She could imagine why. It must have been a shock to start out in ancient Greece but end up in modern-day Massachusetts. Poor Zeus. If he could stop yearning for the past, he might be grateful for such a view. Certainly Lydia delighted in what she saw—a glimpse of the carriage house and, beyond it, the greenhouse. In the other direction was a large meadow at the back of the estate, mirroring the meadows she'd seen earlier. Everywhere were garden beds overrun with bright riots of friendly flowers like zinnias and sunflowers, petunias and nasturtiums, bachelor buttons and sweet peas. Plus, one bed dedicated to a tangle of raspberry bushes. Lydia popped a berry into her mouth and almost swooned. This was her first raspberry eaten fresh, still warm from the sunshine, and she never again wanted to eat raspberries any other way.

Yes, poor Zeus. Why should he be grateful for being stuck staring at raspberries he'd never eat? Lydia picked a few to place at his marble feet.

"As tribute," she told him, then swayed and stomped, being what she thought might look like a Greek maiden from ancient times. "Now, Zeus, you must know Alice pretty well. Do you think she wants to be friends with me?"

Zeus's look of confusion didn't waver, though at least it didn't get worse.

"Maybe, maybe not? It might not be our destiny."

Lydia did a bit of soft-shoe for him, thinking he might like some more up-to-date dancing, then realized that she was hungry—breakfast felt like a lifetime ago. Because it was difficult to contemplate abstract subjects like destiny on an empty stomach, she turned herself around and pointed her dancing feet toward Arundel Hall and, she hoped, Batty and food.

The closer Lydia got to Arundel Hall, the larger it seemed to grow, until she felt teensy, like Jill, Scrubb, and Puddleglum when they reach the giants' castle in *The Silver Chair*. She decided that the mansion was her least favorite part of Arundel, and she wasn't looking forward to sleeping in it.

There was no way to guess where Batty might be in this great fortress, and Lydia wished she'd asked Alice how to get inside. There were plenty of doors, but any she tried were locked. The carved-oak front door— truly tall enough for a giant to go through—was forbidding, but Lydia bravely made an attempt anyway. Locked. She wondered if she'd be circling this unfriendly behemoth, waltzing along terraces, skipping up and down steps, for the rest of her life. How long did it take to die of hunger, and why didn't the Penderwicks use birdsongs to find each other?

But then came rescue: not birdsong, but indeed a beacon that said "Here is Batty" or, as their father said, *"Hic Batty est."* Somewhere a piano was pouring out the score for *Merrily We Roll Along*, the musical put on by Cameron High School when Batty was in tenth grade and one of the stars. She'd played and sung the score so many times at home that the whole family learned it along with her. Mr. Penderwick still sometimes sang the title song when he thought no one could hear him.

Right now, it was just a tiny thread of music, but

once Lydia figured out the direction it was coming from, it didn't take her long to find the source, a large room on the other side of locked French doors. Most of the room had a desolate look, its furniture shrouded in white sheets that made Lydia think of ghosts, and not in a good way. But one part of the room was alive—the corner that held a grand piano, shiny and black, jutting like the prow of an ocean liner. The vast lid was propped up, blocking Batty from Lydia's view, but she could spot Sonata asleep under the piano and Feldspar in front of it, proudly guarding Batty from the eerie furniture. Lydia knocked on the window to get Feldspar's attention—and here he was now, wagging his tail and cleaning his side of the window with his feather duster.

"Tell Batty I'm out here," she said, even though she knew he wouldn't listen. And, indeed, he concentrated on his dusting until the song ended and Lydia's knock could get through to her sister. Batty ran to unlock the door, grabbed Lydia's hand, and dragged her over to the piano.

"I haven't forgotten everything after all—I remember this piano! I think I hid under it once." She let her fingers trail over the keys, picking out snatches of melody. "How were Alice and the sheep?"

"One of the sheep was friendly. I don't know whether Alice likes me."

"But of course you like—" Batty broke off when

she saw her younger sister's frown. "Sorry, I forgot about Deborah."

"I do like Alice, though. And I found raspberry bushes." Lydia gazed around the room—and didn't like it much. Really, there was no guarantee that the white shapes were furniture. Anything could be hidden under those sheets. "Is the whole house like this? Covered up and spooky?"

"I haven't seen all of it yet. Mostly the kitchen, some closets, and here." Batty closed her eyes for a minute, searching through old memories. "You know, I think Mrs. Tifton yelled at me in this room. And Skye and Jeffrey were here, too, but not Hound, and I was terrified because he wasn't there to protect me."

Lydia thought this room suitable for many kinds of unpleasantness. "We should stay out of it from now on."

"This is the music room—I have to be in here. I'll fill it with music and banish the bad feelings."

Lydia thought that taking the furniture covers off would also help. But it was true that if anyone could banish bad feelings with music, it was Batty. She loved music, embraced it, exuded it, lived it, and had a motto that said so: *Musica anima mea est*, which meant "Music is my life." Lydia didn't have a motto yet, though she'd experimented with a few, asking her father to translate each into Latin, as he had for Batty. She'd memorized each, just in case it turned out to be the right one, but so far none had been. For a while, she'd thought about making *Non omnes amo*—"I do not like everyone"—permanent, but it didn't have quite the right energy.

Batty had slipped back into the *Merrily We Roll Along* score, playing and singing "Old Friends." Lydia was tempted to dance along—but not with those white shapes watching, and not while she was getting steadily hungrier. She convinced Batty to shut the piano lid and go eat the lunch their parents had sent along.

The sisters turned lunch into a picnic, sitting beside an elaborate marble fountain. If the water had been on, it would have gushed out of the jugs held by the fountain's three chubby cherubs. Lydia was pleased that the cherubs seemed more cheerful than old Zeus, but nonetheless, she slipped a bit of her lunch into each of the jugs—a spoonful of potato salad for one, carrot salad for another, and broccoli salad for the third. She was too hungry to share any of the rolls with butter, or the peaches and cookies. Nor did she offer the dog snacks to the cherubs—these were essential for keeping Feldspar away from the potato salad, and Sonata from the butter. (They each had their favorites.)

When everyone had eaten their way to comfort, Batty announced that the next activity would be cleaning, and they would begin with the kitchen.

Lydia felt that cleaning should wait until there were more Penderwicks to share the burden. She felt it even more acutely when Batty led her to what at Arundel was called a kitchen, but what anywhere else would be mistaken for a giant's lair that happened to have a bunch of ovens and refrigerators in it. Plus, it wasn't just ridiculously big, it was also, by Lydia's standards, already quite clean enough.

"This looks fine to me," she told Batty. "Maybe a touch of sweeping and dusting, and then we can go explore the gardens and meadows."

But Batty was looking up, up, to the high ceiling, especially into its corners, of which there were many, since the kitchen was not only huge but full of nooks and offshoots, each one with its own set of corners.

"See those?" she said, pointing to several tangles of barely visible, delicate webs. "Where there are webs, there are spiders. We need to find them and put them outside."

Spiders were in the subset of living creatures that Lydia had never taken to, despite Batty's influence. She would never kill one, but she also had no interest in seeking them out.

"Maybe they're happy where they are."

"Next week this kitchen will be overrun with people, and the spiders will definitely not be happy then. Help me look for containers."

After opening and shutting a few dozen cupboards,

Batty found a stack of small plastic containers perfect for transferring spiders from one location to another. Lydia found something she considered more practical—a pile of aprons. She used one to cover her head, and tied two around her waist, one for her front and the other her back. Now she felt safe—a spider would have to have unusually good aim to land on any part of her not protected by aprons.

Spiders aside, Lydia also felt like the aprons had taken her inside *The Sound of Music*, by combining two of Maria's identities. The apron on her head represented Maria the nun, and the ones around her waist, Maria dancing on the mountaintop. Lydia flung out her arms, twirling around and around, while Batty used a chair to clamber up onto the countertops, initiating her search for spiders. It didn't take long.

"Here you go, my lovely, walk into my parlor," she said. "Got him. Lydia, take this one outside and set him free."

Lydia stretched up to receive the container-plus-spider, almost fell when Feldspar rushed over to see if the container held food, exited the mansion through the nearest door, put the container on the ground, and took off the lid. Inside was the tiniest spider she'd ever seen, and also the most terrified—too stunned by the recent cataclysm to move. Lydia had to tap the container to convince him to scuttle away into the forest of grass blades.

"How many spiders do you think there are?" she asked Batty when she got back inside.

"Lots. Hello, darling spider, we've come to rescue you." Batty handed another container to Lydia. "This one's a little bigger than the other one."

"How much bigger?" Peeking inside, Lydia found herself eye to eye with not just the biggest spider she'd ever seen, but a spider so colossal—at least, this is how she'd tell the story later—that it was able to use two of its long-as-pipe-cleaner legs to throw off the lid and the other six to vault out of the container and onto Lydia.

What followed was not a dance Lydia could be proud of. Her jeté of terror was clumsy, the following leaps and dips shaky, and one doesn't usually scream while dancing. Then everything got worse, because the spider disappeared and could have been anywhere. Lydia tore off her three aprons, frantically shook herself—and there it was! The demon spider was crawling up her leg! Lydia flung herself from one end of the kitchen to the other, continuing to scream until the spider shot off her leg and fled into a dark refuge underneath one of the ovens.

"Really, Lydia," said Batty.

"I know." She picked up her aprons and tied them back on. "Sorry."

"Maybe you'd be better off sweeping or dusting in another room where there are fewer spiders. I spotted brooms in that tall cupboard."

Lydia didn't point out that since spiders don't automatically prefer kitchens, they could be anywhere, but she figured that as long as Batty wasn't there, actively encouraging them to show themselves, most spiders would sensibly stay hidden. Still, she had to make a decision about which was scarier—roaming through the mansion alone or getting ambushed by Godzilla spiders.

"Here's another big one," said Batty. "You'd better go now."

Armed with a broom, Lydia set off looking for an un-spooky room to sweep. She took her time, wandering down long halls, making random right and left turns, until she unexpectedly arrived at the mansion's splendid entranceway—on the other side of that immense front oak door she hadn't been able to get through. She'd heard about this place from her sisters—its grandeur, its glowing stained-glass windows that cast rainbows of color. And here was the majestic staircase, winding gracefully into the upper reaches, and crying out to be used as a dance stage.

No matter that Lydia was dressed for *The Sound of Music*. With the broom, she would dance to "Defying Gravity" from *Wicked*, and here she went, upward, one step to the next, humming off-key and gesturing with her broom, just as Elphaba surely would have done had she visited Arundel. Lydia was heading into the final verse, the broom held triumphantly high, when she heard a creak, like that of door hinges in need of oiling. She halted mid-step and watched as the oak door swung open. There, in a blaze of sunlight, stood a woman who appeared to have the right to open any Arundel door she felt like opening, no matter what she'd sworn about staying away forever. If that hadn't given away the woman's identity, there was also this— she looked like she'd just bitten into a sour pickle. For an instant, Lydia could delight in Alice's imitation skills, but very quickly dismay set in, along with the realization that she and Batty were in for a rough time.

"Who are you?" Mrs. Tifton's question was loud and sharp. "And how did you get into my house?"

# CHAPTER SIX
## Even More Spiders

LYDIA DESCENDED THE STAIRS with dignity, refusing to cower like a thief. She knew she wasn't breaking any laws by being on the steps, though she wasn't quite as sure it was legal to be wearing the Arundel aprons.

"I'm Lydia." That was truthful without giving away anything important, like being a Penderwick.

"Lydia *who*? And what are you doing here? Tell me!"

Abruptly, Lydia's courage failed. She needed reinforcements, which she desperately wished could be Jane and Ben, but there was no putting off Mrs. Tifton for a whole day, and Batty was better than no one.

"Excuse me for a minute, please," she said, and turned on her heel to flee the ogress, blindly negotiating the maze of halls—left, right, right, left—and only by luck ending up in the kitchen. Batty was still on the counter, coaxing yet another spider into a container to add to the stack she already had. Even in the midst of the Mrs. Tifton trauma, Lydia took the time to hope none of the new spiders was as large as the one who'd attacked her.

"Batty," she gasped, "Mrs. Tifton's here."

"Ha-ha. Come to me, sweet arachnid. That's my girl." Batty popped on the lid. "One more safe."

"Not ha-ha, Batty. She's really here."

"What do you mean, here?"

And then came the sound of someone walking—*tap tap tap tap*—still faint, but getting closer.

"She's *here*, here?" Batty was white with fear. "Lyds, she doesn't like dogs—hide them, quick!"

Lydia shoved Feldspar through a closet door, noticing too late that it wasn't a closet, but a staircase down to a shadowy cellar. Next went Sonata, sleepily trotting down behind him. As a final gesture, Lydia ripped off the aprons and threw them, too—unfortunately landing one on Feldspar's head. He stopped in confusion, but the *tap-tap*ping footsteps were coming ever closer, so Lydia shut the door and leaned against it, hoping Sonata would help Feldspar work it out.

"They're in the cellar," she whispered to Batty.

"What else is down there?"

"I don't know."

"This is a nightmare." Batty climbed down from the

counter, still clutching a spider-occupied container, when Mrs. Tifton arrived, talking into her phone.

"Why would Jeffrey have invited—?" She paused, frowning. "Yes, Cagney, I do realize I said I'd never come back. But that doesn't mean Jeffrey could— What did you say? A wedding? A *wedding*! *Whose* wedding? Get over here now, this instant!"

She ended her call and glared from one sister to the other. "According to Cagney, you know my son. How did you talk him into handing over my home?"

"Actually, it was Jeffrey's idea for us to come here," said Lydia, hoping to draw Mrs. Tifton's attention away from Batty, whose hands were shaking. The spider must have thought it was in the middle of an earthquake.

"Lydia, I'll handle this," said Batty.

"*Handle*? Excuse me! What you will handle is getting out of here," snapped Mrs. Tifton. "And what's in that plastic box?"

Lydia knew without a doubt that Batty should ignore Mrs. Tifton's second question—that if anything could worsen this situation, it would be bringing the woman face to face with a spider. But Batty wasn't thinking clearly. She opened the container to give Mrs. Tifton a peek at its inhabitant, and Mrs. Tifton did what naturally she would—shrieked, and swatted Batty's hand away, without, thank goodness, dislodging the spider. Lydia didn't think either she or Mrs.

65

Tifton would live through an encore of the spider-on-the-loose episode.

"What on earth are you doing?" gasped Mrs. Tifton. "There's a spider in there!"

"She's rescuing it," explained Lydia. "She believes in equality for all creatures. She doesn't eat meat or fish, and not even insects, though luckily there isn't a lot of opportunity for eating insects. Yet."

Mrs. Tifton stared in disbelief. "Who *are* you people?"

"We met long ago, though maybe you don't remember." Batty didn't sound hopeful about the not remembering. "We're . . . Penderwicks."

"*Pender—!*" Mrs. Tifton's pickle face was in full force. She whipped out her phone and hit redial. "Cagney! You didn't tell me they were Penderwicks! You'd *better* be on your way."

While Batty added the container to the spider-condo tower and Lydia stayed put, guarding the door to the cellar, Mrs. Tifton tapped again at her phone. This time there was no answer, and when she left a message, it made both Batty and Lydia wince, especially Batty.

"Jeffrey, this is your mother. I'm at Arundel with the Penderwicks. The Penderwicks! What were you thinking? Call me!" She hung up and threw herself onto the bench of a cozy breakfast nook.

Batty had gone back to rescuing spiders, doing her

best to pretend that she and Lydia were alone in the kitchen. But Lydia stared openly at Mrs. Tifton, busily adjusting her inner version of the woman—gleaned from her sisters' old stories—to the reality. This Mrs. Tifton was no towering menace. Even in her high heels, she was barely as tall as Batty, and she had less an air of threat than of chronic unhappiness. Now she was on her phone again.

"Mimi, you're not going to believe this. Remember that family I told you about—the people who ran wild here about fifteen years ago? One of the sisters had a big crush on Jeffrey. . . . Yes, them. They're here in the mansion—two of them, anyway. . . . No, not the one who had the crush on Jeffrey. She was blond and these aren't. Mimi, they think they're here for a wedding! . . . I don't know yet, but it couldn't be either of these two—they're not old enough. The brunette is a teenager, and the redhead—" Mrs. Tifton turned to Lydia. "How old are you?"

"Eleven."

"Eleven. The father must have remarried. . . . Hold on, let me look." Now Mrs. Tifton was carefully studying Lydia's hair. "Bright but not garish copper, with golden highlights and some streaks of walnut brown . . . Yes, it's gorgeous, but, Mimi, you don't seem to understand what it feels like to have these people encamped in my home! . . . All right, I will. Bye."

Lydia was doing her best to study her own hair, which isn't easy without a mirror—you can see only what's long enough to pull in front of your eyes. She'd never heard her hair described the way Mrs. Tifton had, and wondered how much of that was accurate. She couldn't ask Batty, who wasn't near enough to have heard—apparently, there were a lot of spiders at the far end of the kitchen. And asking Mrs. Tifton would feel like begging for compliments, so she couldn't do that.

There were other things Lydia also wanted to ask Mrs. Tifton, like how she'd dreamt up the idea about Skye having a crush on Jeffrey. And how had it felt to have the attic cleared out by a thieving husband, and why was she at Arundel, anyway? But she couldn't ask any of that. And yet, she didn't want this silence to continue for too long, not with the dogs wandering the mansion's subterranean regions and capable of barking or howling at any moment. Oh, here was something she could safely ask:

"Do you go to the theater a lot in New York City?"

Mrs. Tifton frowned, looking for hidden meanings but unable to come up with any. "I suppose so. One does."

"Musicals? If I lived there, I'd go to a musical every week to study the dancing."

"Thank heavens," said Mrs. Tifton.

At first Lydia thought that Mrs. Tifton was grateful

that Lydia liked musicals, but that wasn't it. She was thanking heavens for the arrival of Cagney and a woman who Lydia knew was Alice's mom—she had the same quirky smile. Alice had come, too, her eyes no longer red and swollen. She dashed past Mrs. Tifton to join Lydia.

"You can call my mom Natalie if you want," she whispered. "Jack's friends do."

Lydia wanted to point out that not only wasn't she Jack's friend, she wasn't even certain she was Alice's friend, but Mrs. Tifton was loudly proclaiming her woes, which made it difficult to be heard.

"And then she tried to frighten me with a huge spider! Cagney, I need these people out of here immediately."

"I understand it was a shock, Brenda," answered Cagney. "If only you'd told us you were coming."

"It was a spur-of-the-moment trip to see Mimi Robinette. She's having trouble with her ex-husband and wanted to talk to someone with plenty"—she glanced at the Penderwicks, then finished the sentence with an unintelligible murmur—"plenty of hmm-hmm-hmms."

Lydia figured that the hmm-hmm-hmms were Mrs. Tifton's ex-husbands, of whom there had indeed been plenty. She also thought she recognized the name Robinette from the old stories. Hadn't there been a boy named Robinette who Jeffrey's mother was always forcing Jeffrey to play with? Lydia wished she could ask Mrs. Tifton this, too, but then she remembered that the Robinette boy had been a bully, and that Jeffrey had loathed him.

Lydia went back to listening. Alice's mom was asking Mrs. Tifton if she meant to sleep at Arundel. Lydia hadn't even considered that unpleasant possibility. But on this topic, at least, she and Mrs. Tifton were in agreement.

"No, I'm staying with Mimi, but that doesn't mean these people can move in."

"You understand Jeffrey invited the Penderwicks to stay here," said Cagney, "and that we're responsible to him now, don't you?"

"Yes, and I also understand that Jeffrey pays you out of a trust I set up." She dropped her voice. "Maybe we should talk about this in private."

Both Penderwicks would be delighted to be separated from Mrs. Tifton, but they needed to maintain possession of the kitchen, with its doorway down to Feldspar and Sonata. Lydia was wondering how to say so without actually mentioning the dogs, when Batty spoke up. The possible risk to the dogs had given her both courage and a foolproof way to evacuate the enemy.

"I think one of my spiders has escaped." She lifted a lid and looked anxiously inside. "The extra-large one."

Mrs. Tifton was immediately on her feet, deter-

70

mined on a speedy exit with Cagney and Natalie behind her. On their way out, Mrs. Tifton's phone rang—it was Jeffrey—and she began berating him in a voice so angry that Batty went white again and Lydia covered her ears until the woman was outside and no longer within hearing range.

"Did you see her face?" Alice did the pickle face again. "Was I right? Didn't I tell you she makes things more exciting? Jack's going to be jealous he missed it."

"This isn't exciting—it's awful," said Batty. "She's screaming at Jeffrey."

"Mom and Dad will calm her down. They've had lots of practice."

"Then they must be miracle workers. Lydia, make sure the dogs are okay."

"I will, but can Mrs. Tifton force us to leave?"

"Dad and Mom won't let that happen," said Alice. "They said so on the way over."

"I really want to stay," said Lydia.

"Don't think about that right now," said Batty. "Go find Feldspar and Sonata, but don't bring them upstairs until I give you the signal."

Alice followed Lydia down the steps into the cellar. There were no dogs in sight, just large shadowy spaces that led through rough arches into other large shadowy spaces, all of them eerily empty. Lydia wondered if the spookiness in the mansion originated here. She'd learned in school that heat rises. What about spookiness?

71

"Why is it so empty?" she asked Alice. "Did one of the husbands steal everything out of here, too?"

"Dad says there's never been much down here. Too damp and moldy."

"Yuck." Lydia shook off images of mold growing and mutating, becoming sentient beings capable of making forays upstairs to, for example, the bedroom where Lydia was going to sleep. She considered giving this to Ben for a movie idea but decided not to—since she'd end up as a character being killed by mold. Worse, part of the movie would be shot down here, and she hoped this would be her last visit ever.

"Mom said you can be an eastern towhee." Alice whistled three notes—two quick ones, and a third that went up the scale and trilled. *Ly-di-AH-AH-AH-AH*. "Do you like it?"

Lydia liked it very much—her feet itched to dance along. "But, Alice, I only need a birdcall if you want us to be friends. You didn't seem sure before."

"I had to think about it. It wasn't just my parents telling me to be nice to you. Before Jack left, he said you and I could be friends, and I'm tired of him telling me what to do."

"My brother does that, too." Though Ben's bossiness had less to do with Lydia's friends and more to do with dying in his movies.

"But now I'm sure," said Alice, smiling her funny crooked smile. "Forget dopey Jack."

"Friends, then," said Lydia. "Pinky promise."

They intertwined their little fingers, swearing lifetime fealty, then turned their attention to finding the dogs. The most logical strategy would have been to split up and go in opposite directions, but because neither wanted to be alone in those creepy caverns, they stuck together, moving cautiously from one dank space to another, whistling and calling for Feldspar and Sonata. When they came upon one of Lydia's discarded aprons, and then another, they knew they were on the right track. A little farther, and they found Sonata asleep on the third apron.

Lydia prodded her awake. "Whine, Sonata. Feldspar will come for you, if not for me."

Alice helpfully whined to show her how it was done, and here came Feldspar, trotting toward them, proudly carrying—

"An ax!" cried Lydia. "Where did he get an ax?"

"Maybe Mrs. Tifton used it to kill some of her husbands, and then bury them down here." Alice scrutinized the ax for evidence.

"I don't think she's strong enough to kill someone with an ax," said Lydia hopefully, and tried to take the ax away from Feldspar. But it was his prize and he wasn't letting go.

"She could have poisoned them and used the ax to chop them into pieces. Look right there." Alice pointed at the blade. "I bet that's blood."

"Just rust, I think." Lydia gave up the tug-of-war with Feldspar. She could possibly trick him into trading it if she could find his feather duster, but there was no way she was going deeper into the gloom in search of an old feather duster. It would have to lie down here for the remainder of time.

"The husbands could now be ghosts, waiting for their revenge," said Alice. "We could search for them, Lydia."

"But what would we do if we found any?"

"I know tae kwon do." Alice demonstrated.

Alice's tae kwon do looked more enthusiastic than fierce, and Lydia wasn't sure how effective it would be against ghosts. But here came Batty's "ALL CLEAR!" echoing through the cellar. No time for ghost-hunting now, with or without tae kwon do.

The girls each took hold of one dog and coaxed them back to the staircase, picking up the aprons as they went. By the time they got there, the weight of the ax was becoming a problem for Feldspar, until he was doing more dragging than carrying. Still, he wouldn't give it up. The clanging and banging he made on the steps disgusted even Sonata.

The Pelletiers were back inside, without Mrs. Tifton—she was gone for now—and Batty was on the phone with Rosalind.

"It was horrible hearing Mrs. T. shout at Jeffrey— poor guy, trying to have a life in Germany with his mother screeching at him across the Atlantic. . . . Yes, I'm still scared of her. . . . Wait, I'll ask her. Lydia, you're scared of Mrs. Tifton, too, right?"

"Not really."

"You're not?" Thunderstruck, Batty went back to the phone. "She says she isn't, but I think she's in shock."

"I'm not in shock, Batty," said Lydia. "Tell Rosy."

But Batty had hung up and spotted Feldspar. "Why does he have an ax?"

"We think Mrs. Tifton used it to chop up her husbands," said Alice. "And buried them in the cellar, where their ghosts still roam at night."

"Alice, sweetheart, we've had so many discussions about ghosts," said Natalie.

"But, Mom, they could be real. No one can prove they're not."

Even Batty couldn't convince Feldspar to release the ax.

"We'll have to get him out of the mansion," she said. "I don't want him scratching furniture. Especially with Mrs. Tifton roaming around."

While Natalie and Cagney were almost certain that Mrs. Tifton wouldn't be back that day, they couldn't guess what would happen next, only that Jeffrey would do his best to calm her down.

"You should be okay sleeping here," added Natalie. "She wouldn't come over in the middle of the night."

"She could, though," said Alice. "She's unpredictable."

Lydia's concern about sleeping in Arundel Hall was less about Mrs. Tifton and more about her dead husbands, but she was saved from having to face any ghosts that night, at least. Batty insisted they stay out of the mansion while there was any possibility of a Mrs. Tifton reappearance. Cagney and Natalie invited them to sleep at the cottage, but when Batty insisted on not imposing, they suggested Cagney's old apartment in the carriage house. This Batty gratefully accepted.

"It's been empty for a long time, and will probably need some cleaning," said Cagney.

"We're willing to clean, aren't we, Lyds?" said Batty.

More cleaning was definitely not Lydia's first choice, but it would be worth it not to sleep with the ghosts. She put her three aprons back on. She was ready.

# CHAPTER SEVEN
*Bobolinks*

AFTER THE MANSION, THE carriage house apartment felt deliciously cozy and human-sized. The living area had just one piece of furniture, an ancient couch. Off to the left was an alcove for sleeping, and a tiny kitchen. The bathroom was tinier still, and also pleasingly ancient, with a claw-foot bathtub and a blurry mirror. The toilet had a pull chain for flushing. Lydia had never before seen a pull chain—she and Alice took turns pulling it just for the experience, and to hear the gurgling rush of water.

Batty was more interested in the spider colonization, which went far beyond what they'd found in the mansion.

"Generations upon generations of them," she said.

"Go away, Lydia, until I've helped them emigrate. Neither they nor I want you screaming and bounding around like a lunatic."

"It was just that Godzilla one." Lydia didn't want to help with the spiders—she just felt the need to re-establish that she wasn't a complete coward.

"And I've already spotted a few more Godzillas, so you should leave. Alice, will you take her?"

"Come on, Lydia," said Alice. "I'll show you one of my secret places."

Alice wasn't kidding about the secret part. Before they set out, she made Lydia shut her eyes and keep them shut. This wasn't so difficult when they were leaving the apartment, or while they were still on the paved driveway. But once they reached the grass, Alice spun her around three times, until Lydia was not only blind but dizzy, and had lost her sense of direction.

"Take my hand," said Alice. "I'll lead you."

"How far are we going?"

"I can't tell you, but, honest, you'll like it."

Walking along with her eyes closed, Lydia concentrated on her other senses. She felt changes in temperature as they crossed through shadows; she caught whiffs of roses at one point and lavender at another, and heard frogs croaking. At first the frogs sounded far away, but as they got louder—and closer—Lydia found it frustrating not to see them.

"I want to open my eyes," she said.

"It's just the frogs at the lily pond," said Alice.

"Please."

"One glance, that's all."

Lydia opened her eyes to a serene pond, blue from the reflected sky and dotted with round green lily pads, floating plates for white flowers. Hopping among the pads were the frogs themselves, their tongues darting out at passing insects. Lydia would have been happy to stay for hours, but Alice made her close her eyes, then spun her around again. This time Lydia didn't get dizzy, but she did start giggling, which can be almost as disorienting, particularly when the person leading you by the hand is also giggling, and walking in not exactly a straight line.

Still, onward they went without any disasters. Alice did try to scare Lydia by shouting "GHOST!" but everyone knows that ghosts don't come out in the sunshine, so that didn't work. Then Lydia yelled "GHOST!" and that did scare Alice for a minute, because she hadn't yet heard Lydia shout and didn't know how loud she could be.

Soon after that, the sounds changed for Lydia. The croaking frogs had faded away, and now there were more insects—crickets, mostly, and, with her heightened senses, Lydia could hear humming bees. Then the feel of the ground changed. The girls were no longer on smooth lawn—they were crushing small stubbles of

79

growing things. Lydia could now guess where she was, and when she brushed up against high grass, she was certain. Alice had led her into a meadow, the one at the back of the estate.

They stopped.

"From here on, you have to move carefully," said Alice. "Be like the lightest of winds, leaving no trace of your passage."

"It would be easier to be like the wind if I could see where I'm going."

"If you look now, you'll spoil the surprise. Keep your eyes closed and think like the wind. Swoosh, swoosh."

"Swoosh, swoosh." Lydia made her best attempt at thinking like the wind, imagining being midway through a graceful leap. "I'm ready."

They left the path and pushed their way into the meadow itself, a wild place—the Argentinian pampas, the Russian steppes, the Serengeti savannas! The grasses brushed and clung, and flitting bugs protested this invasion of their inner sanctum.

"Two more steps," said Alice. "Okay. Now just stand there, and keep your eyes closed."

There was an interval full of crackling noises—as if Alice was battling a plastic bag—and then another of her muttering to herself. Then she must have sat down, because her voice was coming from somewhere around Lydia's knees.

"Lift your right foot," she told Lydia. "Good. Now put your right foot down and pick up your left. Good. And now you can lie down."

Another thing that isn't easy to do with your eyes closed is gracefully lower yourself to the ground. Lydia ended up going down onto her hands and knees, wriggling into a sitting position, and then, with Alice's guidance, stretching out. The ground was more comfortable than she would have imagined— she seemed to be lying on cloth rather than smashed meadow.

"Open your eyes," said Alice. "This is my secret place."

They were in a nest carved out of the meadow, just large enough for the two of them. Underneath them was a thick blanket, above them were tiny floating seeds that shimmered in the sunlight, and above the seeds was nothing but sky, the girls' private patch of vivid blue. This was a flawless secret place, exquisite and absolute.

"I'm honored to be here," said Lydia, feeling solemn.

"You should be. I keep the blanket in this bag, so it won't get wet." Alice picked up a corner of the blanket to show Lydia the plastic bag underneath. There was also a metal box with a tight lid. "And here's food, in case of emergency."

Lydia didn't want to ask what kind of emergency

81

Alice had in mind, just in case it involved more dead husbands and ghosts. But she was happy enough to eat a granola bar out of the metal box.

Now small rustlings started up, as the animals alarmed by the girls' passage decided it was once again safe to move about. And the birds began to sing, reassuring each other that Lydia and Alice were not to be feared, especially Alice, because they'd seen her before.

"Alice, teach me your chickadee call," said Lydia.

"It's easy."

When Alice whistled the call, it did look easy, but Lydia couldn't get anything to come out of her mouth that sounded remotely like a bird.

"I guess whistling isn't one of my strengths," she said after multiple attempts.

"You can do Jack's call, anyway. It's an owl, so you don't have to whistle."

Both girls hooted like an owl for a while, and that was fun. For the girls, that is—the owls trying to sleep through the day were now confused and grumpy.

"I wonder if I used to be a bird," said Lydia. "I'm always dreaming about flying, and every time, I convince myself that it isn't a dream and that I'm really flying. I feel it in my shoulder and back muscles—as if I had real wings."

"Show me."

Lydia showed Alice what she'd learned from her

dreams, throwing in bits of what she'd gathered from watching videos of *Swan Lake*, though she thought those swans made too much use of their hands and not enough of their back muscles. Alice imitated her— there was just enough space for both of them to be birds. When Alice had the flying down, she whistled again, this time doing a burbling call.

"That's a bobolink call," she said. "We have lots of them. Mom named this Bobolink Meadow Two— the one in the front of the estate is Bobolink Meadow One."

Lydia attempted the bobolink whistle. This time at least she could form the notes, but only in a pathetic hissing kind of way. No bird would be fooled.

And yet—or maybe it was because of Alice—a moment later, a small bird flew over their heads and gracefully settled onto a nearby stalk of grass. He was black and white, with a yellow patch on his head, and kept one bright eye on the girls.

"It's a bobolink." Alice said it almost without moving her lips.

Lydia tried whistling again—and the bird looked at her in disbelief. "You do it."

But before Alice could whistle, the bird was gone.

"I've never seen one so close!" said Alice. "It's you, Lydia! He came to welcome you to Arundel!"

"Do you think so, really?"

"I know so."

Lydia felt solemn all over again, and also determined to be worthy of the bobolink's welcome.

After the excitement with the bobolink, Alice assumed that all the birds in the meadow were delighted to have the girls visit. This caused her to ignore the first few black-capped chickadee calls, thinking they came from actual birds. When eventually she realized that it was her father, she headed home, and Lydia went in the other direction, back toward the carriage house—slowly, unwilling to get there before Batty had completed the spider-removal project. Lingering at the lily pond, Lydia told the frogs about the bobolink, and mentioned that she'd be grateful if they, too, wanted to welcome her to Arundel. None of them took her up on it, and some went so far as to jump into the water in protest of the request. She apologized effusively and waited for them to resurface, but none did, and there was no more excuse for delay.

When she arrived, Batty was releasing several spiders into the wild, and singing "Born Free," an old and sappy song about a lion named Elsa. Lydia danced along, making leaps of freedom, always *away* from the scuttling spiders, until Batty stood up, her containers now empty.

"That was the last of them," she said. "Every spider I could find has been relocated. How was Alice's secret place?"

Lydia leapt back toward Batty, hoping she wasn't inadvertently squishing spiders—they'd already had enough trauma for one day. "Perfect. And, Batty, I was officially welcomed to Arundel by a bobolink! And the meadows are called Bobolink Meadow One and Bobolink Meadow Two, and I saw some frogs at the lily pond."

Batty put down her containers and gave Lydia an inspection, not the full treatment, like if they'd been apart for a month or so—Lydia's height, for example, wouldn't have changed in the last hour.

"You really like it here, Lyds, don't you? Even after Mrs. Tifton said those things about us?"

"Why? We're not leaving, are we? Please say we're not."

"We're not leaving."

"Good, good, good." Lydia spun in circles, one spin for each "good." "I believe it is our destiny to stay."

"I don't know about that, but it turns out I was the only one who wasn't sure we should. I talked to Mom, Dad, and Rosalind, and Jane. Rosalind and Tommy talked to Jeffrey, and Jeffrey talked to Mom and Dad and Skye. Ben fits in there somewhere, but I've lost track. They brought me around by promising I'll never have to see or talk to Mrs. Tifton again. Jeffrey thinks she'll go back to New York soon, but until she does—or until he gets here next week to distract her—I should just stay out of her way. And Jane promised that she and Ben would get here as soon as they can tomorrow, to help protect me. Not that Jane isn't scared of Mrs. Tifton, too—she told me she is—so I'm not sure how much protection she'll be."

"Having been officially welcomed by the bobolink of Arundel," said Lydia, dancing a bit of *Swan Lake*, "I can also help protect you from Mrs. Tifton."

"You're really not afraid of her?"

"I don't like it when she yells, but I don't get scared."

"Lyds, you don't actually like Mrs. Tifton, do you? I know you like everybody—"

"I. Do. Not. Like. Everybody." Maybe she should make *Non omnes amo* her motto after all. "I wish you could remember that, especially since Deborah."

"Sorry, I'll try."

"Thank you."

"And Mom asked me if you're homesick yet. I told her you aren't, so I hope that's true."

"It's true. As long as no Rockettes show up, I'll be fine. Yikes! What's that noise?"

Something or someone in the carriage house was clonking loudly, as if a sink or tub had gone to war with its own metal pipes. And now the sisters heard Feldspar barking, not his weird half bark, but a real one, the kind that meant he had nothing in his mouth. They rushed inside, followed the racket into the bathroom—where there was barely enough room for two people and one emotional dog—and discovered he'd dropped his ax into the bathtub. His barking was meant to convince it to jump back out.

"Quick!" said Batty. "This is our chance to get the ax away from him. Go find something else!"

"Like what?" Lydia was shoved aside as Sonata arrived to find out why Feldspar was so excited.

"Anything!"

Maneuvering herself out of the room, Lydia flew around the apartment in search of the next replacement object. The kitchen cabinets and drawers were empty, and there was nothing lying around the apartment except cleaning supplies—scrub brushes, sponges, a mop, a broom, and four buckets of soapy water. She briefly considered the mop, but that would cause as much trouble as the ax. In desperation, she looked under the couch, and there it was—a lone chair leg abandoned in some distant past, stoically waiting for the rest of its chair to come back.

"Got it!" Lydia rushed into the bathroom and shoved the chair leg right in front of Feldspar's nose, distracting him while Batty grabbed the ax from the bathtub and raced into the kitchen.

"All safe," she called. "It's in the refrigerator now."

Feldspar knew when he'd been bested. He took the chair leg, pretending that doing so was his own idea, and fooling no one.

"That's taken care of, anyway," said Batty.

"What else?" Still buoyed by the bobolink, Lydia thought there was no problem she couldn't easily solve.

"Cleaning, remember?" Batty pointed to the supplies.

Except cleaning. There was no easy solution to dirt. Lydia sighed and picked up a scrub brush.

# CHAPTER EIGHT
## *Too Many Alice Books*

L YDIA SAT UP QUIETLY, careful not to wake Batty or the dogs. The four of them had slept on the floor of the apartment, cuddling in a nest of sleeping bags and couch pillows. It was more comfortable than it looked, not that it mattered much. Lydia and Batty would have slept well anywhere. Hours of cleaning is a good guarantee of a restful night.

She was getting up to see if the eastern towhee she'd heard, calling *Ly-di-AH-AH-AH-AH*, was an actual bird or, as she hoped, Alice. When she got to the window, there, indeed, was her new friend.

"Good morning, Alice," she whispered. "Batty's still asleep."

Alice whispered back. "You're both invited for

breakfast, and Mom said you'd better come right now if you want to see Hatshepsut climbing the stairs."

"I didn't know chickens could."

"So far, only this one can."

While Lydia pulled on her clothes, she contemplated waking up her sister, who would surely want to witness Hatshepsut's display of mountaineering. But Batty was still deeply asleep, and Lydia had learned long ago not to wake up sleeping people, especially when they're not yet full-fledged adults. Now she had to waste precious time looking for a way to leave Batty a note—there was nothing in the apartment—and finally used Batty's own phone to send her a message, then raced out to Alice.

While Lydia had assumed she'd find Hatshepsut climbing the steps to the front porch, the reality was more exciting. The chicken had sneaked into the house and was climbing the stairs to the second floor. When the girls arrived, she was halfway up and determined to go even higher.

"She's probably trying to get to Jack's room. We think he taught her," said Alice. "I'll tell my parents you're here."

"But what should I do?" asked Lydia. "I have no chicken experience."

"Just try to keep Hatshepsut from going farther up."

"Please go no farther," Lydia told Hatshepsut as Alice disappeared into the kitchen.

The chicken threw Lydia a scornful glance and hopped to the next step.

"Wrong way. Please. No, come down, come down."

Defiantly, the chicken hopped yet higher.

"Help!" cried Lydia, and was relieved when Natalie appeared. "She's not listening to me."

"Yes, well, she's a chicken." Natalie plucked the bird off the step. "Come on, old girl. Let's get you back outside."

Lydia followed them into the kitchen, trying to avoid the chicken's scowl—she obviously blamed Lydia for her capture. It was a cheerfully cluttered kitchen, full right now of delectable breakfast smells. Cagney was stirring pancake batter, Alice was rinsing raspberries, and they were in the middle of a discussion about whether or not it was Jack's fault that Hatshepsut kept trying to get upstairs—Alice said yes and her father said no. Having no opinion either way, Lydia looked around and got a surprise bigger even than a climbing chicken—a tapestry hanging on the wall so skillfully and delicately made that Lydia thought it should be in a museum. She moved closer—it showed a meadow much like Bobolink Meadow Two, with a dozen shades of greens and yellows, tiny dots of pink for flowers, and—she stepped closer—a bobolink perched on a long piece of grass!

Alice noticed her looking. "Mom made that."

Lydia pointed at the tapestry. *"That?"*

Lydia was very proud of her own mother, a brilliant astrophysicist, and of her father, too, a brilliant botanist, but neither of them—or any other Penderwick—had the ability to create something people would want to look at.

"Yes. She's an art teacher and also a great artist."

Natalie had come back inside, without Hatshepsut. "She's exaggerating, Lydia."

"She's not exaggerating," said Cagney. "You *are* a great artist."

"Dad met her when they both started teaching," said Alice, "and fell in love with her because of how talented she was, but then he had to beat out the math teacher, the gym teacher, and also Mom's boyfriend from college before he could win her heart."

"Your father made up the part about the gym teacher," said Natalie. "And, anyway, I had to compete with the two English teachers who were nuts about him."

"Not two, Nat, just Brayonna."

"And," continued Alice, "he built her a tapestry loom as a wedding gift. Dad can build anything. He's going to build benches and tables for Rosalind's wedding, not that they'll be as hard to make as a loom. A loom is possibly the most difficult thing to build ever."

"No, it isn't, Alice," said Cagney. "Now you *are* exaggerating."

Alice waved off his protest. "The loom is upstairs, Lydia. I'll show you after breakfast, and I'll show you my room, too. Dad says it's where Batty slept when she was little. Rosalind slept in Jack's room."

"That reminds me, Alice," said her mother. "We got a message from Jack while you were going for Lydia. My phone's over there on the table."

Alice pounced, then read the message out loud. "*'Forgot socks Aunt Carol bought me six pairs having a great great great time.'* Three greats. He's rubbing it in. Look at this picture, Lydia. What a show-off."

Lydia saw a twelve-year-old boy in an ice rink, wearing a Bruins jersey and flourishing a hockey stick. Lydia liked his face—like a young version of his dad's, friendly and used to smiling. But she thought it best not to praise Jack to Alice, and, indeed, Alice was once again downcast, but not as much as the day before, and pancakes topped with raspberries and syrup did an excellent job of perking her up. As did the photo of the girls eating pancakes that she asked her mother to take.

"Thanks, Mom. Please send it to Jack—he loves pancakes," said Alice. "Nyah, nyah, big brother."

Lydia had heard a lot about this room on the third floor, under the cottage eaves. Fifteen years ago, it had been Jane's bedroom, where she wrote one of her best books about Sabrina Starr, the hero of Jane's youthful writings. Now it was Natalie's studio, and nothing like Lydia could ever have imagined. Color was everywhere, in great skeins of wool hanging from hooks, large spools of thread lined up on shelves, piles of bright fabric, and a half-finished tapestry—this one had sheep and was just as lovely as the one downstairs—on the big upright loom. On other shelves were rows of stuffed dolls and animals made of felt, each with its own expressive little face and wearing clothes with itsy-bitsy pockets and buttons smaller than that. The dolls were children of many races, and the animals of many species—an elephant, a fox, a donkey, a pig, a dog, and a chicken. Lydia peered closely—the chicken was wearing a black mask with pointy ears and a black cape. The chicken Alice had named Batgirl!

In one corner was a sewing machine with two more stuffed animals sitting nearby—a baby sloth in a shirt that still needed buttons, and a giraffe in a tutu and one ballet slipper, waiting for the other.

"I told you Mom's a great artist," said Alice. "Come over here—this is her leftovers box. We're allowed to take whatever we want."

The box held scraps of Natalie's raw materials, the hues and textures jumbled together, turning it into a treasure chest. Lydia couldn't believe that such riches were up for grabs, but with Alice's encouragement, she picked out the bits that spoke to her—thin yarn, thick yarn, scraps of silks, even a hank of dyed sheep wool. She didn't know what she wanted to do with any of it, she just wanted it nearby, teeming with possibilities. When both girls had as much as they could carry, they went back down to the second floor, to Alice's room.

Batty's old room now had bunk beds, and a blue dresser with one of Natalie's dolls on top. She wore tiny overalls with ALICE stitched across the bib and showed signs of having been well loved—the hair had definitely been sewn back here and there. Next to the doll was a trophy, a statue of a girl kicking her leg sideways, with the inscription TAE KWON DO ALICE PELLETIER MOST IMPROVED. There was also a bookshelf, where Lydia was glad to see her favorite book—Lewis Carroll's *Alice's Adventures in Wonderland and Through the Looking-Glass*. Back when she was too young to read on her own, her mother and father had teamed up to read this to her, splitting the characters between them, using special voices for each one. Her mother's Red Queen and her father's March Hare were, in Lydia's opinion, of professional quality.

But now Lydia looked farther along the shelf and saw that all the books there had been written by Lewis Carroll. They were of many different sizes, and with many different illustrators, and even in a few languages other than English—she recognized Spanish and German—but every single one was either *Alice's Adventures in Wonderland* or *Through the Looking-Glass*.

"Isn't that annoying?" asked Alice. "My relatives keep giving me copies, except for the relatives who send me the Disney movie. It's like a curse, being named Alice. I'd rather be named, I don't know,

Margarita or Anastasia. Serafina! Wouldn't it be fun to be named Serafina?"

"No one would know how to spell it." Lydia knew this because she herself wasn't sure whether that second syllable was an *e* or an *a*. It could even be an *i*.

"Look!" Alice flung open the door to her closet. "More Alice stuff."

On the floor was a large cardboard box full of more iterations of Alice's adventures—plus several Alice coloring books and paper-doll sets that looked like they'd never been touched. But what was more interesting to Lydia was the back wall of the closet, a puzzling mishmash of scraps of thick cardboard taped together—several layers, it seemed, judging by the bulges and overlaps. Words had been scrawled here and there—*Jack is a creep*, for example, and *I don't want to be in your dumb room anyway*—and rough drawings of female warriors, including Batgirl. There were also several holes that had been repatched and refilled from the back. Lydia could see the formerly sticky side of the tape, now covered with dust and lint.

"Jack made that wall," said Alice. "When we were little, we went back and forth into each other's rooms through the closet, but he started closing it up a few years ago. I bet your brother wouldn't do that to you."

"Ben guards his room like it's Fort Knox." Lydia looked down into the box of Alice stuff. "You told me Jack's always telling Blossom stories about people named Jack, right? Let's read the Alice books to her. They are truly excellent, you know."

"But I'm sick of them."

Lydia was certain that her idea was a great one, and Alice was just as certain that it wasn't. This was the girls' first argument, and it was a good sign for the future that they didn't argue for long and even came up with a compromise. Alice agreed to read a book about an Alice to Blossom, but it had to be a different Alice than the Lewis Carroll one who fell down rabbit holes and climbed into mirrors.

The girls searched through Alice's parents' books for possibilities, and soon were on their way to Blossom with two books, one about a real Alice who'd actually lived, and one written by an Alice, another real person. The girls also had some of their pockets full of oats, to help keep the sheep's attention on the books. Plus, a last-minute inspiration had them shoving Natalie's yarn scraps into any pockets that weren't full of oats.

Blossom came to them more quickly today. She'd remembered Lydia and her high-quality petting. She had not, however, been expecting the yarn, and backed away when Alice tried to tie a blue bow around her neck.

"You would look quite stylish," Lydia told Blossom.

"The other sheep will be jealous," added Alice.

Knowing that the other sheep would not only

*not* be jealous but that they'd also tease her, Blossom backed away farther and was considering leaving altogether.

"Don't go!" cried Lydia. "We're sorry, and we have books."

The promise of books had no effect, but when Alice took oats out of her pocket, Blossom reluctantly returned. Lydia decided that if any reading was going to be done, it had to happen immediately, while Blossom was still focused on Alice's oats. She opened one of the books.

"This book is called *Alice: Alice Roosevelt Longworth, from White House Princess to Washington Power Broker*, and it really happened. Here's how it starts: "'For nearly all of her ninety-six years—'"

"She's paying no attention, and I'm already out of oats," said Alice. "Give me your oats and try the other book."

Passing the oats to Alice was tricky, as Blossom was eager to eat them during the transfer, and did manage to get hold of some. Now time was really of the essence. Lydia quickly opened the second book.

"This book was written by a woman named Alice. It's called *The Moons of Jupiter*, and I hope it's not about science, because Blossom won't understand it." Lydia glanced anxiously at Blossom, who'd already eaten most of the oats. "'Cousin Iris from Philadelphia. She was a nurse. Cousin Isabel from—'"

"I'm out of oats again," said Alice. "And that book didn't sound very exciting."

Lydia stopped herself from saying that the Alice books she'd wanted to bring were extremely exciting, with a near-drowning in a pool of tears, not to mention a queen who cut off people's heads. It was too late for recriminations, and Blossom was already leaving, pleased to have escaped the blue yarn neck bow. She'd gotten only halfway back to her friends when she was startled by a sound she'd never heard before—a loud, sickly moan coming from the other side of the estate. Blossom broke into a trot—racing now for her life.

Alice had never heard that sound before, either. "Do you think that could be a ghost?"

"No ghost," said Lydia. "Just our old van. Jane and Ben are here."

# CHAPTER NINE
## The Next Wave

As THE GIRLS RAN to meet the new arrivals, Lydia warned Alice about Ben's bossiness. She should have done it earlier—running and explaining don't go well together—and maybe she wasn't clear enough, because Alice refused to believe that Ben could be as bossy as Jack. Even a description of Ben's despotic filmmaking methods didn't discourage Alice. She was intrigued that Ben made films at all, as Jack had never attempted anything so creative. Lydia would have to attack the problem from Ben's side. She didn't want him ordering around her new friend.

Batty and the dogs were already beside the driveway when Lydia and Alice arrived, everyone enthusiastically waving arms and wagging tails as their van—dubbed "Flashvan" years ago—appeared, yawing from one side of the drive to the other. Either Jane was asleep at the wheel or Ben was driving. He was still in the learning phase, and too stubborn to let anyone tell him what to do, especially one of his sisters.

When the van stopped with a lurch and a nasty squeal of brakes, Jane tumbled out of the passenger door and onto the grass, looking green. So it had been Ben driving.

"I didn't think I could get carsick that quickly," said Jane. "He's only been driving since the pillars."

"Second gear kept sticking," said Ben.

"That wasn't second gear. That was you." Jane did her best to fend off the dogs, who were delighted to have her stretched out on the ground, making it much easier to search for spilled food. When they realized that she was clean, they tried to lick her face instead, which would have been okay if Feldspar had dropped his chair leg first. "Ouch, Feldspar, knock it off, you big galoot. Hello, you must be Alice."

Alice leaned down to shake Jane's hand. "Mom can't wait to meet you, and Dad said that he remembers you as being excitable."

"I'm still excitable," said Jane, "except when I'm carsick. I can't believe how bad a driver Ben is. I was never that bad."

"Yes, you were," said Batty.

"You really were," said Ben. He was ready to argue

this point indefinitely, but Lydia put a stop to that by leaning into the van and whispering to him.

"Alice is my friend, so don't boss her around or do anything to make her unhappy."

"Like what?"

"Like, for example, when you said my hair's like a trash-can fire, and when I got mad, you pretended it was a compliment."

"It *was* a compliment."

"Just be careful, please." Lydia pulled Alice over. "This is Ben. I told you about him."

"Hello," said Alice.

"What did Lydia tell you?" asked Ben.

"That you keep her out of your room just like my brother does with me."

"That's true. Did she say anything positive about me? Like that I'm smart and kind and overwhelmingly good-looking? But you can see all that for yourself. Right, Alice?"

Alice tipped her head to one side, studying him. "Not particularly. But you sound interesting."

Ben decided to accept this markdown in quality, but only if he could elevate it just a bit.

"Let's say that I'm *very* interesting," he said.

Jane was now testing her ability to stand up. "Good—wooziness dispelled, no thanks to Ben's driving. Lyds, Iantha wants me to make sure you're not homesick."

"Do you get homesick?" Alice asked Lydia.

"No, I don't. Jane, please tell Mom I'm happy. Good grief."

"And no more Mrs. Tifton sightings? Batty?"

"Not so far. Perimeters are secure. I mean, I think they are. She could have slipped in without us noticing."

"We could set up lookouts," said Alice. "That would be fun."

"Trip wires," said Ben.

"No! No lookouts or trip wires," said Jane. "Rosalind told me specifically that we should act normally."

The other three Penderwicks gawked. Even Feldspar reacted, dropping his chair leg onto Jane's foot.

"Not sure what Rosy means by that," said Ben.

Jane wasn't sure, either. "I think she means that we shouldn't *try* to make Mrs. Tifton angry."

"You don't really have to try much," said Alice. "She does it on her own."

"Okay, well, we'll do our best." Jane, already in need of rest from being in charge, leaned against Flashvan. "Now, here's the plan. I'm taking over the carriage house apartment and turning it into my dressmaking center. The rest of you will sleep in the mansion, starting tonight."

"No," said Lydia.

Three Penderwicks were gawking again, this time at Lydia. It was rare for her to utter a plain and unequivocal no.

"Why?" asked Jane.

"Ghosts," said Alice. "That's why."

"Are there ghosts in the mansion?" asked Ben. Lydia could tell he was already getting an idea for a film.

"Of course not," said Batty. "Ghosts aren't real. Lydia knows that."

"But you didn't want to sleep there, either, Batty," said Lydia.

"That was because of Mrs. Tifton, not ghosts!"

"Enough," said Jane. "According to Jeffrey, Mrs. Tifton will not be haunting the mansion from now on, and if there are ghosts, there will be three of you against them, plus the dogs, which should be enough. I'm taking the carriage house. Rosalind said I could, and I am."

Lydia preferred Batty's certainty that there were no ghosts to Jane's belief that three not-even-adult Penderwicks could defeat the ones they ran into, but she submitted. As soon as night fell, though, she'd refuse to be alone in the mansion, not even for a second.

Jane continued with orders. "Batty and Ben, take Flashvan to the apartment and start unloading. Lydia, there's a large cooler with food that needs to go into the mansion refrigerator—please do that now. There are no ghosts during the day, I suppose?"

"No," said Alice. "They walk at night."

Ben grinned, Lydia winced, and Jane decided to ignore the part about walking at night.

"Alice," she said, "if your parents are home, I'd like to go say hello. I think I remember the way—is Jeffrey's hedge tunnel still here?"

"It's Alice's now," said Lydia.

"Forgive me, Alice, of course it is," said Jane. "Do you mind if I use your tunnel?"

Alice was willing to let Jane use her tunnel but not, it seemed, without supervision. The two of them went off together, leaving the three youngest Penderwicks behind.

"Where are these ghosts supposed to be?" Ben asked Lydia.

"Alice said in the cellar."

"But, Lyds, honey," said Batty. "Alice also said that those are ghosts of the husbands Mrs. Tifton murdered! And you know that's not true."

Lydia saw the logic in this, and thought it would be a relief to shake this ghost nonsense, and she would try, she really would. She might even make "There are no ghosts" her motto. She just wished she didn't have to sleep in the mansion.

After wrestling the heavy cooler into the mansion, Lydia felt she deserved a break before transferring the food into the refrigerators. But it occurred to her that if any spiders had escaped yesterday's purge, they might want revenge for the removal of their friends— *they* didn't know Batty had done it for their own good.

There could be squadrons of diminutive paratroopers preparing to attack her from above.

She found another apron to tie over her head, did what she had to do with the food, and escaped. Once again outside, and blessedly free of spiders (or ghosts, but she shoved that thought into the back of her mind), Lydia celebrated with a tango, gliding down the path, the apron now a matador's cape used to both lure and repel her imaginary partner.

"Dance with me, señor! ¡Olé, olé! No spiders in my hair, and we're staying at Arundel! ¡Olé, olé— whoops!" No tango had ever come to so abrupt a halt. Hadn't Jeffrey said his mother wouldn't be haunting the mansion anymore? Nevertheless, there at the end of the path, standing beside the terrace steps, was Mrs. Tifton.

"Good morning, Mrs. Tifton. I was just dancing."

"Hmm." Mrs. Tifton didn't seem certain that Lydia's tango could be called dancing. But she also didn't seem to be furious at the moment—a great improvement over the day before. "Linda, right?"

"Lydia, actually." Lydia bundled the apron under her arm—now was the second time she'd been caught red-handed with Arundel property. "We're still here."

"Yes. I was out-voted." There it was—a hint of the pickle face. "According to Jeffrey, you'll be here for a long time."

"Just until the wedding—a week from Saturday."

Lydia thought that hardly any time at all for experiencing a paradise like Arundel.

"That's a long time to stay in another person's house." Mrs. Tifton inspected the steps to find the cleanest spot, then sat down.

If Mrs. Tifton meant what Lydia thought she meant, Jeffrey had been right about her going back to New York soon. Lydia decided to check: "So you must be going back to New York City soon."

"Why do you say that?"

"Because you won't want to stay at Mrs. Robinette's house for a long—"

"That's different. Mimi's one of my best friends." Mrs. Tifton shuffled through her bag and pulled out a phone. "Who, by the way, has been looking for a new shade of red to try, and my description of yours didn't give her enough to go on, so now she wants a picture. Sit down next to me and turn your head—I'll photograph the back."

· Lydia obediently sat and turned the back of her head to Mrs. Tifton, trying to remember if she'd brushed her hair that morning. "To try for what?"

"Her own hair. What else?" Mrs. Tifton put away the phone. "Thank you. I'm done. When is the rest of your family arriving?"

"Jane and Ben just got here. Rosalind and Skye are coming next week, and Mom and Dad, the day before the wedding."

"Rosalind is the one getting married?"

"Yes. She's the oldest."

"Batty, the spider-obsessed one, is the youngest of the original four—I remember her and her dog. That makes Jane and Skye the middle ones. Are they attached?"

"Attached?"

"To a man."

Now Mrs. Tifton was staring intently at Lydia—apparently, this was an important question, maybe even the reason Mrs. Tifton had shown up. Lydia didn't know why it would be, and she also wasn't sure what it meant to be attached to a man. Skye and Dušek had been together for three years, but Lydia could imagine what Skye would say if anyone described them as attached. *Attached by what, exactly? Cement? Chains?* Lydia stuck with what she could state with certainty.

"Skye says that marriage is an outmoded social construct." Hoping Mrs. Tifton wouldn't ask what that meant, Lydia rushed on. "And Jane has no intention of getting married for a long time, not until she's published her first book, or maybe never. She says artists need to be selfish, and for a woman, that might mean not getting married or having children. Male artists, she says, have always had permission to be selfish, but thank goodness things are changing as the patriarchy is gradually breaking down."

Mrs. Tifton raised her eyebrows at the part about

the patriarchy breaking down—and seemed ready to argue—but Lydia was rescued by the cry of an eastern towhee.

"Alice is looking for me," she told Mrs. Tifton. "Any chance you can whistle like a black-capped chickadee?"

"Excuse me?"

"Never mind." Lydia cupped her hands like a megaphone and shouted, "*Alice, over here on the steps!*"

A moment later, Alice trotted into view. She faltered when she saw who was sitting beside Lydia but quickly recovered, pulling a phone out of her pocket.

"Hello, Mrs. Tifton." She handed the phone to Lydia. "Mom let me borrow this but only for taking pictures, and if I break it, I'm grounded for the rest of my life. Take a picture of me with Mrs. Tifton."

"Whatever for?" Mrs. Tifton asked.

"To send to Jack." Alice squished herself in between Lydia and Mrs. Tifton, forcing Mrs. Tifton to scooch over. "Make it good, Lydia. Jack replied to our pancake picture with one of him and Marcel eating waffles."

While Mrs. Tifton mulled that over, trying to decide if she was being compared to waffles, Lydia stood up to take the photograph. When she showed it to the subjects, Alice declared it just right, but Mrs. Tifton was disturbed by the wrinkles on her neck.

"We could take another, if you want," said Lydia,

though she didn't know how to take a photo without showing Mrs. Tifton's neck wrinkles.

"No, never mind." Mrs. Tifton shifted over to put a little more space between her and Alice. "By the way, do you know if my ex-husband is invited to your sister's wedding?"

After hearing Alice's theory of murdered ex-husbands haunting the basement, Lydia was confused about which, if any, were still alive enough to attend Rosalind's wedding.

Alice was also perplexed. "Which ex-husband?"

"For goodness' sake, Alice, the only one the Penderwicks know well enough to invite to a wedding."

This still didn't give Lydia enough information. Her sisters had gotten to know the awful Dexter Dupree pretty well. But Mrs. Tifton couldn't possibly imagine they'd invite—

"You must mean Jeffrey's dad," said Alice. "Alec."

Alec! Of course. Lydia had known him her entire life. He was part of the Penderwicks' extended clan, not just because he was Jeffrey's father, but because he'd been Uncle Turron's friend long before Uncle Turron married Aunt Claire. With all this shared history, it was hard to remember that Alec had been the very first of Mrs. Tifton's ex-husbands. He seemed an unlikely match for her, being warm, funny, and kind, and also a professional musician. Jeffrey got his talent from that side of the family.

"Yes, I mean Alec," said Mrs. Tifton with a hint of pickle. "Is he invited?"

"Yes," said Lydia. "He's going to help Jeffrey with the music for the wedding. They're putting together a band, with—"

"When is he arriving?"

"Probably next week, I think," said Lydia. "Jeffrey will know better. You can ask him."

"Jeffrey and I don't discuss his father." Mrs. Tifton stood, brushing off nonexistent dirt. "Lydia, I'd like to speak with your sister Jane. Where can I find her to-morrow morning?"

Lydia's mouth dropped open. Ben always made fun of her when this happened, calling her a goldfish, but sometimes when she was startled, she just couldn't help it. She and Mrs. Tifton had, she thought, been getting along well. Why now the desire to meet with Jane? Lydia would bank her life on Jane not wanting to meet with Mrs. Tifton.

"Jane's awfully busy, Mrs. Tifton. I can ask her any-thing you want to know, like about Alec or anything."

"There's more to it than Alec."

"Together, Alice and I can remember a long mes-sage. Can't we, Alice?"

Alice nodded. "When I was five, I knew all the words to *Unicorn Thinks He's Pretty Great,* possibly the funniest book in the world, and I still remember them. I can act out the pictures, too."

"And I know by heart the lyrics to *Into the Woods*, *A Little Night Music, Les Mis*—"

"I don't care what either of you know by heart." Mrs. Tifton's face was moving into full-fledged pickle territory. "I need to talk with Jane. Where can I find her tomorrow morning?"

There was no sense in continuing to stall. Mrs. Tifton was making that clear.

"She's staying at the carriage house," answered Lydia.

"I'll be there tomorrow at ten. Tell Jane."

As the girls watched her go, Lydia couldn't help remembering she'd promised to protect Batty from Mrs. Tifton. At least she hadn't promised Jane the same thing.

"What do you think she wants to talk to Jane about?" she asked Alice.

"Probably, mostly Alec. Dad thinks Alec is her least favorite ex-husband," said Alice, "but Mom thinks that deep down he's her most favorite, that she forces herself to hate him because of how awful she was to him over Jeffrey."

Mrs. Tifton had not only let her own father separate her from Alec before Jeffrey was born, she'd never told Alec that he had a son afterward, or told Jeffrey anything about his father. Jeffrey had ended up finding Alec himself, one summer in Maine, with help from Skye and Jane, years and years ago. This, by the way, had done nothing to diminish Mrs. Tifton's dislike of the Penderwicks.

"Do you think she minds him coming here? Alec, I mean." Lydia was trying to understand the touch of sympathy she felt for Mrs. Tifton. "I might be upset if I were her."

"But if you were her, you wouldn't have been awful to Alec, and none of this would be happening." Alice looked again at the photo of her with Mrs. Tifton. "I don't know if this is exciting enough for Jack, with Mrs. Tifton almost normal. We should have taken another at the end, when she was pickled. Should we try again, the next time she's angry?"

Lydia had no desire to take more photos of Mrs. Tifton. "Send this one—Jack will be impressed."

"Photo, fly up to Canada to impress Jack," said Alice, and sent it.

"I guess we should tell Jane about Mrs. Tifton and tomorrow." Lydia wasn't looking forward to that discussion. "But maybe we don't need to hurry."

"Let's take a detour," said Alice. "I'll show you the greenhouse."

# CHAPTER TEN
## The Rock and the Red Shoe

To AVOID BEING SPOTTED by other Penderwicks, Alice and Lydia took a circuitous route to the greenhouse. They started out by traversing Bobolink Meadow One, where Lydia wondered if Alice was making their trip longer than necessary—some of the mown paths they followed went in obviously wrong directions. But, as in Bobolink Meadow Two, the sights, smells, and sounds were too delicious for Lydia to care how long they stayed.

At the edge of the meadow was a narrow thicket that marked the border of Arundel. Silent and invisible—they hoped—the girls darted through its shrubs and trees until they were directly behind the greenhouse. This last stage of their expedition would put them at their most vulnerable. There was no cover, and, at least at the beginning, anyone looking out a back window of the carriage house would see them. But they made it. A quick dash—crouching to make themselves smaller targets—and they were safely inside the greenhouse, quite pleased with themselves.

It was like being in a large garage, if the garage had been built of frosted glass and, instead of space for cars, there were rows of tables, with pebble paths running between them. The tables were now empty, but Lydia could imagine the welter of color that had once dwelled there. Storage shelves still held stacks of clay pots and tools that no one had picked up for several years. It occurred to Lydia that this would be a great home for spiders, but she decided not to ruin her experience by looking for them.

"Dad used to take care of exotic plants for Mrs. Tifton in here," said Alice. "But since she left, we don't do anything fancy, and nobody comes here. Except me and Jack sometimes."

"I'd like to be a plant living in here," said Lydia, and danced as if she were one—feet together and rooted, body waving gently, face tipped up to the light.

Alice found a few dead vines in a corner and draped them over Lydia to make her more plantlike, then added the yarn that Blossom had rejected, tying it around Lydia's right ear, which tickled.

"Now you're a plant, and *I* want to be something,"

115

said Alice. She wandered through the greenhouse until she found a pile of empty burlap bags, then put one over her head. "What do I look like?"

She looked like a burlap bag with two legs. "A gigantic seed, maybe. Or a rock."

"I'll be a rock." Alice hunkered down, tucking her legs into the bag, until she was a big blob of burlap. "A rolling rock."

She rolled down the aisle, bumping into tables and grumbling about life as a rock. "This is fun. Take my picture."

But since Lydia was a rooted plant, the rolling rock had to come to her, and then there was the problem of getting the phone out of the rock's pocket. The plant was almost knocked over, and the rock got tangled up in itself. This was an unfortunate moment for Ben to show up.

"Should I even try to guess?" he asked.

"I'm a plant." Lydia wanted to convey that any idiot would know she was a plant. "And Alice—"

Alice was now beeping, setting off a newly frantic attempt to untangle herself. Lydia forgot about her roots to tear at the burlap, but Ben simply picked up Alice by her feet and dangled her upside down until the bag fell off. The phone also started to slip out of Alice's pocket, but Lydia caught it in time and handed it to Alice.

"Thank you." Still upside down, Alice looked at the phone. "It's Jack already."

116

When Alice was right-side up again, Lydia and Ben crowded around to see the new photo. In it, Jack looked nervous, as well he should have. Standing beside him was a man who was possibly dangerous, and definitely peculiar. His shirt was inside out, his eyes were shifty, and he was chewing on a cigar.

"That's my brother, on the right," Alice told Ben.

"Who's the creepy guy?" asked Ben.

"My uncle," said Alice.

"I'm sorry." Lydia didn't think him a nice uncle to have.

"Oh, he's not like that usually. He's just goofing for the picture." Alice eyed Ben speculatively. "Do you ever wear costumes?"

"He and his friend Rafael dress up as characters from movies every Halloween." Lydia was bragging in spite of herself. "One year they were Michael and Fredo Corleone—"

"'I know it was you, Fredo,'" said Ben. "'You broke my heart.'"

"—and last year they were the boat from *Jaws*."

"How were you a boat?" asked Alice.

"We painted a big cardboard box," said Ben, "and hacked off a big hunk to make it look like a shark had bitten it."

"You actually *are* very interesting." She took a clay pot from a shelf and handed to it him. "Put this on your head and I'll take a picture."

But Ben had a better idea. He tapped the pot

against the edge of a table until it broke neatly in two. "I can pretend I've just broken it apart with my bare hands."

"Brilliant," breathed Alice. "Like a superhero."

"Not really," said Lydia, but she photographed Ben with his face contorted with superhero strength and the pot just coming apart in his hands. Alice was in the photo, too, gazing at Ben with admiration.

"I'll send it to Jack," she said. "I'll write a message, too. *'This is Ben Penderwick, a better brother than you, and also very interesting. Love, Alice.'* Thank you, Ben. Jack will be devastated that you're here."

"Glad to be of help," said Ben. "And now, to my mission. I'm supposed to deliver you both to the carriage house."

"Why?" asked Lydia. "And how did you know we were here, anyway?"

"I knew you were here because I was looking out the window when you burst out of the thicket—you looked pretty funny, by the way—"

"No, we didn't." Lydia knew they'd looked like professional spies.

"—and why, is because Jane and Batty are fixing lunch."

Although Lydia was getting hungry, she didn't know if lunch was a good enough reason to stop stalling on sharing the Mrs. Tifton news. She'd leave the decision to Alice.

"Are you hungry?" Lydia asked her.

"Starving."

Lydia sighed. Time to face the furor.

"That's not funny, Lyds," said Jane.

"Not even a little bit," added Batty.

"I'm not trying to be funny. It's true."

"It is true, really, Jane. I was there," said Alice. "Mrs. Tifton is coming here tomorrow at ten to talk to you."

Jane put down her sandwich, her appetite gone. "Why?"

"She wants to ask you when Alec is coming to the wedding," said Lydia.

"That makes sense," said Ben. "He *is* her ex-husband."

"One of six," said Batty. "And don't defend her. You have no idea."

"I think she has other things to say, too." Alice did the pickle face, and quoted Mrs. Tifton. " 'There's more to it than Alec.' "

"Is that what she looks and talks like?" asked Ben.

Lydia nodded. "Exactly. Unfortunately."

"This wasn't supposed to happen," said Jane. "I just want to finish the wedding dresses and work on my book. I even had a new idea on the drive here, about the art forger and Degas. But I can't be creative while worrying about Mrs. Tifton."

"It'll probably only be a short meeting," said Alice. "Mom says Mrs. Tifton won't talk long to people she doesn't like, and Dad says my mom should do something to make Mrs. Tifton not like her."

"I'm sorry, Jane," said Lydia. "We tried to get her to give us the message. We offered to memorize it, but she refused."

Jane had stopped listening and was staring at the mess around her. The sleeping bags from the night before were still in the middle of the floor, the dogs had taken over the couch, lunch fixings cluttered the kitchen counter, and an entire van's worth of boxes and luggage was spread everywhere else.

"I can't let Mrs. Tifton see it like this."

"We'll help you straighten up," said Batty.

"And clean," added Jane.

"We cleaned it yesterday," said Lydia.

"It needs to be sparkling clean, I mean. There should be nothing here for Mrs. Tifton to criticize."

"That's impossible," said Alice. "She's like a complaining machine."

"Nevertheless," said Jane.

They were at it for the rest of the day. Lydia stuck with scrubbing—she'd done it once, she could do it again—with Alice as an enthusiastic partner. Ben helped Cagney track down and transport spare furniture that Jane could use, much of it from the cottage basement. Batty supervised the unpacking and organizing. Jane went from one task to another, or sometimes managed two at once, provided food and drink for anyone who lagged, continually thanked everybody, and here and there managed to stop fretting over Mrs. Tifton.

When, finally, the apartment was as clean as it could be, Jane was more grateful than Lydia had ever seen her, more even than when she'd gotten a hundred-dollar tip for a cup of coffee at the restaurant. Lydia was also grateful, in a way. As little as she'd enjoyed the scrubbing, for the second night in a row she'd be exhausted enough to sleep well. And that would be extra helpful and important tonight. Tonight she'd be sleeping in the mansion, with its possible ghosts.

"Just one more song, Batty, please."

"I can't think of any more songs about courage. You're going to have to go to sleep on what I've sung so far."

Batty had been singing songs about being brave, and Lydia had performed dances of valor to each, but she still didn't feel strong enough to get into bed and let Batty turn out the light. Even knowing Batty and the dogs would be right there—they were sharing a room—wasn't quite enough.

"There's that song in *Sweeney Todd*, about prowling demons," she said. "It's kind of about courage."

"'Not While I'm Around'? All right, but just this one."

Batty loved this song and could often be convinced

121

to sing it several times in a row, and dancing to it was a dream—going back and forth between slow movements and quick ones as the mood switched. Lydia had chosen wisely.

"I'm ready," she said, and took her position. "What, Feldspar?"

Feldspar was banging his chair leg on the room's door.

"Is Ben out there?" Batty asked him.

In a show of independence, Ben had chosen a bedroom far away from his sisters. Maybe he'd come for company. But when Lydia shoved Feldspar aside to open the door, Ben didn't come in—Feldspar went out, and disappeared down the dark hall.

"Feldspar, no!" shouted Batty. "Lydia, you grab Sonata, and I'll go after him!"

Grabbing Sonata wasn't difficult, since she was sleeping through the excitement. But remaining there in the room without getting nervous and maybe shrieking took some effort. Lydia was now alone at night in the mansion, exactly what she hadn't wanted to be. And for how long? Long enough to imagine horrors— that Feldspar had made it to the cellar and Batty and Lydia would have to go down there after him, that he'd made it to the empty attic, which would be just as scary as the cellar, that he'd come upon a ghost and attacked it with his chair leg—

Phew. Here came Batty, dragging Feldspar back

122

into the room. He showed no remorse. On the contrary, he was bursting with pride, for he'd run down a new and most horrifying prey and was thrilled to be bringing it back to his den.

"Where did he get that shoe?" asked Lydia.

"I don't know," said Batty grimly. "By the time I found him, he already had it."

Feldspar begrudgingly let them take a look, making it clear that he was going to keep the shoe. He liked it more than the chair leg, the lost feather duster, and the ax, possibly more even than his all-time favorite score from a year ago, Mr. Penderwick's eyeglass case, which thank goodness had been empty when Feldspar swiped it.

The shoe was red leather, with a high heel—higher than Lydia could imagine walking on—thin crisscrossing straps, and, on the toe, a delicate flower crafted from black leather.

"It's got to be Mrs. Tifton's," said Batty. "I can't believe it. Feldspar stole one of Mrs. Tifton's shoes."

"Though probably not right off her," said Lydia.

"I know *that*."

"And look, the heel is broken."

Feldspar let Batty confirm this by wiggling the heel back and forth.

"Did you do this, Feldspar?" she asked.

His look of outrage was convincing. And, anyway, the sisters couldn't work out how a dog could break a heel without leaving teeth marks on it. Their conclusion: Mrs. Tifton had discarded the ruined shoe and left it behind when she moved to New York City.

"So he can keep it, though now we'll have to be extra careful to keep the dogs away from Mrs. Tifton." Batty shivered at the vision of Mrs. Tifton spotting Feldspar with her red shoe in his mouth. "Okay, Lydia, no more excuses, no more songs. Feldspar took the last of my energy, and we're going to sleep."

Being in bed with the lights out wasn't as awful as Lydia had feared. Moonlight filtered in through the windows, and she could hear crickets and, farther away, the deep chorus of the lily pond frogs. This is a nice way to fall asleep, she thought, and maybe I'm almost asleep . . . was that an owl hooting? . . . sounded just like Alice . . . looking for Jack—

Lydia sat up, wide awake again. No owl. Batty's phone was dinging.

"Sorry, I should have turned it off," said Batty, staring at its screen. "I wish I had. Wesley just broke the no-contact rule with a picture."

The only photographs Wesley ever sent were of his dog or his art, but mostly of his dog.

"If it's Hitch, may I see?" asked Lydia.

"Don't you think seeing him will only make you miss him more?"

"I don't care." She put out her hand for the phone. There he was, giant, wonderful Great Dane Hitch.

His face, all nose and eyes, filled the screen. What little background showed around him was blurry, giving no hint of where the picture had been taken. He could have been inside or outside, in Massachusetts or Indiana. It was impossible to tell.

"He isn't wearing his crash helmet in the photo." Hitch and Wesley traveled by motorcycle, with Wesley on the bike and Hitch riding along in his own private sidecar. "Maybe they haven't left Boston yet."

"It's possible," said Batty. "Wesley didn't tell me when they were leaving—and I didn't want to know."

Lydia put the phone closer to her face, hunting for clues. "Hitch looks happy, anyway."

"He always does when he's with Wesley."

"That means it's Hitch's destiny to stay with Wesley wherever he goes." She reluctantly handed back the phone. Batty had been right. Seeing the photo had reawakened the ache of missing Hitch, the regret of not having said good-bye. "And I guess it was my destiny to love, then lose, Hitch."

"And mine." Batty settled back down on her pillow. "Good night, Lyds."

"Good night." But Lydia had another thought. "Do you think Mrs. Tifton is part of our destiny?"

"I think I should never have mentioned destiny to you."

"Or we're part of hers. Unless that's the same thing."

"Lydia!"

"Yes?"

"If you don't stop talking about Mrs. Tifton and destiny, I'm going to find another bedroom and make you sleep by yourself."

"Good night, Batty."

"Good *night*, Lyds."

# CHAPTER ELEVEN
## *Pins and Threats*

THE NEXT MORNING, THE Penderwicks and Alice gathered at the carriage house for one last discussion before Mrs. Tifton's visit. At Jane's insistence, everyone remained outside, temporarily banned from the apartment. She'd stayed up half the night arranging furniture, making sure the place was a hundred percent free from dirt and clutter, and wanted it to stay that way until Mrs. Tifton had come and gone.

First they had to decide where to hide Batty, Sonata, and the bearer of the red shoe, Feldspar. Lydia suggested the greenhouse, Ben and Alice agreed—it was too full of dirt to attract Mrs. Tifton—and that was settled.

Next up was whether or not Jane should be alone

for this portentous meeting. Alice wanted to stay as a representative of the Pelletiers, and Lydia figured that if Alice stayed, she should, too, although Batty and the dogs in the greenhouse would be more fun. Ben wanted to stay because he was curious about a woman who could frighten his older sisters. But Jane said she wanted just Lydia, please. A crowd for backup could indicate weakness on her part, and according to Jeffrey, his mother considered Lydia to be less difficult than the usual Penderwick.

Lydia protested. "I'm just as difficult as the rest of them, aren't I, Alice?"

"Absolutely," said Alice.

"We know you are," said Jane, "but if Mrs. Tifton likes you, great—we can use that."

"Likes me!" objected Lydia. "She didn't even know my name. She called me Linda."

"She used to call me Bitty." Batty shuddered. "I just remembered that and wish I hadn't."

"Try to forget again," said Jane. "Ben and Alice, I want you to be lookouts for Batty, please. Make certain Mrs. Tifton goes nowhere near the greenhouse. If she does, you'll have to distract her somehow."

"How about it, Alice?" said Ben. "Should we throw ourselves in her path and pretend to be mortally wounded?"

Alice fell to the ground, writhing in pain, then abruptly became quite dead. "Like that?"

"Outstanding. Why can't you die that well, Lydia?"

"I'm sure Lydia is good at dying," said Alice.

"No, Ben's right. I'm terrible at dying."

Jane clapped her hands for attention. "We need to take this seriously, folks. Mrs. Tifton is due in fifteen minutes, and Lydia and I have to be prepared. Everyone else, go away. Lydia, take off your shoes. No tracking dirt into the apartment. We'll work on your bridesmaid dress while we wait."

Lydia took off her shoes, and also checked the bottom of her feet—earlier she and Alice had dangled their feet in the lily pond. She wouldn't want to track bits of lily pad into the apartment Jane had worked so hard to whip into shape.

The place truly had been transformed.

"I didn't know you could be so tidy," she told Jane.

"Neither did I." Jane pushed a chair an inch to the left to square it up with the table. "And I doubt I'll ever be able to do it again. The fear of Mrs. Tifton turned me into a cleaning machine."

Most impressive was the gown production area. Jane's sewing machine was on a table, and an ironing board and iron were close by, as were the carefully stacked boxes used to store and transport the half-finished gowns. In the corner were two dress dummies, headless beings that had frightened Lydia when she was little. Now, though, she was used to them and had often danced with them as unwitting partners. The taller of the two was wearing Skye's bridesmaid dress, finished but for hemming. The other, rounder dummy was wearing the top of Jane's dress—the fabric that would become the skirt was still in its box. Jane didn't need dress dummies for Lydia, Batty, or Rosalind. Lydia could be her own dress dummy, and Batty could be both her own *and* Rosalind's—they were the same size and shape, except for the hotly disputed quarter inch each claimed was hers.

"Let's pin your dress onto you, and see how it fits so far," said Jane. "That will make us seem relaxed and blasé when Mrs. Tifton gets here."

"I'm never relaxed when I'm being dress dummy." Lydia had experience—it was like playing statues while someone comes at you with sharp objects.

"I'll be careful," said Jane. "Minimal scratching."

Lydia gave in without more fuss. She loved the dress too much to care about a little pain. Like the other three bridesmaids' dresses, it was a shorter version of Rosalind's pale ivory bridal gown; all of them had skirts of cascading layers of voile, and silk sashes around the high waists. Rosalind's sash would be ivory, and her sisters' would be soft colors—aquamarine for Skye, violet-blue for Jane, dusky rose for Batty, and copper for Lydia. Lydia thought hers the prettiest.

The first scratch came while Jane was pulling the dress over Lydia's head.

"Jane! That didn't feel minimal."

"Sorry. You have to stand really still. No dancing."

"I wasn't dancing. I was only thinking about it." The dress would be wonderful for dancing, light and swirling, the sash blowing behind her—Lydia could see it all in slow motion. "*Ouch!* Worse that time."

"Are you bleeding? I don't want to get blood on the dress."

"Not yet. Maybe we should stop before that happens."

"A short break might be good. But don't move—the pins in the bodice could scratch you." Jane sat on her hands to stop them from shaking. "Do you mind if I practice talking to Mrs. Tifton?"

"Go ahead. I'll be her."

"Good morning, Mrs. Tifton, so nice to see you again—it's certainly been a long time, ha-ha-ha." Jane stopped. "Does my laughter sound fake?"

"Are you asking me or Mrs. Tifton?"

"You!"

"Then it sounds fake."

"I'll try again. Ha-ha-ha." Jane looked to Lydia, who assumed she was still supposed to be Lydia, so nodded her encouragement. "Lydia tells me you'd like to know when your first ex-husband, Alec—no, no, I decided not to say 'first'—when your ex-husband Alec, Jeffrey's dad—"

"You should leave out that part, too. She knows Alec is Jeffrey's dad."

131

"—when your ex-husband Alec is arriving at Arundel, which I'm not completely sure about, but maybe I should tell a lie. I'll say tomorrow because then maybe you'll go back to New York City to avoid seeing him."

"How dare you!" said Lydia angrily.

"What?"

"I was being Mrs. Tifton."

Jane put her face in her hands. "I can't do this, Lyds."

"Talk about your book, then." Talking about writing always made Jane happy.

"Good idea. My book. You already know it's about a detective hunting a time-traveling art forger."

"Do you know how the time traveling works yet?" When Jane had last talked about the time travel, she hadn't figured out the rules. Lydia was anxious to hear when she did, hoping to find the tiniest grain of possibility in them. "Didn't Skye tell you Stephen Hawking could help?"

"And who would help me with Hawking? No, I'm still working on that. But I have changed the name of my detective. She's now Philippa Nel. Do you like it?"

"Philippa! Jane, but that sounds sort of like my name—same number of syllables and with an *a* at the end. Why can't you call her Lydia Nel?"

"Because I'd be thinking about you instead of her."

"What's wrong with thinking about—?" Lydia stopped when she heard a car door slam outside the carriage house. "I think she's here, Jane."

"Stay calm! Be casual!" Jane grabbed another handful of pins. "I don't want to give her the satisfaction of knowing we're waiting for her."

"OUCH!" Jane's aim had been way off. The pin went into Lydia's arm, and was more like a stab than a prick. "I think I *am* bleeding now."

Jane found a scrap of fabric to use for dabbing at Lydia's blood. But then Mrs. Tifton was knocking on the door, and Lydia was left to tend her own wound while Jane ushered the enemy inside and rolled out her prepared speech.

"Good morning, Mrs. Tifton, so nice to see you again—it's certainly been a long time."

"Yes." Mrs. Tifton had cut off Jane's ha-ha-ha before it even began. Lydia thought this was probably a good thing.

She was learning to read the woman's moods. On a scale of one to five pickles, Mrs. Tifton was now at about two and a half. Lydia was torn between trying to take her down a pickle or so and trying to dispel the notion that Mrs. Tifton thought her less difficult than the other Penderwicks. She settled for a tone somewhere between polite dignity and cautious friendliness, and also dropped the bloody scrap of fabric on the floor.

"Good morning, Mrs. Tifton. Isn't my bridesmaid dress gorgeous? Jane's making it."

"Hmm." Mrs. Tifton inspected the dress carefully,

lingering over the narrow tucks in the bodice, which Lydia knew were perfect.

"She's making all the bridesmaids' dresses, and Rosalind's gown, too."

"Even the veil?"

"Rosy isn't wearing a veil."

"A veil is so pretty on a bride." Mrs. Tifton had lost a pickle over the narrow tucks, but her look of disapproval at this etiquette faux pas was almost as unnerving. "Where will the ceremony be held?"

Lydia remembered her sisters' having this discussion. Rosalind wanted an outdoor ceremony, and also didn't want it to be near any spot where Mrs. Tifton had ever gotten married. They'd consulted with Jeffrey, and found that only two of her weddings had been at Arundel, one in the large front hall and one on the veranda.

"The Greek pavilion," said Jane.

Mrs. Tifton seemed to be trying to find a reason to criticize this decision but came up only with weather. "It could rain that day."

Jane had been hovering, waiting for a break in the conversation that would let her give the rest of her speech. But she couldn't let the threat of rain go unchallenged.

"The long-range forecast is good," said Jane.

"Perhaps." Mrs. Tifton looked capable of summoning thunderstorms for Rosalind's wedding.

And Jane looked capable of bopping their guest on the head. "Can I get you something, Mrs. Tifton? Tea, coffee, water, lemonade?"

"Don't bother. I won't be staying long." Mrs. Tifton sat gingerly on the edge of the couch. "I suppose your sister has already chosen a caterer. If not, I could recommend—well, one or two of the less expensive ones."

"We're not having a caterer," said Lydia. "Rosalind, my parents, and the Geigers have been cooking ahead and freezing a lot of the food, and a bunch of Rosy's friends are making cakes."

"It sounds—rustic." Mrs. Tifton closed her eyes briefly to block out the image of un-catered food.

"Rustic." Jane made a rude face at Lydia, who managed not to laugh. At least Jane seemed to be getting over her nerves. "Yes, that sounds right."

"Well, Jane," said Mrs. Tifton. "You're probably wondering why I'm here."

"No, I understand completely. I do." Here, finally, was Jane's chance to go on with her speech. "Lydia tells me you'd like to know when your ex-husband Alec is arriving at Arundel. I don't know the exact day, but it should be sometime next week, because he's going to help Jeffrey with the wedding band."

"And they're professionals, you know." Lydia didn't want Mrs. Tifton to label the band as rustic, too.

Mrs. Tifton waved away the subject of the wedding

band as not worthy of her notice. "It's distressing to have one's ex-husband visiting one's own house for a wedding to which one hasn't been invited."

While Lydia was trying to sort through that sentence, Jane said, "Yes, that's reasonable."

"I'm always reasonable," replied Mrs. Tifton.

"On the other hand," said Jane slowly, working it out as she went. "It is a wedding that one wouldn't want to attend . . . oneself."

Lydia was now completely lost. "Jane, who is 'one'?"

"I believe she thinks I am 'one,'" said Mrs. Tifton.

"Oh." Lydia made an attempt at clarity. "So Jane is saying you wouldn't want to come to Rosy's wedding even if you were invited. Is that true?"

Jane was making more rude faces at Lydia—signaling that she should stop talking immediately and possibly forever, but it was Mrs. Tifton who answered.

"No, Lydia, I do not want to be invited to your sister's wedding. However, thank you for your kind offer, and now, why don't you go outside while your sister and I have a grown-up discussion?"

"I can't move. I'm pinned into this dress." It was obvious that Mrs. Tifton was about to explain the real reason for her visit—Lydia didn't want to miss that.

"You can change out of the dress. I'll wait."

"Mrs. Tifton," said Jane. "I don't want to hear anything you can't say in front of Lydia."

"Even if it's about Jeffrey's financial prospects?"

Lydia would have liked to ask about "financial prospects," which confused her even more than all those "ones" had. But the look on her sister's face—a tight smile barely disguising an angry grimace—convinced her that the time for casual questions was past.

"Mrs. Tifton, I hope you're joking," said Jane. "Jeffrey tells us what he wants us to know. Anything else is none of our business."

"I never joke about serious matters."

Lydia could well believe that. She'd seen no evidence that Mrs. Tifton could joke about anything. She also believed that this conversation was going badly. Mrs. Tifton was quickly closing in on three pickles, and Jane's grimace had given up any pretense of being a smile.

Mrs. Tifton went on. "And Jeffrey can't tell you everything because he doesn't know everything."

"Making it even less of our business. I won't listen." Jane picked up her pins again, and Lydia braced herself for more stabbing.

"Jane, you've made this your business by being here at Arundel, as would any young woman who might want to marry Jeffrey."

A young woman who wanted to marry Jeffrey! Lydia vaulted out of confusion and into mental pandemonium. She knew that Jeffrey had fallen in love a few times in Germany, but she'd heard no rumors of marriage. There had been Barbara and Anke, and, the most recent one, a French horn player—Sigrid.

"Does Sigrid want to marry Jeffrey?" She directed her question at both Jane and Mrs. Tifton, hoping one of them would explain what was going on.

Neither did, or said anything at all, but Jane put her pins back down. Her nervousness had vanished altogether, burnt up by outrage—she was ready for battle. An angry Jane was rare, and Lydia wished more than ever that she hadn't lost the thread of this conversation.

"Mrs. Tifton," said Jane, "it turns out you were right that Lydia shouldn't hear this. Sweetie, go into the bathroom and shut the door."

Lydia thought it unfair to be forced to leave before anything was properly explained. But she never argued with a battle-ready Jane, and the getting-scratched excuse was removed when Jane pulled out the most lethal of the pins.

"Into the bathroom, Lyds," said Jane. "I mean it."

Lydia went, and shut the door behind her.

While she was too honorable to eavesdrop on the conversation in the other room, she also made no attempt not to listen. But Jane and Mrs. Tifton were conducting their argument—if that's what it was—in low tones, and Lydia got none of it. She wandered over to the bathroom window and spotted Ben taking his protection job seriously, standing tall like a sentry

138

awaiting the arrival of the enemy at dawn. Alice was a few feet away, doing exactly the same thing, and now Ben was barking orders at her and they both bent over laughing. If Lydia weren't still in her bridesmaid dress, she would have crawled out the window to join them.

When at last Jane opened the bathroom door, it wasn't to let Lydia exit but to let herself enter, turn on the cold water in the sink, and stick her head under it. Lydia backed away, not willing to have water splashed on her dress, and waited for Jane to come up for air. When she became worried that Jane might be drowning, she turned off the water.

"A towel, please," said Jane.

Lydia handed her a towel. "What happened? What did she want to tell you?"

Jane wrapped the towel around her hair, but not before water streamed down onto her clothes.

"Now you're soaked," said Lydia.

"That's the point, to wash away my anger." Jane rubbed her hair vigorously. "How can Jeffrey be who he is when his mother is such an arrogant fool?"

"Please tell me what she said, Jane."

"She said she's aware that Skye and I are plotting to marry Jeffrey for his money, and that we should stop doing so. One, because he was promised years ago to Mrs. Robinette's daughter Marlene, and two, because she—Mrs. Tifton, not Marlene—will disinherit him if he marries a Penderwick."

Lydia sat down on the edge of the tub. This certainly was a day for decoding peculiar statements.

"She thinks you and Skye *both* want to marry him? Like, at the same time?"

"That wasn't clear, but I got the idea she wouldn't put it past us."

"And if you do, she'll take away Arundel?"

"She can't, but when she gave it to him, she put only enough money in trust to take care of the estate for a while. If she disinherits him, the money's gone, and he'd have to sell. And I don't know if he would care—the point is, she thinks that we care, and only want to marry him for his money."

"But none of us wants to marry him for any reason. You told her that, right?"

Jane applied the towel to her face and mumbled something unintelligible through it.

"What?" asked Lydia.

"No, I didn't tell her that. She wanted me to swear to it, which was beneath me as a woman, and a Penderwick."

That made sense to Lydia, but if she'd been there, she would have taken the easier way forward and simply told Mrs. Tifton that no one wanted to marry Jeffrey. Unless Jane had an ultra-secret love for Jeffrey, hidden so deep in her soul that even she barely understood it.

"You're sure you don't want to marry him, right?"

"Yes, of course I'm sure. A thousand times sure."

"And Skye and Dušek are really happy—"

"Yes, they are," said Jane firmly.

"Then why—?"

"It's a matter of principle, Lyds. Okay?"

"Okay." Lydia knew Jane had lots of principles.

"Thank you," said Jane. "Now I need to tell Batty, then everyone else. Any message for Dad and Iantha when I call them?"

"Tell them I'm not even a little homesick. Can you get me out of this dress?"

"Yes, and then you go find Alice and forget about this nonsense."

# CHAPTER TWELVE
## The New Alien

Lydia was rapturous to be free of pins and back into clothes she could get dirty. "Freedom from pins" would be a good motto, she thought, dancing to the glory of summer sun and fresh air, and making her way to where Ben and Alice were playing sentry.

"Mrs. Tifton's gone," she said. "She thinks Jane and Skye want to marry Jeffrey for his money, and says that if any Penderwicks do, she'll disinherit him."

"She's always threatening to disinherit Jeffrey, and he always does what he wants anyway," said Alice. "Did she also say that Jeffrey's going to marry Marlene Robinette? She loves talking about that as much as about disinheriting him."

"I didn't think any of us did want to marry Jeffrey," said Ben.

"We don't," said Lydia. "Mrs. Tifton made it up."

"She's good at making up stuff," said Alice. "Ben, you ready to see the springhouse?"

Lydia had no idea what a springhouse would be. Not, she figured, a house built on springs, though that would be fun, and she sprang into the air a few times, pretending to be the house, until Alice explained that the only springs involved were the kind with fresh cold water bubbling out of them. She was leading them deep into Bobolink Meadow Two, farther than, and in a different direction from, the secret place she'd shared with Lydia. Eventually, they came to a hollowed-out clearing shaped like a deep cereal bowl. And there was the springhouse: a teensy stone building with a front door, so low that Lydia would have to stoop to go through, and nothing else to see—the back of the house was built into the side of the hollow.

"The spring is inside, and keeps it cool. In olden days, people used it for a refrigerator," said Alice. "When I was little, Jack said he was going to lock me up in there until I froze to death or starved, whichever came first."

"That wasn't very brotherly of him," said Ben.

"Are you *kidding*?" Lydia was indignant. "Remember when you threatened to bury me in the backyard and cover my grave with leaves so that no one would ever find me? Or the time you said you'd push me off—?"

"I wouldn't have really done those things. Calm down, Lyds."

143

"Those weren't brotherly, either," said Alice.

"Thank you, Alice," said Lydia. "And then there was the time he— Ben, what are you doing?"

He'd made an impromptu camera viewfinder with his hands and was staring through it at the spring-house. There was only one reason for him to be doing that—he was thinking about using the springhouse as a film location. Which he definitely shouldn't have been, at least not if he wanted her to be involved in the film. Lydia was not going to die at Arundel.

"He asked me to help him scout film locations," said Alice. "He wants a lair for a frightened alien, and I said maybe the springhouse."

Not just a film, but the alien film all over again! An alien with a plush giant isopod on her head!

"No, no, no, no, no, no, no," said Lydia.

"Lyds, wait," said Ben. "I've had a few ideas on how to fix the script—"

She refused to listen, covering her ears and humming as loudly as possible. "Jingle Bells" was the first song she could come up with—not appropriate to the season, but a good song to use for blocking out brothers. When his mouth stayed shut for ten seconds straight—she counted it out—Lydia stopped humming and opened her ears a little.

"You promised me," she said. "No more dying on film."

"I know, Lyds, but—"

144

"Jingle bells, jingle bells, hum hum hum hum hum." But wait, Alice wanted to say something. Lydia stopped humming again.

"I'll be the alien," said Alice.

Both Penderwicks looked at her, Ben through his viewfinder and Lydia through her fear that Ben would be bossy with Alice and ruin their time at Arundel.

"Can you say *'Qhajnao lo plikna'*?" Ben asked.

"Don't say it, Alice," begged Lydia. "You have no idea what you could be getting into."

"Trust me, Alice," said Ben.

*"Qhajnao lo plikna,"* repeated Alice.

"He'll make you die, Alice," said Lydia.

"I like dying. Wasn't I good at it before?" Alice fell over and died again for them, this one a softer, sadder, more drawn-out death.

"Say *'Shigukna ladarnik,'*" said Ben. "A little deeper this time."

*"Shigukna ladarnik."* Alice used an impressively deep, raspy voice, then stood up and kicked out her right leg. "I can also do tae kwon do."

"Let me see you walk first." He demonstrated what he wanted, dragging his legs like they were too heavy for him. "Earth's gravity is greater than the gravity on your planet, so it's hard for you to move. Pretend you have weights strapped to your legs and arms."

Alice lurched, fighting gravity. Lydia thought she did it too well—more encouragement for Ben.

Desperate, Lydia clung to his arm, fighting for her friend's happiness.

"Ben, if Alice does this, you can't boss her around like you do me."

"Directors need to be bossy. Think of James Cameron."

"If he's a famous director, who cares—you're not."

"Yet."

"And you don't have an alien costume, anyway. Unless you brought that giant isopod with you, and that kept falling off and ruining the shots."

"Mom will make a costume," said Alice.

"Alice, no!"

"But she *likes* doing it. She made me a porcupine costume for a school play, and she made Jack a cricket costume. That wasn't for a play. He just wanted to be a cricket."

Lydia was temporarily distracted, trying to see the boy in those photographs dressed like a cricket. "Recently?"

"No. When he was five," said Alice.

Ben took back the conversation. "How about this, Lyds? I'll need a sound technician on the shoots. Do that, and you'll be there to monitor my level of bossiness. Deal?"

This gave Lydia pause. Ben had never before let her even touch the equipment, let alone use it on an actual shoot. She'd always thought that being behind the camera would be more fun than being in front.

"Alice, are you absolutely, positively sure you want to do this?" she asked.

As an expression of certainty, Alice kicked out her left leg, then died again, even more impressively than the last time. Lydia surrendered, and Ben took charge. He gave Alice a list of alien phrases for her to memorize, announced that the first shoot would be that very evening at dusk, and sent the girls away so that he could think great thoughts.

Natalie made one last adjustment to the alien, then sat back on her haunches.

"What do you think, Lyds? Good enough?" she asked.

"Much, *much* better than good enough." Lydia now considered Natalie to be an actual genius. "Ben is going to want you to do costumes for every one of his movies."

The alien wanted to witness for itself what the fuss was about. "Let me see, too, Mom, please."

Natalie circled the creature, taking photographs that showed every detail—the leotard and tights decorated with chicken feathers, the enormous woolly head with amber eyes on either side of its face, and the misshapen hands, which had been Lydia's own creation. She'd started with a pair of Cagney's work gloves, stuffed them with tissue paper to stiffen them, then painted them orange and purple, colors appropriate for aliens.

147

"Here you go, Alice." Natalie held the camera in front of the alien's mouth—it had a camouflaged slit to let Alice see the outside world—and scrolled through the photos.

"I'm magnificent." Alice's voice leaked, muffled, through a small hole in the neck. "I didn't know I could be so magnificent."

"Honestly, sweetheart, I find you more magnificent in your natural guise, but I'm glad you like the costume."

"I love it. Thanks, Mom, and please send the best photo to Jack. No, don't! Let's wait and send him some of the movie. That will be much more impressive."

The costume had taken most of the day to put together, and Lydia had been with the Pelletiers throughout the process, even staying for dinner, eating while putting the final touches on the gloves. And now it was close to sunset, and Ben would soon be arriving with his film equipment. How pleased he would be with this costume! But first they had to get Alice out of Natalie's studio and down the stairs, slowly and with great caution. Alice's vision through the alien's mouth was limited, and until she got used to the heavy head, it could easily tip her over. Natalie guided her from the front, while Lydia helped balance her from the back, and they were doing well until they came upon a chicken on the steps. It was Hatshepsut, again attempting to storm the second floor. Terrified by this sudden apparition, she started squawking and flapping her wings, making such a fuss that Cagney heard her from out back, where he'd been sawing wood for wedding-ceremony benches and tables, and came inside to see what was going on.

"You're being absurd," he said to the chicken, and scooped up Hatshepsut, who buried her head under his chin, in the mistaken belief that what you can't see doesn't exist. "But, Alice, my dear, you are a star."

"I know." Alice was inspired by his praise to try a tae kwon do kick, but her mother stopped her in time, and the rest of the journey down the steps was uneventful.

Ben's reaction, when he arrived, was all that could be hoped for. At first, too impressed to speak, he stared and stared at Alice through his viewfinder—a real one this time, in a real camera—until even she got tired of being gazed upon.

The camera was only the beginning of the equipment Ben had brought with him. There was also a wireless microphone with a transmitter and receiver, a bunch of wires, a tripod for the camera, and a headset, which he put onto Lydia's head, making her feel professional. He also assigned her tripod-carrying duties, which made her feel less professional and more like she was stuck with a heavy hunk of metal that dug into her arms, but she wasn't going to complain. Not when Alice was so pleased to be the dying alien—almost as pleased as Lydia was not to be.

The sun was low in the sky, stretching and distorting

the film crew's shadows as they set out toward their first shooting location. Alice's shadow was the most peculiar—a long, skinny body topped by a gargantuan sheep's head—and was made even more so when she bumped into a bush and dislodged the head.

"Careful, Alice," said Ben, readjusting it.

"Sorry. *Qankla*."

"What?" Lydia thought Alice might be speaking Alien, but when you can't hear because you're wearing headphones, Alien and English sound a lot alike, especially when it's coming out of a small hole in the throat of a giant fake head.

"*Qankla*," said Ben. "It's the alien apology."

"*Nikaj*," said Alice.

"What?" asked Lydia again.

"Let's take off the headset, Lyds." Ben did it for her, since she hadn't heard him. "Just wear it around your neck until you need it."

"How am I going to die?" asked Alice. "I can't drown—that would mess up the head. The wool would come off. I could eat something that poisons me because it's Earth food."

"The death scene isn't tonight. It will be the last scene we shoot, so don't worry about it now," said Ben. "Okay, everybody stop."

"Say please," said Lydia.

"Directors don't say please to their crew!"

"You said I could make sure you're not too bossy."

Ben sighed. "Alice and Lydia, please stop right here."

They'd reached the cottage side of the hedge tunnel. As Ben clipped on Alice's microphone equipment, he explained what would happen next. He and Lydia would leave Alice there alone, and set up the shot from the other side of the hedge. When they were ready, they'd yell for her to begin, and she would come through the hedge tunnel and see Zeus.

"You're scared and confused and looking for a friendly native, except you don't know what the natives look like, so for all you know, this big white thing could be one of them. You'll say hello to him."

"*Quch ladare*, Zeus," said Alice.

"Good, but you don't know his name; and act more scared. Remember, you're light-years away from home."

"*Quch ladare*," repeated Alice more softly. "Scared like in *ET*, except ET ended up coming back to life. Maybe I can come back to life after I die?"

Ben made sure her microphone was securely attached. "We're not doing *ET*. My movie is noir, and full of despair, a metaphor for adolescence. *ET* was a hopeful movie about a boy finding a friend, with ET basically standing in for a magic pixie dream girl."

"That's a female character who's in a story just to help the male character get better or happier," Lydia told Alice. "Jane explained it to me. She's against them."

Even hidden inside her alien head, Alice managed to look confused. "Wasn't ET a boy?"

"Forget ET," said Ben.

Lydia cut in. "Say please to her."

"*Please*, Alice, forget ET." Ben dumped a coil of wires on top of Lydia's tripod to pay her back. "And now we're off. Alice, stay here until I give you the signal. And when you do go through the hedge tunnel, be careful of your head. Please."

Ben led Lydia through the tunnel, past Zeus—who had never before been in a movie and wasn't sure he liked the idea—and about a hundred feet farther, where they set up the equipment. When his camera was in its place on the tripod, Ben handed Lydia the wireless receiver—"hold it up high for the best reception," he told her—and put her headset back on. Suddenly there was an alien breathing right into Lydia's ear. Grinning, she gave Ben the thumbs-up. This sound-technician thing was going to be fun.

He nodded, then shouted, "Mic check, Alice! Say something!"

"Testing, one, two, three," Lydia heard through the headset. "*Quch ladare*, Lydia. Tell Ben I'm ready."

"Alice is ready," she told Ben.

He flicked switches on the recording equipment. "Alice, we're rolling! Please begin your scene!"

On the other side of the hedge, Alice launched into a sad little whimper, interspersed with bits and pieces of alien-speak. Lydia could hear it all, every ragged breath, and it was done so well she almost forgot that it was Alice she was listening to, and not a terrified being trying to survive on this outlandish new planet.

When Lydia heard the shriek—just a little shriek, as if the alien had been startled—Lydia's first thought was that Alice was improvising. Maybe the alien had spotted a bird. Okay. A bird could startle an alien who had just arrived on Earth. But surely that was enough improvising. Alice should now be going back to the script. It was time for her to come through the hedge tunnel.

Instead, she was shushing someone. That wasn't in the script, either, and it made no sense in terms of improvisation. And now there was a kind of thump. Had Alice just covered the microphone, trying to keep Lydia from hearing her? Lydia put her whole self into listening, even shutting her eyes to help her concentrate on sound. She heard a man laughing. Who *was* that? If it was Cagney, why would Alice be turning it into a secret?

There was the man's laugh again, and although it definitely wasn't a Cagney laugh, it did sound familiar. Oh! Could it be?

Lydia took off her headphones. "Alice has gone off script, and I think she's talking to Jeffrey."

Ben kept on shooting. "She couldn't be, because

153

he's not coming home until next week. Go back to your job."

Lydia felt like making him say please, but she was too interested in what was happening at the hedge, because here, finally, came the alien emerging from the tunnel, big head first. Would someone else come through? Yes, and it was a man. He was still too far away for positive identification, but if Lydia had just been handed a million dollars, she'd have bet it all on the man being Jeffrey Tifton.

"It's him. I know it." Lydia disentangled herself from the equipment and sprinted toward the traveler come home to Arundel.

# CHAPTER THIRTEEN
## Music at Midnight

LYDIA HUGGED JEFFREY FEROCIOUSLY, as a thank-you for arriving a week early, and to express her passionate love for Arundel, which she couldn't do in words because Alice was talking on and on, her giant head wobbling and swaying.

"As soon as he heard his mom was here yelling at Batty, he changed his plane ticket, he even had to get a guy to substitute for him in his band, and flew all through the night like a superhero—better even than Ben busting up that clay pot—"

Jeffrey tried to stem the flow. "Don't exaggerate, Alice. Hi, Lyds."

Lydia had to content herself with another hug, because Alice was still talking.

"—was on his way to say hi to Mom and Dad when he spotted me at the tunnel and thought, What the heck is that, and do I need to protect my friends from it—"

"I didn't say that, either. Be quiet for a minute, Alice. Here's Ben!" Jeffrey greeted the latest arrival. "Great to see you!"

"It really is you. Wow." Ben elbowed Lydia out of the way so that he could hug Jeffrey next. Lydia was too happy to care.

Alice rattled on. "—but of course it was only me, and I asked him about his girlfriends—"

"Stop," said Jeffrey. "Alice, I mean it, stop. You have to let me speak for myself."

"Okay, but—"

Jeffrey lunged at her, trying to figure out how to put his hand over her mouth.

"Right there," said Ben, pointing to the hole in the alien's neck.

"Thanks." He blocked the hole. "Can she still breathe?"

"Through the eyes, probably."

"Good." He grinned happily at Ben and Lydia. "Hi, again. Good to see you—and, Lydia, you've made quite the impression with my mother."

"She doesn't really think I'm not as difficult as my sisters, does she?"

"I'm afraid so, Lyds."

"Tell her I am, please."

"I'll try, but she doesn't always listen to me." Jeffrey cautiously uncovered the alien's neck hole. "Have you calmed down yet, Alice?"

"I was calm before," she said. "And you said there are no current girlfriends, because Sigrid—"

Jeffrey grabbed the alien head. "Can I get this off her? I have a small hope that seeing her will make her easier to control."

Ben and Lydia helped, and soon Alice emerged, red-faced and wet-haired from the heat inside the head. "—and also, Jeffrey stopped at the Robinettes' on the way here to tell his mother—"

"Alice, I will tell my own tale." He clapped his hand over her real mouth and held it there firmly. "When I got off the plane, I got Jane's message about Mom's insane marriage threats. So I stopped by to re-assure her that I don't want to marry any of you, and I promised to spend time with her tomorrow afternoon, and I told her she should try to relax until then."

"And not come here to yell at us?" asked Lydia.

"I was more diplomatic than that, but yes. I also told her that none of you wants to marry me. That's still true, isn't it?"

"I don't," said Lydia.

Alice was desperately trying to give her answer through Jeffrey's hand.

He cautiously uncovered her mouth. "Yes?"

"I don't want to marry you, either," she said. "And I never did, and never will."

"I might think about marrying you, Jeffrey," said Ben, "but not if you're going to be disinherited and broke."

"That's the spirit," said Jeffrey. "Now, where are your sisters? Should I surprise them, too?"

Everyone agreed that he should surprise them. The film crew plus Jeffrey set off for the carriage house, looking for Jane. Ben kept whispering for them to move quietly, like thieves in the night, and everyone did try, except when Alice realized that Ben and Lydia hadn't heard the whole story about the end of Sigrid as a girlfriend and Jeffrey threatened to stifle her again, and when Lydia was too happy about Jeffrey being at Arundel to keep from dancing and humming "What a Wonderful World," until Ben threatened to take away her job as sound technician.

When they were within yards of the carriage house, Jeffrey called a halt, and whispered to Lydia, "Go take a peek inside before I burst in. Make sure Jane isn't at work on her novel."

This was wise on his part. When Jane was lost in her fictional world, she didn't like being startled out of it. She said that the best ideas could be lost that way, never to be recaptured. Lydia crept to the window. Jane wasn't writing—she was at the ironing board, pressing an ivory-colored sash—and she wasn't alone.

Batty was in the apartment with her, being the dress dummy for Rosalind's gown.

This was the first time Lydia had seen Rosy's wedding gown on a person instead of a hanger. How splendid it was, its elegant simplicity, its classic flow of lighter-than-air voile. And how regal and grown-up Batty was in the dress, her dark curls pinned up like Rosalind's would be for the wedding.

Lydia waved the others over, but with a cautious finger to her lips. Even Alice made the trip without any noise, and now they could all see the dressmaking scene in the living room. Jeffrey leaned down to whisper in Lydia's ear.

"I thought Rosy wasn't here."

"She's not." Lydia saw that he was staring at Batty. "That's not Rosy."

He took a step back in surprise, then forward again, as if to make sure he understood what he was seeing. At the same moment, obeying some quiet command from Jane, Batty turned to face the window and caught Jeffrey's eye. For what seemed like a long time, the two stared at each other with matching confusion. Until, slowly, Batty smiled, her smile the first warm day of spring, with the daffodils and violets bursting into bloom. She opened her arms and reached toward Jeffrey, and without another word, he went inside.

• • •

It was almost midnight, and Jeffrey and Batty had already gone through much of the Gershwin songbook, most of *Les Misérables*, the latest Norah Jones album, and a bunch of early Kinks songs. Now they were almost at the end of *A Little Night Music* and showed no signs of stopping. They always produced this great outpouring of music after they'd been apart for a while, sharing new songs, ideas, and musical viewpoints.

Jeffrey had been Batty's introduction to music—he started her on the piano when she was only five. By the time she was eleven, she was calling him her *mentore* (Italian for "mentor"), avidly learning whatever he could teach, following any musical lead he gave her. In the last year or so, Jeffrey had begun to reject the term *mentore*, declaring that Batty was his equal now. Each time he said so, Batty tried to argue, but he always managed to steer her away from dispute and into music, and laughter. Laughter and music—these dominated Lydia's memories of Batty and Jeffrey together.

And dancing to their music. Lydia always danced for as long as she could keep up with them. And tonight she had the added joy of the new ballet skirt Jeffrey had brought her from Germany, a pale lilac one with silver threads woven in. He'd brought one for Alice, too, which made it even more special. But now Lydia was tiring and wanted to go to bed. At home, in Cameron, she would simply have done so. But she was in Arundel Hall, and couldn't go upstairs, not as long as Batty was sitting on the piano bench with Jeffrey, singing. Because that would have meant going up alone. Jane was back at the carriage house, and Ben was already in his room, looking at the alien film footage. That left no one but Feldspar and Sonata, and they wouldn't leave Batty.

But there was hope for Lydia. Batty and Jeffrey were on the last verse of the last song of A *Little Night Music*. Surely they would stop now.

"*Hamilton!*" said Batty. "We haven't done *Hamilton* yet."

"Ready, and . . ." He played the opening chords on the grand piano.

"No!" Lydia leapt at them from across the music room. "No *Hamilton*. Batty, please stop and go upstairs with me to bed."

"Is it that late already?" asked Batty.

"Almost midnight!"

"According to Alice, the mansion has ghosts," Batty told Jeffrey. "This makes Lydia reluctant to sleep alone."

"Don't laugh," said Lydia.

"I'm not." Jeffrey frowned to emphasize his non-laughter. "Did Alice give details or just make generalizations?"

"She said the ghosts are in the cellar." Lydia decided not to mention that they were supposedly his mother's ex-husbands.

"I didn't know about the cellar. When I was little, I thought the ghosts were in the dining room."

"Jeffrey," said Batty. "You're not supposed to encourage Lydia's fears."

"Or increase them," added Lydia. She hadn't yet seen the dining room, but it was probably on this very floor of the mansion, even closer than the cellar was to her bedroom.

"You're right. I was very little at the time, though." Jeffrey slid off the piano bench. "Let's visit the dining room. If we don't find ghosts, will you be less nervous?"

Lydia couldn't promise that. She could only promise that if they did find ghosts, she would never, ever sleep in the mansion again. And since she also couldn't stay alone in the music room while the other two went off to the dining room, in a few moments she found herself creeping through the halls of Arundel, in pitch darkness, because Jeffrey said that turning on lights would scare away ghosts, nullifying the experiment. He went first, leading Batty by the hand, and Batty held Lydia's. Lydia would have liked to have the dogs behind her, to separate her from the darkness, but Feldspar was out in front, his red shoe at the ready to repel any ghosts, and Sonata stayed close to Batty, whether to protect or be protected, Lydia didn't know. Either way, this made Lydia last, and vulnerable to being sneaked up on.

"We've reached the dining room," said Jeffrey. "I'm

going to push open the door, and we will quietly look around for ghosts. Ready?"

"What do we do if we find any?" asked Batty.

"Sing them something eerie. Bowie's 'Space Oddity,' maybe."

Batty started to giggle, then choked into coughing when she tried to stop. Lydia couldn't decide whether she wished Jeffrey and Batty would take the ghosts more seriously or if their frivolity was a relief. In either case, she didn't want anyone singing "Space Oddity," a sad song about an astronaut alone in his spaceship.

"If an astronaut dies in space," she asked, "can his ghost come back to Earth to haunt people, or would he be stuck out in space forever with no one to haunt?"

Lydia had meant this as a sincere question, but it had the unfortunate effect of making Batty giggle harder, and it was a while before everyone was quiet enough for Jeffrey to open the door.

The dining room wasn't as dark as the halls. Windows let in stray moonbeams, some landing on white dust sheets covering the furniture, others picking out the faces in the portraits. They weren't friendly faces, mostly stern and taking themselves seriously, but at least they seemed to be staying in their frames. Except for one in the corner that might actually be empty— the moonlight showed just a dark rectangle with no one inside it.

"Look over there, in the corner," she hissed. "One of the portraits is empty."

"That should be my great-great-aunt," said Jeffrey.

"If she's not in there, where is she?" Lydia couldn't spot anything that looked ghostlike.

"This is spookier than I thought it would be," said Batty.

"I never did like this room," said Jeffrey. "Maybe Alice is right about—"

Suddenly Batty was yelping and letting go of Lydia's hand, leaving Lydia alone in a dark room through which a ghost was now drifting toward the empty frame, accompanied by a scraping noise that didn't sound like chains or bones but was nonetheless distinctly unpleasant. Lydia fell to the floor and curled up into a ball like a threatened hedgehog, wishing she weren't in her ballet skirt, because the moonlight could pick out the silver threads and make her easier to see.

"I just turned the lights on, Lyds," said Jeffrey. "It was only Feldspar getting tangled up in a dust sheet."

"What about your great-great-aunt?" Lydia spoke into her own stomach, because she wasn't uncurling until she knew it was safe out there. "Is she back in her frame?"

"Yes, if she ever left it. The moonlight probably tricked us."

Lydia distrusted Jeffrey's casual assurance. "What's Batty doing?"

"Clinging to me in terror."

"No, I'm not," said Batty, but when Lydia stopped being a hedgehog and could see again, she was pretty sure Batty had just un-clung herself.

More important, the great-great-aunt was indeed back where she should have been, but Lydia still didn't trust her.

"She's smirking at me," she said. "She enjoyed terrifying us."

"Don't take it personally," said Jeffrey. "She always smirks."

With the dining room lit up, it seemed safe enough to Lydia. Maybe the great-great-aunt ghost had been her imagination, but—holy bananas!—who were those people painted onto the ceiling? Alice hadn't mentioned this crew, lolling around, wearing togas and eating grapes. They probably weren't more of Jeffrey's relatives, though they might have been friends with lonely old Zeus, stuck outside in the gardens.

"Who are these guys?" she asked Jeffrey.

"No one important. My great-grandfather's idea of culture."

Batty looked up. "The grape man! I remember him. Was I in this room when I was little?"

"My eleventh birthday party," said Jeffrey.

"Your birthday! Now I remember—mostly I tried to slide under the table to hide from Dexter. I seemed to spend a lot of that visit hiding under things."

"There was a lot to hide from."

"Not from you, though," she said. "You were my hero."

"Yup, that's me," said Jeffrey. "Okay, so no ghosts. Ready for *Hamilton*, Batty?"

"Jeffrey! Batty!" cried Lydia. "You're not going to start singing again, are you?"

"We didn't find any ghosts, honey," said Batty.

"But you were scared, too!"

"No, I wasn't. Not really."

"Yes, you were."

"No, I—"

"Stop," said Jeffrey. "I have an idea."

He took Lydia upstairs to Ben's room, and informed Ben that Lydia was going to sleep in his spare bed until Batty came to fetch her. Ben protested. Then Jeffrey described the sound-recording equipment his father would be bringing for the wedding and said that Ben would probably be allowed to use it. And Ben gave in, with one condition—that before morning, Batty would come collect Lydia and take her back to their own room.

"Because waking up with Lydia here would be unacceptable."

Lydia was still trying to come up with a good retort when she fell asleep, curled up on his bed, dreaming about ghostly great-great-aunts wearing togas and eating grapes.

# CHAPTER FOURTEEN
## *Surprises*

"**B**ATTY DIDN'T COME GET me until two in the morning, and she was still singing—in French." Lydia yawned hugely, then sang, "*Ne me quitte pas,* blah-blah-blah-blah-blah. What am I going to do? Ben won't let me into his room every night, no matter what Jeffrey says."

"Sleep in my room from now on," said Alice. "You can have either the top or bottom bunk."

"Really?" What a relief to never again sleep in the mansion.

"Actually, I do prefer the top bunk, so if you wouldn't mind the bottom—"

"No, I mean, do you really think I can stay with you? Wouldn't your parents mind?"

"They'll like it. They've decided you're a good influence on me."

Lydia thought that being a good influence made her sound as boring as being a person who liked everyone (except she didn't). But if that was what she had to suffer to get out of the mansion, she'd accept it.

Both girls were in their new ballet skirts, swishing along on their way to see Blossom. Alice was carrying the oats in a bag—the skirts were without pockets—and Lydia was carrying Natalie's phone, plus two books, in another bag. Alice knew about only one of the books, *Practical Magic*, written by an Alice for grown-ups. The other, sneaked in by Lydia, was a copy of *Alice's Adventures in Wonderland and Through the Looking-Glass*. She was hoping to convince both Alice and Blossom to love it. Unless—she stopped walking—that could be considered being a good influence. No, she decided, and started walking again, quickly, to catch up with Alice as she entered the field.

They'd decided to begin the visit with a dance, the best way to show Blossom their new skirts. This was the first time the two of them had danced together seriously, and anyone other than sheep would have appreciated the vision—the beautiful skirts, the fusion of ballet and tae kwon do, the paean to freedom and friendship. But to Blossom, the oat carriers seemed to have gone crazy, spinning around like bugs trying to escape a water trough. She stopped halfway across the field, apparently planning to chomp on grass until they became less buglike.

The dancing a failure, the girls moved on to the second part of the entertainment. Alice took out oats, Lydia took out *Practical Magic*, and Blossom came the rest of the way over, accepting the oats and ignoring the book.

Undeterred, Lydia opened it. "Blossom, although the book reading didn't work out last time, we're trying again."

"It was Lydia's idea," said Alice.

"And a good one." She started to read. "'For more than two hundred years, the Owens women have been blamed for everything that has gone wrong in town.'"

"Skip to the conversation," said Alice, giving out oats. "I like conversation."

Lydia skimmed through the beginning pages. "There's none for another five and a half pages."

Alice groaned. "Then go on with the boring part."

"'If a damp spring arrived, if cows'— Blossom, be careful!"

Blossom had just stomped one of her hooves, nearly squashing Lydia's right foot in the process.

"Maybe she doesn't want to hear about cows," said Alice.

"I'll skip the cows."

The phone in Alice's bag dinged. A new photo had

arrived from Jack, the first since the girls had sent him the one of Ben being a garden-pot-breaking superhero. It showed Jack and Slapshot jumping off a dock and into a lake. The lake was enough of a taunt—Arundel had no lake—but Jack had upped the sting with a message. *Ben Penderwick does look interesting, but you don't. Ha-ha.*

"Now it's war," said Alice. "Lydia, we have to be fascinating in the next photograph. Think. It's important."

Lydia put away *Practical Magic* and pulled out *Alice's Adventures in Wonderland and Through the Looking-Glass.* "I know you don't like this book, but I think a photograph of Blossom listening to us read it would be fascinating."

"But she won't listen! Look at her." Blossom had wandered off to practice stomping where there weren't feet in the way.

"You said she didn't want to hear about the cows. There's a sheep in this book. Don't you think she'd like to hear that?"

"No!"

"Please."

Alice did Mrs. Tifton's pickle face—rating of two—but relented. "Do you promise that if this doesn't work, we'll think of something better for Jack?"

"Yes, I promise. Get ready. I'll start right where the sheep shows up." Lydia cleared her throat and began to read. "'"Oh, much better!" cried the Queen, her voice rising into a squeak as she went on. "Much be-etter! Be-etter! Be-e-e-etter! Be-e-ehh!" The last word ended in a long bleat, so like a sheep that Alice quite started.'"

"Blossom's actually coming this way!" whispered Alice.

Not wanting to break the spell, Lydia kept reading. "'She looked at the Queen, who seemed to have suddenly wrapped herself up in wool. Alice rubbed her eyes, and looked again. She couldn't make out what had happened at all. Was she in a shop? And was that really—'"

"She is! Oh, Lydia!"

"'Was it really a *sheep* that was sitting on the other side of the counter?'"

It definitely was really a sheep bumping her head against the book. Once, twice, she bumped her head. Alice whipped out her mother's phone and photographed the scene.

"Switch!" said Lydia. "You read, and I'll take a picture for Jack!"

They changed places so smoothly that Blossom didn't notice—all her focus was on this book that miraculously contained not just Alice but an actual sheep.

"'Rub as she would,'" read Alice, "'she could make nothing more of it: she was in a little dark shop, leaning with her elbows on the counter, and opposite to her was an old Sheep—'"

"Got it!" crowed Lydia, and just in time, too. Blossom's concentration was waning.

Alice sent the photo to Jack, along with a message— *This is Blossom not Big Papi and she's my sheep now. Love, Alice*—and the girls celebrated with another dance, more vigorous than the first, and including wild calls of victory. Bothered by the noise level, Blossom began her long trip to re-join her friends on the other side of the field.

The girls toned down their shouts, hoping that Blossom would be less disturbed and more grateful for the introduction to the cultural arts. She did look back at them once, but by then they were paying more attention to someone in the distance, calling for Lydia. She didn't recognize the voice. It definitely wasn't either of her sisters.

"It's Mrs. Tifton," said Alice. "She's here again."

"But Jeffrey told her to stay away."

"Lydia, *Lydia!*"

"She didn't listen to him," said Alice. "Mostly she doesn't listen to anybody."

"Why would she be looking for me?"

"Maybe because she's sure you don't want to marry Jeffrey. I'll come with you. She knows I don't want to marry him, either."

"Nobody does," said Lydia. She could almost feel

sorry for Jeffrey for how little any of them wanted to marry him.

The girls followed the voice out of the sheep field, toward the hedge, and through the tunnel. Lydia didn't know the polite way to handle this situation. As in, how to act with the woman who the day before had scolded, threatened, and enraged Jane enough that she almost drowned herself in the bathroom sink. Lydia decided it would be best to follow Mrs. Tifton's lead.

Mrs. Tifton seemed to be pretending yesterday hadn't happened.

"I've been calling for you," she said. "Natalie said you were out here but didn't know where."

"We were visiting my sheep," said Alice. "Blossom, who used to be Big Papi."

"We have a picture, if you want to see her, Mrs. Tifton," added Lydia.

"No. Do you know where Jeffrey is? He's not answering his phone."

"He told us he's seeing you this afternoon," said Alice.

"I know about this afternoon, Alice."

The last time Lydia had seen Jeffrey, he was still asleep on the music room couch, having crashed there after his music marathon with Batty.

"He might be asleep," she said. "That would explain why he's not answering his phone."

"He shouldn't be asleep. It's almost eleven."

173

"Mom says he has jet lag," said Alice. "He flew in yesterday from—"

"Alice, please." Mrs. Tifton already knew that, too. "I'd look for him myself, except that he's asked me not to barge in on your sisters again. I thought 'barge' was a bit of an exaggeration."

Lydia spoke up before Alice could start arguing about Mrs. Tifton's method of entering Penderwick-occupied territory. "We'd be happy to go look for him."

"Thank you. I'll wait on the terrace. Tell him I have good news about Marlene."

Marlene. That was Mrs. Robinette's daughter, the one who was theoretically marrying Jeffrey. Lydia longed to know what the good news was but didn't want to risk setting off Mrs. Tifton's pickle levels, which so far today had been pretty low. She took Alice's hand, and off they ran.

The search for Jeffrey led Lydia farther into the mansion than she'd yet been, or than she would have gone if it had been night and she'd been alone. And when they couldn't find him anywhere on the first floor, nor on the second floor, Alice urged her up and up until they got to Jeffrey's old bedroom, on the third floor.

He was out in the hall waiting for them.

"Good morning, rhinos," he said. "I heard you coming from miles away."

"Your mother's waiting for you on the terrace," said Lydia. "She has news for you about Marlene."

"Good news," added Alice. "What could it be?"

Jeffrey clutched his head. "I have no idea. Batty, Jane!"

They popped out of his room. Jane was in the middle of unfolding a sheet, and Batty, of stuffing a pillow into a pillowcase.

"Trouble?" asked Jane. "Jeffrey, stop doing that. You'll tear your hair out."

"My mother's outside, with some nonsense about Marlene."

"Your lovely betrothed," said Batty.

That didn't do Jeffrey's hair any good. "Just keep the dogs up here until I tell you she's gone."

"What about me and Lydia?" asked Alice. "Do you want us to go with you for moral support?"

"That's kind of you, Alice, but I can do this."

The four of them watched him walk away, his reluctance showing in every dragging step.

"Poor guy," said Jane.

"Yes," said Alice. "He suffers. Jack thinks Jeffrey might marry Marlene one of these days just to get his mom to stop bugging him about it."

Batty shook her head. "That's never going to happen."

"Come in, Lyds and Alice," said Jane. "We're helping Jeffrey settle."

Jeffrey's old bedroom was the first place in the mansion where Lydia felt comfortable. It was normal-sized, for one thing, and the furniture was functional instead of fancy. There was a piano, but it was a battered old upright Lydia wouldn't worry about banging on. And there were no ghosts—she was definite about this. If ghosts did happen to exist, they wouldn't come in here. The atmosphere was too friendly.

Jane stood by one of the windows, pointing out to a massive tree. "Behold! The legendary tree Skye and I once used for a perilous escape."

"You climbed down *that?*" Lydia had heard this story—about her sisters climbing out the window and down that tree, all to avoid detection by Mrs. Tifton—but she'd never imagined the scope of their adventure. Just looking down at the ground from here made her dizzy.

"It was Skye's idea," said Jane.

Alice was greatly impressed. "I'd like to try."

"No!" cried Batty from the other side of the room—she was making up the small bed with clean sheets. "You'd be killed."

"Skye and Jane weren't," said Alice.

"Which was a miracle," said Jane. "And we did get stuck halfway down. Your father had to get a ladder to rescue us."

Lydia pulled Alice into the middle of the room, away from the temptation of the window. Now they were closer to the closet, which was open and, going by the amount of noise emanating from it, inhabited.

"Feldspar's in there, hunting," said Batty.

"Maybe we should—" said Jane.

"Right." Batty went into the closet and reemerged, Feldspar in tow. He was carrying a new token of his hunting prowess, a crumpled bundle of wispy black-and-orange fabric. A scarf? A kite? Lydia leaned in for a closer look. It had wires meant to hold the shape, but they'd been bent, making it impossible to know what that shape had been. In several places, the fabric had been torn, then carefully mended.

Before anyone could identify this whatever-it-was, Jeffrey returned. He was no longer clutching his head, but he did look weary.

"My mother is gone. Apologies, everyone."

"What was the news about Marlene?" asked Lydia.

"She's coming home next week to visit her mother. According to *my* mother, this will give me the opportunity to properly woo her."

"So it will," said Batty, plumping the pillow on the bed.

"Batty, please." He clutched his head again, then noticed Feldspar's newfound object. "Did you find that in the closet, buddy?"

"What is it?" asked Lydia.

"Batty should know. Batty, you don't remember?"

But Beethoven's *Eroica* was playing somewhere in the room, and Batty was searching for her phone. Lydia found it on a bookcase and tossed it to her.

"Hello?" said Batty.

Somehow—this was impossible—her phone was still playing the *Eroica*. But, wait, no, Alice had just found another phone, this one on the piano bench. Jeffrey claimed it, and she handed it over.

"Hello?" said Jeffrey.

It's difficult to listen to two simultaneous one-sided conversations. If Lydia and Alice had decided who would pay attention to which, they might have understood more. As it was, they got only that Batty was explaining to someone that she was Batty, not Jane, and why had this person called Batty if she was looking for Jeffrey— She was talking to Mrs. Tifton! That was strange.

And Jeffrey seemed to be talking to Wesley— Wesley! Why?—explaining that he was Batty's honorary older brother, and—

"Holy cow!" said Jane. "They've switched phones. Lyds, Alice, help me!"

Each girl snatched a phone and gave it to the correct owner, then went back to trying to decipher the new but still simultaneous phone conversations. Now Jeffrey was explaining to his mother about identical ringtones—no, they hadn't known—and declining an invitation for dinner with her and Mrs. Robinette. And Batty was telling Wesley that she hadn't mentioned Jeffrey would be at Arundel so soon because she hadn't known he would be, and she hoped Hitch was having a good trip, but no, please don't say hello to him for her.

"Who's Wesley?" Alice asked Lydia.

"He's Batty's ex-boy—"

Lydia was interrupted by the sound of banging on an old-fashioned typewriter.

"Jane's phone," she said.

"This is extraordinarily exciting." Alice started taking photos of everyone.

If two simultaneous conversations are confusing, three are Babel. Lydia got that Jane was talking to Skye and that Jane knew without a doubt—she said it three times—that Skye was kidding. And then Jane went into the closet and shut the door, and Lydia couldn't hear her anymore. That left only two conversations, and then, after Jeffrey had also refused an invitation for cocktails and firmly told his mother good-bye, only one: Batty's with Wesley.

"You didn't tell me you were . . . No, it's sweet of you, but . . . I guess so, if you could leave it at the entrance to Arundel . . . No, I don't want to know when you'll be here. Just let me know when you're gone again. . . . Yes, he's the one who taught me music when I was little—I've told you about him. . . . No! . . . Yes . . . Bye."

"He sounds like a nice guy," said Jeffrey when she hung up. "And when did you steal my ringtone?"

"Maybe you stole mine."

"Is Wesley coming here?" asked Lydia. This was vitally important, and ringtones weren't. Because if Wesley was coming, Hitch was coming, and Lydia might be able, after all, to give him a final farewell kiss on the nose. Oh, she did hope so.

"Sort of," said Batty. "He's going to stop here on his way out west, to drop off a wedding gift he's made for Rosalind. 'Drop off' as in 'leave it at the entrance and go on his way.'"

"Who's Wesley?" asked Alice again.

"Batty's ex-boyfriend," said Lydia. "They just broke up, and he has this amazing dog—"

"Lydia, please," said Batty.

"Sorry," said Lydia, then whispered to Alice. "I'll explain later."

Batty had turned her attention back to Feldspar, still proudly in possession of his crumpled black-and-orange treasure.

"Jeffrey, you think I should know what this is?" She leaned in closer. "Let it go, Feldspar. That's right. I'm sure this isn't as good as your red shoe."

To everyone's surprise, he did let go, and watched while Batty untangled the mess, straightening bent wires, gently smoothing fabric.

"You must remember," said Jeffrey.

"You're sure? Oh!" Her face lit up. "My wings! Lydia, remember the stories about my butterfly wings?"

Lydia did remember the stories—of how Rosalind would mend the wings whenever Batty ripped them, and how Skye would go nuts whenever the wires poked her. And there were many pictures, too, not just the gum-in-the-hair one, in which little Batty stared into the camera, a shy but determined butterfly.

"But, Jeffrey, why did you have them? Wait—did I give them to you when we were leaving Arundel? I think so, and you said— What *did* you say?"

"Good-bye for now."

"Yes. Good-bye for now. And it was good-bye for just then, wasn't it? How wise you were."

Alice was once again trying to ask questions—and who could blame her?—but now Feldspar was barking at the closet, wanting to get inside to retrieve his red shoe. He barked and whined, and Sonata, who'd been asleep under the piano bench, woke up and barked with him. Lydia tried to reach the door to open it, which Feldspar himself kept from happening by blocking her way.

And then the door swung open by itself. No, no—Jane had opened it from the inside. In all the excitement over Hitch and butterfly wings, Lydia had forgotten about Jane's conversation with Skye.

Jane looked first at Jeffrey. "Skye says she and Rosy have talked to you about this and you don't mind the added chaos."

"It's not that much more chaos, and I'm delighted for her, and we'll have fun," he said. "Come on, Batty, let's see if these wings still fit."

Batty stuck out her arms. "What chaos?"

"Jane will tell you." He slipped the wings on her. "Yes, they fit."

"What chaos, Jane?"

181

"I'm still trying to take it in. It seems that Dušek and Rosy have been pushing this for a while, and Skye finally decided that since she'd never want to arrange one for herself, she should take advantage of this one, especially since Dušek's family was already planning to be here. So she said yes."

Batty flapped her wings in frustration. "Yes to *what?*"

"A double wedding."

# CHAPTER FIFTEEN
## The View from the Roof

LYDIA AND ALICE NEEDED a long conversation before Alice was caught up on the history of Skye and
Dušek, who were now getting married, and of Batty
and Wesley, who were separated for good. Lydia began
with Batty and Wesley—about Wesley being an artist,
and being as wonderful as he was irritating, and about
how he and Hitch had come together. When Hitch
was a puppy, he was called Bruno by a terrible and ir-
responsible owner, who first let him get hit by a car,
then decided to discard him because one of his front
legs was ruined. That was when Wesley had stepped
in, paid to have the bad leg removed, and given Hitch
his new name to go along with his new and better
life. Alice said she hoped she could meet them when

Wesley dropped off Rosalind's gift. Lydia hoped that, too, but knew they'd have to be lucky to catch Wesley. He'd have no reason to linger at Arundel, not with Batty unwilling to see him.

The Skye and Dušek story was less complicated, even the part about this abrupt marriage. It was typical of Skye, Lydia told Alice, to be as casual about social occasions as she was serious about science, and gave the example of Skye's high school prom, which she decided to attend only at the last minute, then went dressed in a lab coat from chemistry class.

"It's strange, though, suddenly to be having two sisters getting married," she added. But Lydia was already getting used to the double-wedding plan. Once she could accept the idea of Skye getting married at all—outmoded social constructs, et cetera—it didn't matter much when it happened.

"I don't think I'd want to have a double wedding with Jack," said Alice.

"Unless you liked the person he was marrying."

"What kind of loser would marry Jack?"

Of everyone who had to adjust to this new, double-wedding reality, Lydia and Alice were the least affected. Back in Cameron, Rosalind and Iantha had to add calming down the father of the brides to their already long lists of tasks. In California, certainly Skye had some organizing to do, though it was hard to figure out what that would be, since the real work was being done here in Massachusetts. And here at Arundel, Jane frantically ordered fabric for Skye's wedding gown—the one she had a mere week to produce—and Natalie moved her own sewing machine into the carriage house to help Jane. Cagney had to increase his output of benches and tables for the ceremony, to accommodate newly invited, extra guests. Ben was recruited to help him. As was Batty, whenever Jeffrey had to abandon music to placate his mother—and to keep her from dropping in again—which was more often than he or anyone else would have wished. The rest of the time, he and Batty settled down to serious preparation for the wedding music. No more goofing around with old Kinks songs.

Lydia and Alice did try to aid in the efforts. They performed inspirational dances for Batty and Jeffrey, throwing out what they thought were excellent song suggestions, until even Feldspar was sick of them and whined at them to leave. They helped with the dressmaking at the carriage house until Natalie caught them matching a bodice to the wrong skirt and suggested they please move along. The girls' last attempt was at carpentry, but Cagney sent them away from the tables and benches, too, when Lydia almost drove a nail through her thumb. After which they went blithely back to doing whatever they wanted. Especially now that Lydia was sleeping in Alice's room—on the bottom bunk—and they could be together all the time.

Most evenings they spent with Ben, shooting the alien movie. Alice became ever more believable as the alien, and Lydia learned to anticipate and follow Ben's directions so well that she stopped noticing when he didn't say please. The girls' days were for everything else. Blossom saw a lot of them, as she ate oats and listened intently to the Lewis Carroll books, even the parts with no sheep.

Buoyed by this success, Lydia tried to talk Alice into reading to the chickens, too. Alice refused, but did teach Lydia about gathering their eggs and changing their hay, a more practical way to get to know them. Lydia also learned to catch and carry Hatshepsut, who continued to break into the cottage to pursue her quest to reach the second floor. And one rainy day, the girls raided Natalie's scrap box for even more treasures to weave, braid, and tie into colorful concoctions, with no purpose but to please. Natalie said that was one definition of art, and that pleasing was both important and enough. This gave Lydia a new way to think about her dancing, though she did wonder if dancing to please *herself*—rather than other people—counted as art. If not, she thought, maybe someday she'd learn to make real art with fabric and color, just like Natalie did.

While that rainy day was one of Lydia's favorite's,

Alice's favorite days were less about creativity and more about recklessness. And about outdoing Jack, especially after he sent her the photo of his handstand on the ice at the hockey rink, his skates high in the air, while Marcel maneuvered a puck around him. That day, she shimmied up onto the roof of the greenhouse so that Lydia could take a picture of her up there. It was an excellent picture, and when Alice managed not to break the glass roof panels, she proclaimed her desire to conquer other heights. Lydia argued against this plan—she didn't like heights—but gave in when Alice agreed to stay away from roofs more than one story high.

The one-story rule kept the mansion's roof off-limits, even though Alice was certain she could get up there by climbing out an attic window. But the porch roof of the cottage and a lower portion of the carriage house roof both turned out to be low enough for climbing, and Alice did. Lydia refused to join her, but she was willing to take pictures for Jack.

The chicken house was low enough, even for Lydia. Climbing onto it meant waiting until the bench-and-table builders were on lunch break and not there to stop the madness. The chickens weren't so lucky—since they stayed home for lunch, they were forced to witness this invasion. None of them were pleased, except for Hatshepsut, who climbed up next to the girls, and got herself into the picture sent to Jack.

Eventually, there was only one remaining roof-climbing possibility, the Greek pavilion, but Lydia and Alice couldn't agree on whether it qualified as being one story high.

"There is the floor," said Alice, pointing, "and there is the roof, and there is nothing in between. One story."

"But it's an extra-tall story," said Lydia. "And the roof is curvy and made of metal, so it will be slippery and hard to balance on. You said let's climb up to touch the roof from below. You didn't say anything about standing on the roof itself."

"I know I didn't, but, Lyds, think of how I'd look up there, right in the center." Alice struck a pose, feet spread, hands on hips, chin in the air, her ballet skirt billowing around her. Alice thought the ballet skirt added class to the photos.

Lydia couldn't deny that Alice would be an excellent addition to the top of the pavilion—like a Greek Peter Pan about to do ballet—but she didn't want Alice to get killed, and she also didn't want any harm to come to the Greek pavilion. This was Wednesday, and the wedding was Saturday, and Lydia couldn't see her sisters getting married in a pavilion with a smashed roof.

"The ladder is already right here." Alice was kind not to mention that she'd been damaged in the process of getting the ladder to the pavilion, and that it had been Lydia's fault. While the girls had scaled pre-vious roofs by using chairs and ingenuity, a roof this high demanded an extension ladder. They'd secreted this one out of the cottage basement—almost, but not quite, getting caught by Cagney—and lugged it all the way here. Aluminum ladders aren't heavy, but the long ones can be tricky to maneuver when the person at one end isn't paying enough attention, which hap-pened when Alice got whacked in the knees because Lydia had been distracted by a bobolink call.

"Okay," she said. "But only if we do it so that if you fall, it will be into a bush and not onto the hard ground."

"Not roses, though," said Alice. "They have thorns."

Lydia found a hydrangea bush that would do, one heavy with blue-and-purple blooms. It would be a shame to smash the flowers, but at least the bush was at the back of the pavilion, where it wouldn't be seen during the wedding ceremony.

"I'm ready now," said Lydia. "I'll steady the bottom of the ladder."

"Thank you. Now I will climb. 'I will climb and not fall' would make a good motto." Lydia had told Alice about her search for a personal motto, and Alice had eagerly joined in, translating her own choices into pretend Latin. "*Climbiamamius and not fallimakius!*"

Lydia liked the part about not falling but was still

nervous as Alice went up the ladder enthusiastically, not a good thing when you're wearing a long ballet skirt.

"Steady, Alice, stay in the middle of each rung."

*"Lydia isimus my friendimus!"*

"Slow down, the ladder is shaking!"

The top of Alice's head was now level with the pavilion roof, which put Alice's feet at just about a normal one-story height.

"Take a picture, Lyds," she said. "Before I get onto the roof."

But Lydia refused to let go of the shaky ladder, clinging to it with both hands. This meant she couldn't operate the camera, and also that she was directly beneath Alice and couldn't see anything but layers of ballet skirt. Alice leaned sideways to give Lydia a better view of her, the ladder swayed dangerously, Lydia screamed, and Alice straightened back up.

"You have to come down now," said Lydia.

"But once I'm on the roof, you can let go of the ladder and take the picture."

"I've changed my mind about you going onto the roof. You're going to give me a heart attack."

"Please, Lydia. Just think how impressed Jack will be."

"Jack will not be impressed if you break your limbs, which is the most likely outcome."

"I can see so much from up here. There's Blossom."

Alice turned her head. "And Mom is on her way to the carriage house—sewing time."

"Please come down, Alice."

"Not yet." She looked toward Bobolink Meadow One and the lane to the mansion. "Here comes a man on a motorcycle."

A motorcycle! "Does it have a sidecar?"

"Yes, and some guy's in it. Wait a minute, I'm not sure—that is, whoever's in the sidecar is wearing a helmet, and he's got a crazy big nose."

"Come down, Alice!" shouted Lydia, almost tipping the ladder with her urgency. "No longer a request! Down, now!"

Alice was on her way down already—spurred to action by Lydia's vehemence.

"Why?" Down and down and down. "What's happening?"

"Just hurry. Hurry, hurry, hurry, *hurry!* That's got to be Wesley—he rides a motorcycle—and the guy with the big nose is Hitch!"

# CHAPTER SIXTEEN
## *Hitch*

Lydia was thrilled that her destiny with Hitch was changing. Not the part about loving then losing him—she was still going to lose him—but at least now she had the chance to bestow a final farewell. *If* she could get to Wesley before he dropped off Rosalind's present and left again. Lydia didn't think destiny would be so unkind, but wasn't willing to trust in anything, not with a kiss on Hitch's nose at stake. Spurning the paths that wandered idly across Bobolink Meadow One, she plowed right through the long grasses, taking the most direct route to the Arundel entrance. She pushed herself to run her fastest and encouraged Alice to do the same. And both girls shrieked as they ran— Alice's shrieks were superb—imploring Wesley not to leave until they reached him.

Victory! When the girls came charging out of the meadow, they saw—

Not Wesley—that was true. But his motorcycle was there, pulled over to the side of the lane, and so was Hitch. Hitch, still in his sidecar, his giant solemn face topped by a safety helmet. Lydia threw herself onto him and kissed his big nose.

"I love you, I've missed you, I'm so glad to see you," she cried. "Alice, Alice, come meet him! I know he's big, but he'd never hurt anyone."

Alice was hanging back. "I know that. It's just— Do you think he'd mind? He's never met me."

Lydia should have remembered that Hitch could have this effect on people. Her dad called him *Canis regalis*, "royal dog," and even in his goofy helmet, Hitch maintained his stately air.

"I'll introduce you. Hitch, this is my friend Alice. Alice, this is Hitch, and he's very affectionate. I promise."

That was enough encouragement for Alice. She kissed Hitch heartily, and then also mentioned to Lydia that there was a man lying down on the ground, on the other side of the motorcycle. And so there was.

"Hi, Wesley," said Lydia. "I'm glad we caught you. Did you hear us shouting?"

"Couldn't have missed it." He looked up at her, crinkling the corners of his eyes. This, Lydia knew, meant that he was smiling on the inside. "Is this the entrance to Arundel?"

"Yes, the pillars are." Bundles of all shapes and sizes were stowed on the motorcycle and in the sidecar. She wondered which held Rosalind's gift. "What are you doing down there?"

"Checking the clutch cable."

Wesley was always checking something on this ancient motorcycle. He'd once had a better bike but had sold it to pay the vet for removing Hitch's ruined leg.

"This is my friend Alice. She lives here."

"Hi, Wesley," said Alice. "I like your dog."

He nodded his agreement.

"He never says much," Lydia whispered to Alice. "Don't take it personally."

"I won't. It's nice when people don't talk all the time."

"Wesley, can we let him out of the sidecar?" Lydia wanted to make the most of her short time with Hitch.

"He'd like that."

Lydia showed Alice how to unlatch the sidecar door, and out stepped Hitch, who stretched, then made it clear that he'd like them to take off his helmet. His grunt of thanks afterward, and the way he shook his ears, compelled Lydia to kiss those ears while Alice lavished affection on his nose; then they changed places and kissed him some more. Meanwhile, Wesley sat up long enough to produce a dog bowl from one of his bundles and handed it to Lydia, along with a jug of water for Hitch. The girls shared the task of filling the water bowl, splattering a few drops on Hitch during one of the jug transfers, but he was patient with them, and glad to quench his thirst.

"Lyds," said Wesley.

He'd stood up, wiping his hands on his jeans. There were no crinkling eyes, and his shoulders drooped.

"What's wrong?" she asked.

"The clutch cable is broken."

Lydia didn't know what a clutch cable was, or how one could break. But Wesley did all his own motorcycle repairs. She'd once watched him replace the muffler. He'd let her hand him the tools, though a few times she had to fight Hitch for the privilege.

"You can fix it, can't you?" she asked.

"Only if I find a replacement." Wesley was soon on his phone, talking to someone named Charlene.

Alice whispered to Lydia. "If he can't, they have to stay here. They can sleep in Jack's room."

Lydia had already had this thought and dismissed it. Batty didn't want Wesley at Arundel and Wesley didn't want to be here. That had to override any private longings for an extended visit with Hitch.

Now there was a new problem—Flashvan was headed toward them, blundering its way down from the mansion. Its menacing swerves indicated that Ben was driving. But Lydia wondered if it could be Batty, losing control of the steering wheel because she'd just spotted Wesley. If it was Batty, Lydia wanted to get to her before she got to them, to explain the situation. She started running up the lane, hoping that whichever sibling was driving was paying enough attention not to run over her.

The van stopped, squealing and shuddering, and without hitting Lydia. It was Ben.

"Wesley's here," she said, climbing in.

"I see him, and I heard you two yelling for him a few minutes ago—so I grabbed this fancy transport to come say hello. By the way, Alice can really shriek, can't she? Like sonic distortions of the universe."

"His clutch cable is broken."

"That doesn't sound good."

"He's trying to find a new one. What should we do if he can't?"

"Hmm?"

"Alice wants them to stay— Ben!" He wasn't paying attention. "Hello! This is a possible crisis!"

"I just had a genius idea, Lyds. Wouldn't it be great to put Hitch into the last scene of the film, when Alice is dying? The huge dog mourning the little alien?"

"We can't—" She stopped, overwhelmed with trying to figure out who would want what, who would stay where, what was best for Hitch, what was best for Batty, and what Charlene was telling Wesley at this very moment. She would let nature take its course, let the chips fall something, something, whatever that expression was. Her father probably had a Latin phrase for it. "I'm staying neutral."

"About?"

"Everything. Let's go see if Wesley found a clutch

cable, and we will walk. I don't trust you not to crash the van into his motorcycle, and then there would be extra problems."

"I thought you were going to stay neutral."

"Not about this."

When they reached the others, Wesley was getting off his phone, and Alice was taking photos of Hitch and explaining at great length her ongoing rivalry with Jack. When she finally took a breath, Hitch edged away to greet Ben the way he always did, with their own personal ritual. Hitch stood on his back legs, his one front leg draped over Ben's shoulder, as Ben wrapped his arms around Hitch. And for long moments, the two stared at each other with mutual affection and respect.

"Hey, Wesley," said Ben when they were through. "Motorcycle problems?"

"Some, yeah. I can have the part shipped as soon as I know where I'm staying. I'm sure there are camp-grounds around here."

"Forget campgrounds," said Alice. "You can stay in my brother Jack's room. He's in Canada, so you wouldn't have to share."

"Batty wouldn't like that," he said.

"It's a big estate, Wesley," said Ben. "If you and Hitch stay on the cottage side, you could never run into Batty. Of course, it would have to be her decision."

"And Alice's parents'," added Wesley.

"My parents will say yes," said Alice. "Lydia, they'll say yes, won't they?"

"I'm staying neutral." Though it was getting ever more difficult to pretend she didn't want Hitch staying here. "Alice, don't pinch me. I have to."

This got an eye crinkle from Wesley. "Is Rosy here?"

"She's coming tomorrow, with Skye," said Ben. "And Skye and Dušek are getting married, too. Double wedding."

"That's great. Good for Skye. How about Jeffrey, the guy who answered Batty's phone. Is he here?"

"It's his house, so yes. He and Batty are putting together the wedding band."

Wesley gazed off into the distance, seeking some lost horizon.

"Why don't I go talk to Batty?" said Ben. "And Jane and Jeffrey. See what they think."

"Don't forget my parents," added Alice. "Tell them about using Jack's room."

"I'm outnumbered here," said Wesley. "Lyds, you sure you want to stay neutral? You could even this up for me."

"But she wouldn't even it up," said Alice. "She wants Hitch here—"

Lydia interrupted. "Wesley, would you mind if Alice and I took Hitch for a walk while Ben is talking to people?"

"We can take him to the cottage and show him Jack's room," said Alice.

"Go ahead," he said. "But don't promise him he

can sleep there. I don't need any more opposition to my campground plan."

On the way to the cottage, the girls argued about Lydia's neutrality. Alice said that Lydia should put her entire soul into keeping Hitch with them for as long as possible. Lydia tried to explain about her loyalty to Batty, and that took them on a conversational detour about loyalty to siblings—Alice wasn't sure how much of it Jack deserved. Then there was another detour about whether dogs should sleep on bunk beds, and particularly on Jack's. Because neither girl knew the answer to either question, Alice asked if Hitch could climb steps with only three legs, Lydia assured her that he could, and by then they'd forgotten their disagreement, and were happy to watch Hitch enjoying the new scenery and smells.

Another thing they'd forgotten was the possibility of finding Hatshepsut on the stairs. They did. Not only was this one of her days for climbing, but she'd gotten farther than ever before, and had been positive she could finally reach the second floor. While she squawked furiously, horrified at the sudden apparition of Hitch, he seemed pleased to see her, cocking his ears in an attempt to understand chicken language. This further enraged Hatshepsut—she wanted to be feared, not understood—making her squawk louder than ever.

"I'll go get her," said Lydia. "You hold him back."

Alice grabbed Hitch's collar with both hands. "I'll try, but don't count on it."

Lydia ran up the steps and scooped up Hatshepsut, who finally quieted down and retreated with wounded dignity, tucking her head under Lydia's arm. Lydia was pleased to be trusted that way, except that having a chicken under her arm turned out to be ticklish.

"Be still, at least," she told Hatshepsut. "When you move, you tickle more."

"Lydia, I can't hold him," said Alice.

Hitch's interest in the chicken had only increased when Lydia picked her up. Deciding he wanted a closer look, he'd already dragged Alice up several steps.

It wasn't hard to choose between letting Hatshepsut get more upset and letting Alice be knocked around on the stairs. "Save yourself! Let go of him!"

Alice did let go, and Hitch pressed onward. To be fair, it was his only choice. Because he was too big to turn around on the stairs, the only way back down was backward, which is difficult enough for a dog with four legs, but nearly impossible for one with only three.

"Dad!" screamed Alice. "If you can hear me, we need help!"

Cagney came right away. He'd brought along a hammer, in case Alice's cry for help meant she needed rescuing from a terrifying intruder. At first this seemed to be true—his young daughter and her friend hemmed in by a gigantic beast—but then he noticed that Alice wasn't frightened and that Lydia was giggling. The tickling had started up again.

Cagney put down his hammer. "Alice, where did you get that horse?"

"He's a dog, not a horse," said Alice. "Could you take Hatshepsut from Lydia, please?"

"She's tickling me," added Lydia.

Cagney's phone beeped. "Nat? Alice has gotten a horse stuck on our steps."

"He's not a horse!" protested Alice.

Her father waved at her to be quiet. "Batty's ex-boyfriend? . . . Stay here? It's fine with me."

"Mr. Pelletier, Wesley can build and fix things," said Lydia.

"Carpentry?"

"Anything."

Cagney went back to the phone. "Ask if he'd mind helping with the benches and tables. . . . Great. Let me know what happens." He hung up.

"Is Wesley staying with us?" asked Alice. "I love Hitch very much."

"Hitch is the horse?"

Hitch took a moment away from Hatshepsut to gaze sadly at Cagney.

Cagney nodded back at him. "My apologies. I do know you're a dog. Here, Lydia, hand Hatshepsut over to me."

Her eyes shut, preparing for death, Hatshepsut

was successfully passed across the dog to the shelter of Cagney.

"Thank you," said Lydia, glad to be done with the tickling.

"You're welcome. Now, truth time, Alice. I understand that Hitch belongs to Batty's ex-boyfriend, but why is he on our stairs?"

"We're showing him Jack's room, in case he and Wesley end up sleeping here."

"I suppose that makes sense. Don't let him eat Jack's furniture."

Cagney took Hatshepsut outside, and Hitch docilely followed Lydia up the stairs to the second floor.

"There's my room," Alice said as she came up behind them. "It's right next to Jack's room, so we'll be very close to you at night."

He allowed himself a polite glance, just in case there was more livestock in there.

"*If* he stays here," said Lydia.

"Right. Oh, Lyds, I have an idea. Take Hitch into my closet and wait."

Lydia understood right away. They would show him how they could communicate by knocking on the wall between the closets. Maybe they'd work out a code. One knock for "hello," two for "meet me in the hallway." *If* he stayed.

But once in the room, Lydia had trouble distracting Hitch from the alien costume, resting on the floor next to Alice's bureau. The tights, especially, were a lure, with their glued-on chicken feathers. To get Hitch into the closet, Lydia told him a white lie, though it could have been true, she just didn't know if it was—that the feathers had been taken not from Hatshepsut, but from Nefertiti.

At last he believed her, and went into the closet just as a chunk of cardboard flew off the wall, barely missing Lydia. It looked like Alice wasn't going to be content with a knocking code—she was over there tearing open a hole.

"Won't Jack be angry?" asked Lydia, ducking a wad of tape.

"I'll fix it before he comes home." Alice's face appeared at the hole. "Hello, Hitch. This is going to be our secret communication spot while you stay here."

"*If* he stays," protested Lydia. "Don't raise his hopes."

Hitch stuck his nose through to Alice, dislodging another piece of cardboard. This seemed to please him—his madly wagging tail was banging against anything nearby, including Lydia. She tried to think of a way to make him less happy, but before she could, he'd backed away from Alice and was kissing Lydia in gratitude for—what?—letting him bust up cardboard?

"See how much he loves it here?" asked Alice through the hole. "He just has to stay."

Lydia knew she should argue, but Hitch's kisses were ruining her ability to remain neutral. She kissed him back, and let herself hope with all her heart that he and Wesley would end up visiting for a while.

# CHAPTER SEVENTEEN
## *Death of an Alien*

IT HADN'T BEEN EASY to dislodge Wesley from his campground plan. He didn't want to intrude on the Pelletiers, or on Batty. But Ben had fought hard to persuade him to stay at the cottage, and Natalie had fought along with Ben, knowing that Cagney would appreciate the extra help with tables and benches. Jane said she was fine with whatever Batty decided. And when Batty let it be known—with Jeffrey acting as intermediary—that she didn't mind having Wesley and Hitch at the cottage as long as they stuck to that side of the estate, Wesley surrendered to the majority.

Lydia and Alice learned all this when Ben delivered Wesley to the cottage and introduced him to Cagney. Ben also brought Lydia a note from Batty.

*Give Hitch a kiss from me. I wish I could see him, but it tore my heart saying good-bye to him last time and I can't do it again. P.S. I feel the same way about Wesley, not the part about wishing I could see him—because I don't— but that I can't see him for the same reason I can't see Hitch. P.P.S. Don't try to tell me that Wesley's broken clutch cable has anything to do with destiny. It doesn't. Hugs.*

Even Charlene with the clutch cable was working in the girls' favor. Her delivery service couldn't get it to Wesley until the next afternoon—by the time he'd completed the installation, it would be too late to get on the road again. He and Hitch would be at the cottage for another forty-two hours, nearly eternity, and for much of it, Lydia and Alice would have Hitch all to themselves.

While Wesley went to work on benches and tables, Lydia and Alice went on their first adventure with Hitch. They took him to the stream that cut across one corner of the estate, far behind the cottage, hidden behind rough brush and trees.

All three walked boldly into the water and enjoyed doing so, except that Alice thought the stream would be better if it were deeper. This led to the idea of building a dam, which Hitch embraced enthusiastically, sitting down in the water and using his one front paw to dig mud. As quickly as he could dig it, the girls used it to build a dam wall.

"It's beginning to work," said Alice. "Look, the water is getting trapped."

"We're like beavers," said Lydia.

"Dig, Hitch, dig!"

And Hitch continued to dig, and the dam wall continued to grow, until the girls realized that if they went much farther, they could cause a flood. But once they explained the situation to Hitch, he was just as happy to help knock down the wall as he had been to help build it. Everyone got filthy in the process and had to be hosed down by Cagney and Wesley when they went back to the cottage. But not until after Alice had asked for a photo to be taken and sent to Jack, along with this message: *This is Hitch, the world's greatest dog, and he's here with me, not you. Ha-ha. Love, Alice.*

That was when Hitch noticed the chicken pen, which appeared to be deserted. He sat down and stared into it anyway. And stared. And stared.

"They're hiding from you," Alice told Hitch. "There's nothing to see."

"Wouldn't you rather do more exploring?" asked Lydia. "Oh, wait, here comes somebody."

It was Cleopatra VII, poking her head out of the little henhouse. Hitch started forward eagerly, and she instantly withdrew.

"This is a waste of time, Hitch," said Alice.

But now Hatshepsut strutted out of the henhouse.

It seemed that she'd decided to stop being intimidated by the huge dog. Either that or she was showing off for her friends. Or, possibly, her small chicken brain had misplaced the memory of her former encounter with him. The why didn't matter to Hitch. He was simply pleased to see Hatshepsut again, and decided to watch her for as long as she was there to watch. She climbed up onto the roof, he nodded his approval, she flapped her wings—which he thought delightful— she turned her back on him, he didn't care. And so it went until Alice and Lydia got bored. As much as they loved Hitch, watching him watch Hatshepsut wasn't their idea of a good time. They decided to put together more fabric and yarn creations while they waited, and this is what they did. Hitch continued to be so intent on Hatshepsut that he didn't notice the decorations that kept being tied to his collar, until he was superb, an extravaganza of color.

"*Canis regalis*," said Lydia. "Now he needs a crown."

Alice pulled out a piece of yellow fabric. "Let's make him one."


"Death!" Alice pulled on one leg of her alien tights. "I haven't been thinking about it nearly enough."

Ben had scheduled the alien shoot for sunset, and it was getting close to that now. He'd wanted Alice to mull over death ahead of time, to get herself in the right frame of mind. Lydia didn't believe Alice needed encouragement to think about death.

"Death, death, death," said Lydia. "There, that's plenty."

"I guess so." Alice started putting on her leotard. "Do you think Batty might change her mind about seeing Wesley and fall back in love and then Hitch can stay even longer?"

"No. And, anyway, the wedding is in three days, and then we'll all be leaving."

"I don't want *you* to leave, either."

Lydia preferred not to think about it. "Let's pretend I'm not."

The alien head would wait until they got downstairs. They carried it together, handling it like the precious object it was. It had survived the shoots leading up to this one—no point in causing damage now, before the very last scene. When they safely reached the first floor, Alice knelt, making it easier to receive her cranial burden.

"Is it straight?" asked Lydia.

"Little bit to the right. Yes, there." Alice stood up, an alien complete. "Cold, lonely death. Go see if Wesley's in the kitchen."

Wesley knew the shoot was coming—he'd agreed to come along, to help Hitch with his part—but he hadn't yet seen the glory that was Alice the alien. Lydia went to the kitchen to make sure the time was right for the unveiling. Natalie was hand-stitching the hem of a bridesmaid dress, Cagney was drinking coffee, and Wesley was stretched out on the floor beside the dishwasher, which was no longer in its usual place, but out from under the counter and on its back. Hitch was being Wesley's assistant, sitting patiently nearby, with a screwdriver in his mouth. His collar was still bedecked with yarn from earlier that day, but he'd refused the crown, indeed burying it beside the chicken coop.

"Wesley heard a rattling noise in the dishwasher," said Cagney.

"He seems to know as much about dishwashers as he does about carpentry," added Natalie.

Lydia recognized the metal toolbox on the floor near Wesley. After he'd fixed both the refrigerator and washing machine at home, her father had dubbed him the Appliance Whisperer. *Machinarum susurrator.*

"He knows about everything," she said.

"No, I don't." Wesley held up a teeny tiny button. "Here's what was rattling. It was caught in the pump."

"Nat," said Cagney. "Have your stuffed dolls been using the dishwasher again?"

Natalie took the button and pocketed it. "I've told them and told them, but they don't listen. Thank you, Wesley. I feel foolish."

"Don't. I found a chip of mica in the Penderwicks' washing machine filter."

"Ben's," said Lydia. "Not mine."

Ready to reassemble the machine, Wesley put out his hand for the screwdriver. Hitch passed it over and, his job done, went to stare out the back door. He'd done this off and on through dinner, looking always for Hatshepsut, or any other chicken who might show her face.

As Cagney and Wesley shoved the dishwasher back under the counter, a muffled cry for Lydia came from the hall. The alien was weary of waiting.

"Sorry!" called Lydia. "You can come in now."

Alice leapt into the room. "Behold, Wesley! I am Alice the Amazing Alien!"

"Terrifying," said Wesley.

"I'm not just terrifying." Alice let the head droop to one side. "I'm also tragic."

"Come over here, honey," said her mother. "Looks like one of the ears needs a few more stitches."

"Are we ready for the shoot?" The alien turned toward the back door. "Hitch?"

Wesley snapped his fingers and Hitch left his chicken-surveillance post.

"We're ready," said Wesley.

When they left, the sun was going down, and twilight was thickening around them. Wesley and Lydia walked on either side of Alice, helping her navigate the terrain she could barely see through her eyeholes. Hitch followed, his ears cocked, listening to the day birds announcing the coming of night, a thousand

210

and one cicadas practicing their scales, up and down, up and down, and the *hoo-hoo* of an owl, a night bird warning the small meadow creatures that his hunt would soon begin.

"*Hoo-hoo,*" imitated Alice.

Hitch trotted up, staring at her alien head, then sniffed at the chicken feathers on her legs, then stared at her alien head again. He seemed to be trying to fit the sound of the owl in with the feathers of a chicken, not to mention the head of an alien.

"It's just Alice," said Lydia.

"Now I'll be a raven." Alice *caw-caw*ed throatily, as if a frog had turned into a bird. "Jeffrey can make that sound on his clarinet."

Even more perturbed by the raven than the owl, Hitch poked at Alice with his big nose until Wesley snapped his fingers. Hitch dropped back and returned to listening to actual birds.

"He seems like a nice guy," said Wesley.

"Jeffrey?" said Lydia.

"Nice!" Alice's voice exploded out of the alien head. "He's like a perfect human being."

"No one is perfect," said Lydia, but then couldn't think of anything wrong with Jeffrey. "He has a clump of hair that used to stick up. I've seen it in old pictures."

"Hair can't count, because what about bald—"

Alice tripped on a fallen branch but was rescued in time by Wesley.

"He taught Batty music when she was young?" he said.

"Piano, mostly," said Lydia. "I mean, he got her started on it when she was five, and from then on, he was always kind of her mentor—she called it *mentore*. That's Italian."

She started to sing "*mentore*, oh, oh," to the tune of a song called "Volare." It was a good song for a moonlit night, and she was inspired to dance along. And then Alice joined in with the singing—she knew all the words, and just substituted *mentore* for *volare* at the appropriate spots—and tried a few dance steps, too. Until she almost tripped again.

"Careful," said Wesley.

"My mom likes that song," said Alice. "My dad says it's because she dated a guy named Angelo in high school."

Lydia heard what could have been a quiet chuckle, and looked quickly at Wesley. There were crinkles around his eyes, so it could have been him. Or it could have been another bird or beast.

"What are you giving Rosy for a wedding gift?" she asked him.

"One of my mobiles."

"You mean, like Batty's? Oh, I love that. Alice, you should see it, all these adorable Hitches of different sizes, hanging from wires, spinning around. Lucky Rosalind!"

"Rosy's has flowers instead of dogs. I'm going to make a mobile for Skye, too, once I get settled out west." He pulled a piece of wood out of his pocket and handed it to Lydia. "What do think of this?"

It was a goofy little star, chunky around the middle, its rays spread out unevenly. Wesley had given it as much personality as the tiny Hitches on Batty's mobile. This star was optimistic and also humble, yet still aware of its importance in the universe.

"I like it very much," she said. "You are a great artist."

"I just make things."

Lydia tried to show Alice the star, but no matter where she held it, it was either too close and looked like a blob or too far away and looked like nothing. Lydia was still trying to find the happy in-between when a peal of thunder came rolling out of the west. She and Wesley checked the sky. It was still clear, the rising moon shining brightly, but dark clouds were gathering. No time left for chatting or singing. Rain was coming.

The death scene had originally been planned for the springhouse. But because of Batty's edict about Hitch and Wesley sticking to the cottage side of the estate, Ben had moved it to Blossom's gate. While the springhouse would have been better, nothing would beat having Hitch in the scene.

When they arrived, Ben already had the tripod and

camera set up several yards from the gate. Lydia was now experienced enough to get her own equipment ready, connecting the headset to the receiver, and the receiver to the camera, while Ben attached the microphone to Alice.

"Are you prepared to die, young alien?" he asked.

"Yes, I am reeking with death."

"Excellent."

"Can I do anything?" asked Wesley.

"Stand by," said Ben.

"Stand by, *please*," said Lydia. Ben didn't need to say it to her or Alice anymore, but Wesley was a guest.

Ben ignored her—there was the thunder again.

"Alice," he said, "you're going to start on the other side of the gate, just inside the field. The sheep aren't there, by the way. I checked."

"They're in the barn for the night," said Alice, mistress of at least one of the sheep. "Duh."

Ben ignored the "duh" also. It was beneath him, as a serious director. "When I start to roll, you stumble out of the gate. You're exhausted, starving, you can barely stand up. You teeter, look up at the moon— your home is light-years beyond it—and then you die."

"What do you want Hitch to do?" asked Wesley.

"Keep him out of the shot until Alice dies— please—then he should go to her, realize she's dead, and be sad about it. Alice, take your place."

Wesley repeated the instructions to Hitch, who

214

listened carefully. But although the alien did her part perfectly, dying tragically, Hitch remained unmoved. Lydia wondered if Alice's earlier owl and raven calls had turned him against her.

Again they went through the scene, with Ben keeping a careful watch on the clouds as they advanced steadily on the moon, and still Hitch had no interest in being Alice's costar. Wesley commanded, Lydia begged, Ben kept shooting, Alice kept dying, and Hitch only yawned.

Alice sat up, and tried again to make Hitch understand.

"I've met no one on this planet. I know I'm dying and will never see my home again. Imagine how you would feel if you were stuck here and Wesley was up there, beyond the moon," she said. "Wesley, do you think he gets it?"

He shrugged. "Hard to tell."

"Alice, back to your starting position," said Ben. "If this one doesn't work, we'll have to wrap for tonight. Ready? And . . . rolling."

Somehow Alice managed to improve her performance. Her fall, her dying, were truly heartbreaking. There she lay, the broken alien who would never get home, whose family and friends would never know what fate had befallen her. So tragic was the scene that Lydia forgot she was watching Alice and felt a tear on her face. But no, it was a drop of rain, and then more drops, and more, splattering down on the tragi-cally dead alien. And then, at last—though they'd all stopped expecting or even hoping he'd do so—Hitch got into character. He approached Alice, snuffled mournfully at her lifeless body, even tried to lick her woolen face to revive her. But he'd come too late and, realizing it, howled his grief up into the rain.

# CHAPTER EIGHTEEN
## *The Wedding Veil*

Aᴛ ʙʀᴇᴀᴋꜰᴀꜱᴛ, Lʏᴅɪᴀ ᴀɴᴅ Alice asked if they could introduce Hitch to Blossom. Wesley gave permission—he'd be busy again today, building benches and tables, and fixing his motorcycle when the clutch cable arrived.

"What happens if Lydia and I ambush the delivery truck bringing the clutch cable, and then you can't fix it?" asked Alice.

"I'd order another."

"Please don't ambush the delivery truck," said Cagney. "I'm too busy to bail you out of jail."

"Well, at least you're staying until tomorrow, Wesley. Thank you." Alice hugged him enthusiastically. Lydia didn't think she'd ever seen Wesley so surprised.

Hitch went outside with the girls but, like the day before, decided to stare into the chicken pen for a while. Cleopatra I, Nefertiti, Batgirl, and Cleopatra VII once again decided to hide in their house until he was gone. And Hatshepsut once again ventured out, where Hitch could see her, but this time flaunted her courage by climbing onto the chicken house roof, her eyes bright with challenge.

"Hitch wants her to come closer, I think," said Lydia.

"She won't." Alice pulled out her mother's phone and shook it, as if doing so would help it receive a message. "Still nothing from Jack."

Ben had sent Jack a clip from last night's death scene, along with a message from Alice: *This is me in a brilliant film and you will never do better ever ever ever ever forever I am the champ. Love, Alice.*

"He might not even have seen it until this morning," said Lydia. "It'll take him a while to top it."

"He can't top it. That's the point. He should just admit defeat and surrender."

The Jack familiar to Lydia—the one in photos— didn't look like he'd admit defeat easily. But Alice was right. How could he possibly do better than the alien death scene?

"Hitch," said Lydia. "You can come back to Hatshepsut later, but now we're going to meet a sheep."

"Much more fun than a chicken," added Alice.

But he wasn't ready to leave, and Lydia was getting impatient. Skye and Rosalind were arriving soon—and Alice had promised to watch for them from atop Blossom's wall. Relief arrived via Nefertiti. Having forgotten about the dog, and wondering where Hatshepsut was, she blithely hopped out into the sunshine. Hitch woofed a happy hello, and Nefertiti descended into a hysteria so intense that Hatshepsut had to get off the roof, herd her back into the house, and stay there to keep her calm. Thwarted, but resigned, Hitch turned away from the pen, and the three companions set off.

Once they reached the gate, it took a while to convince him to look through it. He was too busy snuffling over the site of the previous night's shoot, paying particular attention to where the alien had died. But when he did look up, he seemed pleasantly surprised to see Blossom and her sheep friends roaming the field. His snuffling took on a new urgency.

Now that Hitch was intrigued, the girls had to overcome Blossom's probable unwillingness to meet the giant dog gawking at her through the gate. Alice would climb to the top of the wall, where she could both watch for Rosalind and Skye and perform a tae kwon do dance for Blossom, one that would demonstrate the safety and normalcy of the situation—that is, despite the dog. Meanwhile, Lydia would enter the field bearing both oats and *Alice's Adventures in Wonderland and Through the Looking-Glass*, hoping this

double treat would tempt Blossom once she'd been reassured by Alice's tae kwon do dance.

"Ready?" asked Alice.

"Ready."

"Initiate plan." Alice headed toward the built-in
ladder that would let her climb to the top.

Lydia said, "Hitch, I'm going through this gate, but
you can't yet. And back up a little, so that when I
close the gate, I don't smoosh your nose."

Hitch blinked at her without backing up, then
went back to staring at the sheep. Lydia slipped past
him and closed the gate as carefully as she could—
apologizing, since a little nose smooshing was impossible to avoid.

"Yoo-hoo, Blossom!" she called, throwing oats into
the air. "Oats! Oats for you!"

Alice was already on top of the wall, confidently
running back to just above where the gate was. "You
didn't tell me what color Rosalind's car is."

"Yellow." Lydia opened the Alice book. Since
they'd already finished with the sheep in the book, she
was going to read her favorite part, about the mad tea
party. "Hitch, this is for you, too, if you want to listen.
'There was a table set out under a tree in front of the
house, and the March Hare and the Hatter were having tea at it: a Dormouse—'"

"Blossom isn't paying any attention," said Alice.
"Show her the oats again."

"Oats, Blossom!" Lydia tossed another handful. "—'a Dormouse was sitting between them, fast asleep, and the other two were using it as a cushion, resting their elbows on it, and talking over its head.'"

"That did it. She's looking at us now," said Alice.

"Are you remembering to watch for my sisters?"

"Yes. No yellow car yet."

"'"Very uncomfortable for the Dormouse," thought Alice; "only, as it's asleep, I suppose it doesn't mind."'"

"Now Blossom's walking this way."

"'The table was a large one, but the three were all crowded together at one corner of it. "No room! No room!" they cried out when they saw Alice coming. "There's *plenty* of—"'"

"Yellow car!" shouted Alice. "Yellow car, yellow car! You go! I'll take care of Hitch!"

Rosalind stopped the car just as Lydia launched herself through the passenger window, landing on Skye. Her sisters dragged her the rest of the way in and stuffed her between them.

"Let me look at you," said Skye.

Skye's inspections were different from Batty's, with less gazing into eyes and more action, like messing up her hair and poking her to make her giggle. It wasn't the most intimate of greetings, but it came as a relief to Lydia. If this was an indication, getting married wasn't changing Skye. Except that maybe she looked even happier than usual. Batty had once told her that Skye hadn't always been so light-hearted, but in Lydia's memories, Skye was usually smiling. If she wasn't, it was because she was thinking about astrophysics, but that wasn't a lack of happiness, just a seriousness of purpose.

"Dušek must truly be your destiny, Skye," she said.

"What's this talk of destiny? Is our Princess Dandelion Fire growing up?"

There was no easy answer for this question, as Lydia had never before grown up, so didn't know what it felt like. But she figured that reading books to a sheep probably wasn't a sign of impending maturity.

"I don't think so."

"Good." Skye kissed her twice—once on each cheek. "We're certainly not in a hurry for it, right, Rosy?"

"Right, because if Lyds is growing up, we must be ancient."

"And feeble." Skye sucked in her cheeks and hunched over, suddenly ancient and feeble.

"Now let *me* look at you." Rosalind took Lydia's face in her hands. "Iantha told me to make sure you're not homesick."

"I haven't been homesick for even a minute. I told her I wouldn't be."

"I think she just misses you, Lyds," said Skye.

"As does Dad," said Rosalind. "I heard him calling the cat Lydia the other day."

"Asimov probably didn't like that," said Lydia. Asimov had a strict sense of propriety.

"When Dad realized his mistake, he apologized profusely—*Mihi ignosce, feles*—and gave him an extra helping of cat food."

Skye was hanging out the window, taking in Bobolink Meadow One.

"Rosy, wasn't this all lawn when we were here?"

"Yes, don't you remember? We'd just arrived, and Hound threw up on Jane's sneakers, and Cagney appeared, pushing a wheelbarrow across the grass."

"And you fell—kaboom—into a big old crush."

"*What?*" Lydia had never heard anything about Rosalind having a crush on Cagney.

"Don't believe Skye," said Rosalind. "She was too busy getting Jeffrey in trouble to pay attention to what I was doing."

"False," said Skye. "Not the part about getting Jeffrey in trouble—I did that."

"Cagney is Alice's *father.*" Lydia thought her sisters must be talking about a different Cagney.

"We know, honey," said Rosalind. "But he was only nineteen back then, and I was a dippy and over-romantic twelve, and he never knew, and he's never going to find out unless someone opens their big mouth again."

"I will be as a black hole, keeping secrets bound to me," said Skye. "And we like Alice very much, yes?"

"Yes," said Lydia. "Even Ben does."

"High praise," said Rosalind. "Skye, show Lyds that thing you have in the back."

Skye reached for a plastic bag, out of which she pulled a piece of white tulle that seemed to go on and on, and then there was another piece of white tulle, and then Skye impatiently dumped the bag upside down and shook until the whole thing fell out—a bridal veil, layers and layers of the tulle attached to a tiara that was only slightly less garish than a child's dress-up crown. She crammed the tiara onto her head, with the tulle going every which way, including into Lydia's face, which made it difficult to see but not so difficult that she didn't know this was the least Skye-like adornment she'd ever seen. Maybe getting married was going to change Skye after all, and not necessarily for the better.

"Gorgeous, right?" asked Skye.

Lydia pushed the tulle out of her eyes and turned to Rosalind for reassurance.

"Don't worry—it's a joke," said Rosalind. "She found it at a thrift store and was wearing it when I picked her up at the airport."

"You were almost fooled, Rosy," said Skye.

"I wasn't even the tiniest bit fooled." Rosalind plucked the veil off Skye and tossed it aside.

"Did Jane tell you Mrs. Tifton thinks brides should wear veils?" asked Lydia.

"She does? In that case—" Skye put the veil back

on. "So tell us, Lyds. We're dying to hear how you managed to charm the woman."

"Charm her! Who said that?"

"The word is that Mrs. T. doesn't loathe you like she does the rest of us," said Rosalind. "And we are amazed, and wonder how you did it."

"I didn't do anything. She got the wrong idea about me from the beginning."

Skye flapped her veil. "That you're nicer than the rest of us? *That* wrong idea?"

"Yes, that very horribly wrong idea," said Lydia with finality. She didn't want to discuss this anymore.

"We'll stop teasing." Rosalind kissed Lydia's cheek. "We know and love you, Lyds, exactly the way you are."

"Anyway, Jeffrey's kept her away for days now, and we hope she won't come back."

"And how are Wesley and Hitch?"

"Hitch is, you know, adorable. And wait until you see what Wesley made for you, Rosy." He'd given Lydia a peek into the bundle that contained Rosalind's mobile. The flowers were just as endearing as Skye's wooden star, and also as different from it as Rosalind was from Skye. "He's making one for you, too, Skye, but he can't finish until he goes west."

"He didn't need to give us wedding gifts," said Rosalind. "I hope he knows that."

Lydia thought that Rosalind should remember how

difficult it was to figure out what Wesley did or didn't know. "He likes to make things."

"And imagine, Rosy," said Skye, "if all the Penderwick ex-boyfriends gave us gifts. Jane's alone would overwhelm us with swag. What do you think your Oliver would give us?"

"He's not my Oliver."

"I thought he gave people ugly flower arrangements," said Lydia. That was the story she'd heard— part of the night she stabbed him with the quesadilla.

"Right. That wouldn't do," said Skye.

"And none of anyone's ex-boyfriends are as nice as Wesley," added Rosalind. "Skye, we need to ask Lydia our favor, so please get serious."

"I'm too happy and excited to be serious. It turns out to feel good, this getting married thing."

"Take off your veil, anyway. Maybe that will calm you down."

"Veil off," said Skye, whipping it from her head. "I'm serious now."

Lydia couldn't think of any favor her older sisters might ask of her. And when they did ask it, her mind went blank.

"What do you mean, choreograph the procession?" There had been no previous talk of a procession. "You mean for the wedding? The day after tomorrow?"

Rosalind nodded. "An easy routine, nothing too sophisticated, since none of the rest of us can dance like you can."

Sophisticated! With so little time to come up with a routine and even less time to teach it to her sisters, none of whom except sometimes Batty were good at listening to her. Or, in Skye's case, listening to anyone.

"Rosy and I have picked out a song," said Skye. "'Dance Me to the—' I hear the dogs."

All three could hear the dogs. Someone must have told them that Skye had arrived—not the sister who loved them the most, but the sister who took them on the best runs—and they were effusive in their welcomes. Jeffrey, Jane, and Batty were trying to keep up with Feldspar and Sonata. Ben was outpacing them all, closing in on his favorite sister, armed with his camera.

Skye was already putting her veil back on.

"We haven't finished asking Lydia—"

"Hold on!" Skye yelled out the window. "I'll be right there!"

Jeffrey and Jane slid to a halt, which Lydia at first thought was a polite response to Skye telling them to hold on. But now she saw that wasn't it at all. Jeffrey had a soccer ball, which he now triumphantly spun on his index finger, showing off like a basketball star.

"Skye!" he called. "Jane and I challenge you! Two-on-one slaughter!"

"Wait, Skye, don't go yet," said Rosalind.

But Skye was already out of the car and tearing away, her veil floating behind her. She flung herself first at Batty, for a long, joyous embrace, then at Ben, for a less demonstrative but still loving hug, then turned her attention to Jeffrey, who kicked the soccer ball to Jane, who trapped it and dribbled it away, shouting an interesting variety of threats and taunts. And the dogs raced circles around Skye, and Ben shot footage, and Batty laughed, and away they all went, up the lane and out of sight.

"I should have expected this. Instant regression," said Rosalind. "So, Lyds, what do you think about choreographing the procession? Just the five sisters—Ben will be shooting the ceremony—and Dad, but he won't come into it until the end."

While Lydia had gotten past her shock, she still thought this a nearly impossible task and preferred to refuse it and go back to Alice and Hitch with no responsibility weighing on her. And yet, she couldn't help envisioning a sprightly dance across the lawn, the light dresses with their different-colored sashes swishing and swaying to the music.

"I'll do it," she said. "But everyone will have to listen to me."

"We'll listen," said Rosalind. "I promise."

# CHAPTER NINETEEN
## Dancing in the Dark

L YDIA AND ALICE STOOD on the top step of the Greek pavilion, looking out over the stage for the wedding procession. The benches weren't in place yet, but Cagney had marked where they'd go with strips of tape. These were to have been a help with the rehearsal that was supposed to be taking place right now, but all the tape had been trodden on, torn, and displaced, because none of Lydia's sisters was listening to her, or looking at her, or doing anything they were supposed to do.

"Maybe we should put Blossom into the procession," said Alice. "She pays more attention than your sisters do."

"You might be right," said Lydia. "And Blossom can't play soccer, which would be another advantage."

229

She'd thought this morning's two-on-one slaughter would be enough soccer for the day. But while she was hiding out with Alice and Hitch, designing the procession, people had started pouring into Arundel. A bunch of Geigers had arrived—the groom himself, plus his older brother Nick, Nick's wife Laura, and their two small children. Then came Dušek, with *his* family—his parents, two brothers, his brothers' wives, and four young children who belonged, in some combination, to the brothers. And since the Czechs were avid soccer players, an after-dinner scrimmage had sprung up. Here, where the rehearsal was supposed to be taking place. Jane, Skye, Ben, and Dušek, plus Laura Geiger, were representing the USA, the others the Czech Republic, and there was much shouting and laughter and scores being argued over in English and Czech.

Jeffrey's dad, Alec, had arrived today, too, bringing his saxophone and his small black-and-white dog, Dyson. Dyson had started the evening by calmly resting in Alec's saxophone case, but the soccer playing had become too much for him, and now he was frantically trying to keep up with Feldspar, impossible for a dog with such short legs. Feldspar himself was determined to be part of the game, trying to kick the ball with his red shoe. Sonata was following Dyson, making sure he didn't get stepped on and, in the process, bumping into the players, and sometimes tripping them.

Then there were the children. The young Czechs

had joined with the young Geigers to form a roving piratical band, with Nick theoretically in charge. Just now, he was leading them in a wild race around the pavilion—his youngest, two-year-old Georgia, riding on his shoulders—and encouraging them all to yell whatever they felt like yelling. Georgia could come up only with "Cookie, cookie," which was very cute, but Lydia did not appreciate the additional noise.

"Even Hatshepsut would pay more attention," said Alice. "We could put her and Blossom both into the procession."

"Let's use *all* the chickens," said Lydia recklessly. "Why not? Anything would be better than this."

Batty, at least, wasn't playing soccer, but neither was she thinking about wedding processions. She was off to one side with Alec and Jeffrey, singing along while they played an infectious old swing song, "In the Mood," but wait—Jeffrey had put down his clarinet and was now dancing with Batty. Lydia had rarely seen Batty dance with such joyous abandon, which didn't seem fair, since Lydia couldn't dance right now, not while she was still figuring out how to control this chaos.

And Rosalind? The eldest Penderwick, the most responsible, the kindest and most thoughtful? The one who'd promised that everyone would listen to Lydia? She'd sneaked off with Tommy to hide behind the pavilion, where they thought they couldn't be seen.

"They're kissing again," said Alice.

"They've been kissing since they were twelve. You'd think they could take a break." Lydia knew she sounded bitter, but that's how she felt right now. She'd worked hard, her choreography would make for a beautiful wedding procession, and her sisters were acting like unruly children.

"Do you want me to try to get everyone's attention?"

"Do you think you can?" Because calling for attention and looking stern had no impact whatsoever—Lydia had been trying that for ten minutes now.

"Dad says it's only for emergencies."

"This is an emergency."

Alice took a deep breath, then let out a series of shrill battle cries, each a combination of whistle and scream, far more alarming than any sound black-capped chickadees or eastern towhees had ever produced. On the first call, dozens of terrified bobolinks rose out of Bobolink Meadow Two and fled Arundel. On the second, five small children fell to the ground, and Georgia started to wail, clinging in terror to her father's head. On the third, Alec's saxophone stopped mid-phrase, Batty and Jeffrey stopped dancing, the soccer ball stopped moving, Rosalind and Tommy stopped kissing, and everyone stared up into the sky, expecting to see—what? Skye later said she'd expected a spaceship crashing to Earth. Ben had hoped for a Nazgûl escaped from Middle-earth.

"Modified bald eagle," said Alice. "Works every time."

Except for Georgia's sobs and the soothing voices of the parents racing toward stricken children, Lydia's audience was now silent. She clapped her hands to get everyone to look at her instead of the sky.

"Thank you for your attention, everyone. That was Alice, being a bald eagle. She can do many birds."

Alice obligingly did a bobolink for them. Several people looked relieved and clapped. Jeffrey, however, was trying hard not to laugh. When Lydia glared at him, he turned his back to her so that she couldn't see him laugh.

Lydia went on. "I apologize for interrupting, but my sisters have an important rehearsal, and we're already late getting started. Rosalind, Skye, Jane, and Batty, please move forward for procession practice. Jeffrey and Alec, I'd like you to stay, but to play procession music only, please. The rest of you may watch if you'd like, but quietly, please."

"Impressive," said Alice.

Impressive or impolite? Lydia wasn't sure, but at least everyone was sorting themselves out. The children were borne away to bed, Jeffrey and Alec looked over the sheet music for the wedding song, "Dance Me to the End of Love," Tommy and Dušek loped off together, and Ben set up his camera—he wanted to practice shooting before the real event.

And finally, Lydia's four older sisters gathered in a clump, ready to work.

"Sorry, Lyds," said Rosalind. "Now we're listening."

"Well, try to *keep* listening," Lydia said.

"Or else," added Alice, who thought she wasn't being stern enough.

"No laughing, Jeffrey," said Lydia, who knew he was about to.

"Never," he said, laughing.

She attempted an expression of wounded dignity but didn't dare wait to see if it worked.

"Rosy, you asked for a dance down the aisle. But the song is long and beautiful, and the aisle is short—Cagney marked it with tape, which you've wrecked by playing soccer on it."

"Here's some," said Jane. "A little piece of it, anyway."

"You'll have to make do with that," said Alice.

Lydia went on. "Therefore, I've expanded the procession route. Before the music begins, the five of us sisters will file out of the carriage house in a straight line. When we reach the rose arbor, we'll get into formation, with me in front, alone, and two pairs behind me, Batty and Jane, then Skye and Rosalind. When we're ready, I'll give the signal to Jeffrey and Alec, they'll start to play, and we will dance—in formation—from there to the end of the aisle, where Dad will join us and escort Rosalind and Skye."

"It sounds wonderful so far," said Rosalind.

"Hear, hear," said Batty.

"The dance itself is quite simple, a pattern of steps that repeats every four measures. The only part that might confuse anyone—"

"Me," said Skye.

"Shh," said Jane.

"—will be the spin. It's not a spin on one foot. Skye—no!"

Rosalind caught Skye before she fell over in the middle of an attempted spin, and this time it was Batty trying to frown at Jeffrey, who had stopped even pretending not to laugh, and at Alec, too, who was joining in, but Batty was too happy to pull off a real frown and therefore had no effect on Jeffrey. Because Alec was an actual adult, he managed to stop laughing, but Lydia was almost certain she saw him hiding a smile behind his saxophone.

"Sorry," said Skye.

"*Not* a spin on one foot," Lydia repeated. "It's really using four tiny steps to make a tight circle. I'll show you in a minute, and when you get comfortable with that, I'll show you the other steps, and we'll put it all together. First, Alice, the bouquets, please."

Alice gathered up the bunches of wildflowers they'd put together and handed one to each sister.

"These are just for practice," she said. "You can drop them and it doesn't matter."

"I didn't realize we'd be carrying bouquets," said Skye. "Was I supposed to order one for myself?"

"It's taken care of," said Jane. "The Pelletiers are letting us raid their gardens tomorrow morning—we'll each make our own."

"Getting married is a lot of work."

"Not that *you* did much of it," said Jane. "Ahem."

"I know, Jane. I'm sorry," said Skye. "I'll pay you back somehow—maybe I'll make your wedding dress."

"That would be a real treat, Jane, a dress made by Skye," said Batty. "Remember when she tore her dress for Nick's wedding, then tried to glue it back together?"

"Didn't happen," said Skye.

"Did," said Rosalind and Jane.

"*Attention!*" Lydia clapped her hands again. "Watch carefully. This is how you turn."

They practiced until dark—the lightning bugs were blinking love messages, the bobolinks had warily returned to their meadow, and the owls were swooping across the sky. There had been significant progress. The sisters were keeping time with the music, no one had bumped into anyone else for fifteen minutes, Skye was remembering to lead with her left foot going into turns, and, most important, they seemed to be enjoying themselves. After Lydia announced that there would be another rehearsal the following night, on the very eve of the wedding, the crowd dispersed.

Because Alice had left a while ago—Lydia couldn't blame her for wanting to get back to Wesley and Hitch—Lydia trudged to the cottage alone and worn out, wondering why anyone would willingly choose to be in charge of people. And yet, as tired as she was, she knew that if everything went well on Saturday, the procession would be lovely, and she would be proud.

Before she could actually see Alice, she could hear her describing the highlights of the rehearsal, to Hitch, probably. But it turned out that Wesley was there, too—the three of them sitting in a row on the porch.

"I was telling them about my eagle cry," said Alice when she spotted Lydia. "They heard it over here."

"I'm sure people heard it in lots of places," Lydia answered. "I wonder what Blossom thought."

"Hitch thought I was a dragon, didn't you, boy?"

Hitch looked up at the sky and said, "Woof."

"Hitch understood me!" crowed Alice. "He's looking for more dragons."

But Lydia had heard a faint hoot before the woof.

"He was woofing at an owl," she said, and sat down next to Alice.

"I say a dragon."

The girls looked to Wesley to say who was right, but he only shrugged.

"He's a dog," he said. "Alice, go back to describing the rehearsal."

"I did my eagle cry—"

Wesley interrupted. "You were telling me why you did it."

"I already mentioned the soccer, kissing, and cute little Georgia."

"And Batty's dancing with Jeffrey," said Lydia. "She was just as disruptive as my other sisters."

"Right, I forgot that part. Alec was playing his sax, and Jeffrey kept twirling Batty around."

"And you left out the dogs, Alice. They were a big part of the chaos."

"I've never seen Batty dance," said Wesley.

"How could I forget the dogs! Hitch, we've got another dog over there named Dyson," said Alice. "Maybe Wesley can build a platform for you to wear on your back for Dyson to ride on. Or we could borrow Georgia. She'd be small enough to ride on Hitch, don't you think?"

"Except when she sings," said Wesley. "She dances a little when she sings, but not full out like you're describing."

"What do you mean?" asked Alice. "We haven't seen Georgia sing or dance."

"I meant Batty."

"You're right, Wesley," said Lydia. "Batty definitely wasn't dancing the way she does when she sings. Alice, let's show him."

It took them a while to straighten out who would

be Jeffrey and who Batty, but Lydia took on Jeffrey once she realized that Alice wouldn't be able to lead her the way Jeffrey had led Batty, especially for the twirling—Alice kept letting go of her and yelling "SPIN!" which isn't how it works.

"Like that," said Alice when they finished and sat down again.

"Sort of. They probably looked better together than we did," said Lydia.

"That's because they've known each other longer," said Alice. "Did you know that when Batty was here the first time, she kept talking about marrying Jeffrey? Dad told me."

"She was only four." Lydia yawned. "Skye says that when Ben was four, he wanted to marry *her*."

"When I was four," said Alice, "I wanted to be a dinosaur and stomp on Jack. What about you, Wesley?"

"I wanted a dog." He put his arm around Hitch.

"Have you heard from Jack yet?" Lydia asked Alice.

"Nothing. He's still trying to get up the nerve to surrender," she answered. "Mom said that it might be nice for both Batty and Jeffrey. Getting married, I mean, not surrendering."

Lydia thought that this was ridiculous. "She's only nineteen."

"Not *now*, when she's older," said Alice. "They could turn Arundel Hall into a music school. Jeffrey talked about that once, and I said I thought it was a good idea. By then, I'd be old enough to be a role model for the children. I could teach them tae kwon do and about life."

Lydia tried to picture Jeffrey and Batty running a music school that included Alice as a tae kwon do instructor, but she was too worn out for such flights of fancy.

"Lydia, you could teach dance," added Alice. "Dad could teach birdcalls, Mom, weaving, and Jack—I don't know what Jack could do. Ice hockey on the pond in winter, I guess. Wesley, you could teach art, and Hitch could be the school mascot. Hitch, would that be fun?"

Apparently, Hitch didn't think it would be fun. He turned his back on Alice and blew woefully into Wesley's ear.

"It's okay, Hitch," said Lydia. "None of this is going to happen, and you'll be out west by then, anyway."

"But not yet, not yet!" said Alice. "Wesley, why leave tomorrow morning? Why not stay all day again? Please, please, please?"

Wesley didn't seem to hear her. He was staring at his lost horizons again.

"Wesley?" Alice nudged him.

"Hmm?"

"What were you thinking?" asked Lydia.

"Just figuring something out."

"What?" asked Alice.

He not only crinkled his eyes, but actually almost smiled, too. "None of your business. You two want to take Hitch for a walk? I have a call to make."

"Yes, please," said Lydia. "If Hitch agrees."

"He will." Wesley snapped his fingers, and Hitch stood, ready for a walk.

As the girls and the dog ran across grass and dodged trees, their shadows playing tag, Lydia's weariness melted away. The moon was sailing close to Arundel, with no rain clouds to block its dazzle tonight. It seemed a magic moon, larger and brighter than the moon that lived over Lydia's home. No, that was silly—she did a silly dance, quick steps and wiggling arms—of course Cameron had the same moon as Arundel. Still, it would be fun to compare moons when she went back there. She'd pay close attention to the one here at Arundel for the rest of her stay. That would give her tonight's moon, then tomorrow's, then the moon on the night of the wedding—

Three moons. That was all she had left.

Lydia stopped dancing—struck, paralyzed, by a sensation of no longer being here, this night, now. A feeling that she was instead living inside a memory, of a precious place and time, one lost and greatly mourned. As strange as this was, Lydia knew what was happening to her. It could be nothing else: Already she was homesick for Arundel, and could hardly bear it.

# CHAPTER TWENTY
*Good-byes*

Wesley had told Lydia and Alice he'd be leaving at sunrise. Alice set her alarm to make sure they'd be awake in time for good-byes, but they didn't need it. They were pulled out of sleep by Hitch and Wesley having one of their rare disagreements. Hitch was chomping at the hole in Jack's closet, making it even larger, Wesley was telling him to stop, and Hitch kept on doing it anyway, until he could stick his entire head and his one front paw into Alice's closet.

This was an entertaining substitute for an alarm, and both girls giggled sleepily until they were awake enough to remember that Hitch was leaving forever, that this was their last chance ever to talk to him in the closet. They tumbled out of bed, crowded into the closet, and kissed him and rubbed his ears and chin until Wesley coaxed Hitch out and told the girls it was time to go. Hurriedly, they put on shoes, then followed Wesley and Hitch downstairs into the kitchen, where Wesley left a thank-you note for the hospitality and Hitch looked out the back door at the chicken pen. All but one of the chickens were tucked away, dreaming in their house, but there was Hitch's favorite, perched on her roof, glaring at him. He blinked at her, and Lydia gulped back a sob—Hatshepsut would miss Hitch, too.

Because motorcycles are too loud for daybreak, the first part of Wesley's journey was made pushing his bike from the cottage to the entrance of Arundel. The girls helped by shoving the sidecar, and wished Hitch didn't look so pleased to be leaving. When they reached the pillars, there was a solemn ceremony of putting on Hitch's helmet and settling him into the sidecar.

"I don't want to say good-bye." Lydia's sob escaped now. "I wish you hadn't come here, and then I wouldn't have to."

"Don't say that, Lydia." Alice climbed onto the sidecar to hug Hitch.

Wesley pulled two crumpled balls of newspaper from his pocket, and handed one to each girl. "Sorry about the wrapping job."

Alice delved into hers first and found a small

wooden Hitch. He was wearing his helmet and looked every inch a *Canis regalis*. Alice clasped it to her heart, and Lydia hoped very much that hers was just the same. Until she opened it. Wesley had carved a Hitch for her, too, but this Hitch had Hatshepsut sitting on his head. Again, Hitch looked like a king, but Wesley had carved Hatshepsut to look just as regal, and Lydia had to stop crying to laugh at these two beasts, finally at peace with each other.

Then the girls hugged Wesley—it was Lydia's first time ever—until he gently pulled away and put on his helmet. Lydia started to cry again, and Alice draped herself across the sidecar, burying her face in Hitch's neck.

But there turned out to be one more person coming to see Wesley and Hitch off, someone who had changed her mind about telling them good-bye. Lydia sensed her coming—it was their sisterly bond—and turned to watch her racing down the lane, so swift she was almost flying, her feet bare, her hair streaming out behind her. She was coming to tell Wesley she still loved him, to beg him to stay, to say she would go west with him—Lydia thought these things, and knew none of them was true.

"Look," she said, and now Wesley, Hitch, and Alice watched with her until the late arrival was there, bent over, her hands on her knees, catching her breath.

"Hey, Batty," said Wesley.

She held up her hand—she couldn't talk yet—and

they waited respectfully, all except for Hitch, who tried to climb over Alice to get out of his sidecar to Batty. Wesley rescued Alice from trampling-by-dog, then talked quietly to Hitch until he calmed down, and until Batty could tell them why she'd come.

"I won't hug you, Wesley, or Hitch, either. But—" Batty flew to Hitch and hugged him fiercely. "All right, I couldn't help that. Darling, darling Hitch! But mostly I came to say thank you."

"What for?" asked Wesley.

"I don't know. Maybe I shouldn't thank you." She smiled, and he smiled back—a real smile, not just a crinkling of the eyes. "No, I mean, thank you for giving me the Hitch mobile—I'll treasure it—and for making wedding gifts for Rosalind and Skye. And—oh, thank you for being you. That's all, I'm done. Good-bye—take good care of Hitch for us, and have a safe trip."

"Wait, Bats, wait. I want to tell you—" Wesley paused. "You're going to be happy."

"I'm already happy."

"I know." He mounted his motorcycle.

"Then what did you mean? *When* did you mean?"

Wesley shook his head and started the engine, drowning out any further questions. But he was still smiling, and willing to give a wave—though more like a salute—before roaring off, taking himself and Hitch onto the open road, heading into their great adventure.

Batty stomped her foot. "He drives me so crazy!"

Lydia wanted to say that Wesley driving Batty crazy was another reason he couldn't be her destiny, but she was too busy crying. Neither Wesley nor Hitch had looked back as they zoomed away, not even once, and that was possibly the saddest part.

Alice was also crying. "Life is horrible."

"No, no, no." Batty gathered them both into a hug. "Life isn't horrible, but I understand why you're sad, and I apologize for bringing Hitch into your lives only to have him leave again."

"And Wesley, too," said Alice. "He's a great artist."

Then they showed Batty their wooden Hitches— she looked at them for a long time, turning them over, taking in every detail.

"And, anyway," said Lydia. "You're crying, too, Batty."

"Just a tiny bit. I'll feel better when I get more sleep. Let's all go back to bed—later, we can start the day over again."

The next time Lydia woke up, it was because Natalie had come into the room to feel their foreheads and make sure they were still alive.

"Good morning," whispered Lydia when it was her turn.

"You've both slept so long, you missed breakfast. You're not getting sick, are you?"

"No. We were up early to say good-bye to Wesley and Hitch."

"Ah." She stroked Lydia's forehead again, this time for comfort.

"Life is horrible," said Alice from her bunk.

"Sometimes it is." Natalie now stroked Alice's forehead. "I know you've been waiting for a message from Jack—and I've got one for you. Maybe that will cheer you up."

"It won't."

"I'll read it to you anyway. *'Marcel and I are going to impress you so much you'll never try to best me ever again.'* Actually, now that I think of it, that probably won't cheer you up. What's he talking about, Alice?"

"I don't know. He's the least of my problems today. May I have the phone?" Alice took the phone and started typing. " '*You're the least of my problems.*' Do you want to add anything, Lydia?"

"Just say hi."

Alice kept typing. " '*And Lyds says hi. Love, Alice.*' "

"Now, Alice," said Natalie, "we need to figure out what you're going to wear to the wedding."

"I don't care. Whoa—wait, Mom!" Alice dove off the top bunk and attempted to block the closet door. "Don't look too hard at the wall in there, please."

Natalie reached around her to open the closet door and look inside. "As if I could miss *that*."

"I'll fix it before Jack comes home."

"Good." Natalie disappeared deep into the closet, somehow getting past the unwanted Alice books, movies, and games.

"She's looking for dresses back there," said Alice, and climbed back onto her bunk for protection. "This could be a problem."

Natalie had reappeared, carrying two dresses. One was yellow, with a grass stain on the back, and the other blue, with a gaping tear near the hem.

"How did you manage to rip this?" she asked.

"When our class went on that field trip to Tanglewood, I may have tried to do some tae kwon do on the bus."

"And the grass stain on the yellow one?"

"It was Jack's fault for daring me to—umm. It's too small for me now, anyway."

Natalie groaned. "I guess we have to take a shopping trip."

"Shopping! I hate shopping!"

"Alice, the wedding is tomorrow, and you need a dress. You cannot go in shorts and a T-shirt."

"I could wear the ballet skirt Jeffrey gave me."

Both girls' skirts were dangling off the dresser, sprinkled with oats from the last time they'd fed Blossom.

"No," said Natalie.

"But, Mom, I just lost Hitch, and it's almost my last day with Lydia, and her cousins and parents are coming and I want to meet them. No, no, please, no. Life is already horrible!"

"So are those dresses," said her mother. "And the sooner we go shopping, the sooner you'll get back."

• • •

This was Lydia's second trip of the morning to the pillars. This time she was riding in Natalie's car, sticking by Alice until her actual departure. She couldn't tell which of the two Pelletiers dreaded it the most, especially as the shopping list had expanded to include new shoes for Alice—she'd outgrown the only pair of non-sneakers she owned.

"I could go with you," she told Alice, though she herself was no fan of shopping.

"That's nice of you, Lydia," said Natalie, "but you should be here to greet your cousins."

"Don't rub it in, Mom. Her cousins are very interesting, and I won't be here!"

"They'll be here when you get back," said Natalie.

"Just please remember everything that happens, Lyds, so you can tell me what I missed," said Alice.

Lydia got out of the car and waved good-bye. It was early in the day for the number of good-byes she'd already suffered through, but then Alice would be returning today, unlike Hitch. She started back up the lane with a dance of farewell for him—taking long steps, hovering, tentative, wrapping her arms around herself, and letting her head droop. She did much of this with her eyes closed—sadness did that to her—so was caught by surprise when she saw a woman up ahead of her, standing by the side of the lane. She hadn't been there minutes ago, when Lydia passed by in Natalie's car—had she fallen out of the sky? Despite knowing this to be impossible, she couldn't help glancing up, on the lookout for a passing glider or hot-air balloon. That would be a great story to tell Alice.

"Hello, Lydia," said the woman.

"Mrs. Tifton?" Lydia went closer to make sure. Yes, it was Mrs. Tifton, wearing a sort of disguise—a wide-brimmed hat and large sunglasses. "You weren't here a few minutes ago."

"I may have happened to be behind a tree." She adjusted her hat. "I heard a car and didn't know who you were until you were gone."

So Mrs. Tifton's first reappearance at Arundel after six days—six peaceful, pickle-free days—involved wearing a disguise and hiding behind a tree. Lydia didn't want to deal with this on the same morning she'd said good-bye to Hitch and Wesley, and would do her best to get it over with quickly.

"Well, Mrs. Tifton, this is probably the last time we'll see each—"

"I thought it might be my ex-husband."

Lydia needed a moment to interpret Mrs. Tifton's interruption—to work out what the "it" was that might have been an ex-husband. Probably Alec, since surely she wouldn't be adding *another* ex-husband to the discussion after all this time. And wouldn't it be easier for her to avoid Alec simply by staying away, rather than hiding behind trees and hiding her car— where *was* her car?

"I don't see your car. How did you get here?" she asked.

"I came in Mrs. Robinette's car. I'm waiting for her to come back from dropping Jeffrey off at the mansion. We took him out for coffee to warn him that Marlene is in a serious relationship and hopes to be engaged soon."

Mrs. Tifton paused, apparently expecting a comment from Lydia.

"That's nice for Marlene, I guess."

Pickles ensued. That wasn't the right response. "Not if she's going to marry Jeffrey, it isn't nice."

Lydia refused to fill another pause, sure she'd get it wrong again. And she herself didn't particularly care who Jeffrey ended up marrying, as long as he was happy with her. And as long as she liked music and got along with Penderwicks. And Pelletiers. And dogs.

Mrs. Tifton gave up on Lydia and continued on her own. "We didn't make much headway with him, so Mimi's giving it one last try now. She thought he might be more receptive without me there. Sons and mothers, you know."

Lydia had a sudden vision of her own mother sneaking around in disguise, and sending her friend to pressure Ben into doing something he'd sworn never to do. No. It was impossible, even more so than the hot-air-balloon theory.

"If you're feeling sorry for me, don't," said Mrs.

Tifton sharply. "By Sunday, you'll all be gone and I'll have Arundel to myself."

Lydia didn't need to be reminded of that, and didn't appreciate Mrs. Tifton doing so. Still, determined to stay polite to the end, she held out her hand for a friendly handshake.

"Good-bye, Mrs. Tifton," she said. "I guess I won't be seeing—"

"Here comes Mimi! Thank goodness."

A sleek car pulled up beside them, driven by a woman whose hair was a familiar shade—the exact red that Lydia saw when she looked either in the mirror or at Ben. The woman leaned out the car window and said, "Brenda, you can take off the hat and glasses. The coast is clear."

"You didn't see Alec?"

"Nowhere in sight. According to Jeffrey, he's busy setting up sound equipment for the band. Did you know they're putting together an actual band for the wedding, Brenda? Drummer, double bass—"

"I don't care." Mrs. Tifton took off her hat and used it as a fan. "Mimi, this is Lydia, the one whose hair you copied."

"Yes, of course. I recognize her hair from the photo. Come closer, Lydia, let's see how my stylist did."

Aha! This was why Mrs. Tifton had taken a picture of her hair. Lydia had heard about imitation being a form of flattery, but it seemed more bizarre than

252

flattering to see her hair on a stranger. She inched toward the car, not wanting to get too involved in this comparison—Mrs. Robinette looked excited enough to demand a lock or two of hair.

"What do you think, Brenda?" asked Mrs. Robinette.

"Not bad. He missed the walnut streaks, I think. Give me your phone—I'll take another shot of Lydia's. Any luck with Jeffrey?"

"None. He continues to swear he'll never marry Marlene."

Lydia turned to let Mrs. Tifton photograph the back of her head, and concentrated on listening and remembering the conversation for Alice.

"Marlene should have come with us," said Mrs. Tifton, taking the picture. "She would have been able to sway him."

"Yes, well—" Mrs. Robinette paused, then rushed on. "Brenda, we may want to give up on this. Marlene seems to like this new man very much."

"Give up! You'd let her lose Jeffrey for some stranger named Gus?"

"Gary."

"Whatever. Let's get out of here."

Lydia was very much in favor of their leaving—she wasn't interested in Marlene, Gus, or Gary—and was beginning to edge away when an amplified voice came floating down from the mansion.

"Testing, one, two . . . is this thing on? Jeffrey?"

It was Batty. They'd gotten the sound system up. Other voices—male—could be heard, but just barely.

Batty answered the faint voices. "Any requests? Yes, good one, Jeffrey. Let's start off with some classic Roy Orbison."

And she started to sing, just Batty, without accompaniment. Jeffrey had asked for "Running Scared," a song about love and loss, but with a triumphant ending. Since it was one of Batty's favorites, Lydia had heard it dozens of times. Even the presence of Mrs. Tifton and Mrs. Robinette couldn't stop her from humming and swaying.

"Who's that singing?" asked Mrs. Robinette. "Is that the sister who's after Jeffrey? Jane, right?"

"No!" Lydia startled Mrs. Robinette, who hadn't expected such a loud "no" to come out of someone who hadn't yet said anything. "Jane doesn't want to marry Jeffrey! And *she* sings flat."

"Sorry, I'm confused. Brenda, is it Skye who's after him?"

"No, it's Lydia who's confused. Jane *is* after him." Mrs. Tifton flashed a pickle and a half at Lydia, daring her to protest. "Apparently, Skye's now getting married, too. I suppose she's not wearing a veil, either."

"The brides aren't wearing veils?"

"And the wedding feast is a kind of family potluck."

"That could be nice, I guess." Mrs. Robinette's face

said different. "It's too bad about the veils, though. I'm sure Marlene will wear one."

Mrs. Tifton got into the car and slammed the door. "I'm ready to leave now."

But Mrs. Robinette was again listening to Batty.

"Then who is singing?" asked Mrs. Robinette.

"My sister Batty," said Lydia.

"The teenager," said Mrs. Tifton. "The one with the thing for spiders."

"She's quite talented, isn't she?" said Mrs. Robinette.

If Mrs. Tifton hadn't already slammed her door shut, she would certainly have done it then.

"Let's go, Mimi!"

Lydia waved good-bye for as long as she could see the car, determined to be stoically polite until the very end.

# CHAPTER TWENTY-ONE
## The Rest of the Family

As Mrs. Robinette's car disappeared into the world beyond the pillars, a bobolink poured forth a song of gratitude.

"Yes, I know I should feel happy and grateful," said Lydia in reply. "That was the last time I'll have to see Mrs. Tifton and her pickle faces."

But she didn't feel happy. It wasn't just missing Hitch, although that was bad enough. It was also—and here it was again, the crushing wave of grief and yearning she'd felt the night before. Overwhelmed, Lydia let herself tip over into Bobolink Meadow One, facedown and in the dirt. She was leaving Arundel soon. Each new good-bye brought that departure closer, as did each new person to arrive. Once Lydia's entire family was here, there would be little time left—only the rest of today, then tomorrow—and then on Sunday, she'd have to go home. No more bobolinks, frogs, chickens, or sheep. No more fresh raspberries or climbing on roofs and sending pictures to Jack. No more Natalie and Cagney. No more Alice!

She started to cry. I'm watering the meadow with my tears, she thought, leaving a trace of myself behind. A few more tears, and she was also watering a beetle, frightened by the unexpected deluge.

"Sorry, beetle," said Lydia. "I'm spreading around my bad day, aren't I? That's not fair."

The beetle disappeared without accepting her apology, and Lydia rolled over and sat up. Somewhere out on the lane, Donny Hathaway was singing "A Song for You." Lydia knew only one person likely to blast this out of his radio—Uncle Turron, who'd declared it one of the best songs ever recorded. Lydia never knew if he really meant this, or if he just enjoyed infuriating Enam and Marty, who believed that "What's Going On" was far superior to "A Song for You." Lydia herself thought the two songs equally wonderful, especially when Batty sang them.

She jumped to her feet and followed the Asaberes up the lane, and toward the mansion. There would be plenty of time later to mourn Arundel.

"Uncle Turron, Uncle Turron!" Lydia leapt at him and was lifted into the air, giggling and managing an arabesque while she was up there.

"Oof," he said, pretending to stagger, bumping into the Asabere van. "You're getting too big for this."

"You say that every time, Uncle Turron."

"Keep her up there," said Ben, who'd come out of nowhere with his camera. "Marty, you go in close, and I'll get the wide shot."

And now there was Marty, too, hovering around his father's feet with a second camera.

"Hurry up, guys," said Uncle Turron. "I can't do this forever. And—down."

"Hey, Lyds," said Marty. "Ben said I can help with the wedding video. He's going to teach me about shooting a documentary."

"Don't let him boss you around, Marty," she said.

"I'm his assistant. If he doesn't boss me, I won't know what to do."

Ben put his arm around Marty. "And that, little sister, is how I should be treated. Now, let's redo the shot. Lydia, run a little slower this time, before Uncle Turron lifts you up."

"Tell them no reshooting, Lyds," said Uncle Turron. "Since we gave Marty that camera for his birthday, I have to do everything three times. Like brushing my teeth."

"That was a great scene, though, Dad," said Marty, "when the electric toothbrush went crazy and got toothpaste in your eyebrows."

Lydia and Uncle Turron did end up redoing the

scene, but only once, because after that, the dogs arrived and distracted the filmmakers. Blakey Asabere, the smallest of the pack, was in the lead. Dyson came next, then Sonata, and finally Feldspar, being the rear guard with his red shoe. Ben told Marty they were now shooting the stampede, and off they both went, after the dogs.

Now Enam showed up, carrying not a camera, but instead a black T-shirt. This he held at arm's length, as if it were about to bite him.

"Dad, whose idea was this?" He held up the T-shirt so that Lydia could see the back, where ENAM AND THE E-SHARP BAND was printed in large white letters.

"Naming the band after you was Alec's idea, and the rest was a team effort," said Uncle Turron.

"What team? No one asked me."

"We wanted it to be a surprise. Your mother suggested Enam and the Adorables and Enam and the Post-Teenagers. I wanted Enam and the Eligibles. The E-Sharp Band was Jeffrey's idea—he said it would be the least embarrassing. What do you think? Nice, right?"

Enam didn't think it was nice. "Lyds, would you like to have my shirt that I will never wear?"

Lydia wanted the shirt very much. Her mother sometimes wore an old, faded Bonnie Raitt T-shirt she'd gotten as a teenager, and this was almost as cool as that.

"Yes, but are you sure you don't want it? I think it's great, Enam."

"You have always been far too upbeat and positive."

She didn't think he was being fair to criticize her positivity, since it was precisely that characteristic that had gotten her over his desertion. But she took the shirt and pulled it on, covering what she was already wearing, a boring blue shirt without a band name.

Uncle Turron said, "Maybe we should have gone with Enam and the Hard-to-Pleases."

"You're hilarious." Enam slid his double bass out of the van. "Lydia, if I run away after the wedding, may I come live at your house?"

"Sure. We have lots of room."

He stalked off, lugging his huge double bass.

"It's his first public gig, and he's nervous," said Uncle Turron.

"Do you think he'll want his shirt back when the rest of the band put theirs on?"

"Keep it—we've got plenty of them." He pulled a set of bongos out of the van and handed them to Lydia. "Now go say hello to Claire. She's somewhere in that mansion with your sisters."

Lydia danced the bongos into the mansion and to the music room, where Jeffrey and Alec were pounding out Bruce Springsteen songs. She put the bongos down but couldn't leave or stop dancing, because now they'd begun "Thunder Road," and she couldn't help dancing to that—no one can—until the end of the saxophone solo, when she managed to pull herself away and go in search of her sisters and Aunt Claire. She found Batty first, standing on a counter in the kitchen, trying to coax a spider into a small container.

"Nice shirt," said Batty. "Is that our band name?"

"Yes. Batty, why are you hunting spiders again?"

"It's just this one, I promise. I saw her up here, realized I'd stolen away her friends, and decided to put her outside, too, give her a chance to find them. Here she comes, right into my box. Thank you, Ms. Arachnid, I hope you won't regret it." She put on the lid and climbed down. "Are you feeling better, Lyds? About Wesley and Hitch, I mean."

"A little." Without planning it, or even thinking at all, Lydia crinkled up the corners of her eyes at Batty. Huh. It felt good—no wonder Wesley did it—and it also expressed just how she felt, that she was feeling a little better, and thank you for asking, but a full smile would be too much for the circumstances.

"Oh no, you don't, Lydia Penderwick. You are not going to torture me with ex-boyfriend imitations." But Batty was laughing. "How did you do that—look just like him?"

"I'm not sure. Wait." It took Lydia a few tries to get it back, and by then, Batty was doing it, too.

"Wesley's legacy," Batty said. "Come, let's take this poor spider outside. That's where everyone is, with Aunt Claire."

Rosalind, Skye, and Jane were lounging on the

terrace steps, looking like goddesses to Lydia. She rarely thought of them this way. Last night at the rehearsal, for example, they'd been the opposite of celestial. But today they were serene and cheerful, and the sun was so bright on them, and Rosalind had tucked a nasturtium blossom into her hair. Aunt Claire was on the steps with them, also looking to Lydia like a goddess, if goddesses could be comfortable and favorite aunts. Or maybe it was just that Aunt Claire was so much better than Mrs. Tifton and Mrs. Robinette were at being a grown-up woman.

"Come over here," she called to Lydia. "They tell me you've been the rock of Arundel."

Lydia squeezed in between her aunt and Jane. "That's an exaggeration."

"What's Batty doing, Lyds?" asked Rosalind.

Batty was crouched on the grass, singing "Born Free" again.

"Rescuing a spider. She's been doing a lot of that."

Skye called to her. "Batty, hurry up. Aunt Claire has photos to show us."

"One minute!" She finished the song and joined them. "This spider was particularly grateful."

"How could you tell?" asked Skye.

"She could tell because Batty is simpatico with all living creatures," said Rosalind.

"Even older sisters." Batty kissed Skye on the cheek.

Batty looked as goddess-like as the others. Lydia closed her eyes, imagining Zeus being so drawn to her

262

sisters that he left his pedestal to stride—heavily—across the gardens in search of them. But then maybe those weird people on the ceiling of the dining room would come, too, and that would be unpleasant.

She opened her eyes again. Aunt Claire was handing out photos to her sisters.

"Hi, Mom," Rosalind said softly to hers. "We miss you."

"Dad looks terrified in mine," said Batty. "Was he?"

"Terribly," said Aunt Claire.

"Mom doesn't look scared," said Jane. "She looks deliriously happy."

"And she isn't wearing a veil," said Skye. "Nuts to you, Mrs. T."

Lydia leaned over to look at Jane's—it showed their father at his first wedding, to Elizabeth, mother to the older Penderwicks. Lydia had seen photographs of Elizabeth before, but only with her small daughters. None had shown her quite this young, or on her wedding day. And looking so much like Skye. Lydia had always known how much Skye looked like her mother—everyone knew that—but the resemblance today went much farther. It was the radiance, the joy, they shared.

"If she were here," said Aunt Claire, "she'd be so proud of all of you."

"Don't cry, Aunt Claire," said Jane. "If you do, I will, too."

"And I," said Rosalind.

263

"If your mother were here, she couldn't be proud of *me*, though." Lydia knew this was obvious, but still thought it should be said. "Since *I* wouldn't be here."

"Maybe in a parallel universe, you would," said Skye. "Stephen Hawking—"

"Not today, Skye," said Rosalind in such an older-sister tone of voice that the others laughed at her, forgot about crying, and then they all went back to the photos, wondering how their mother had put up with the fashions of the times.

Lydia briefly considered the parallel universes—maybe she'd ask Skye another time—but for now she was content to snuggle against Aunt Claire. She could hear the music from the band, not just Alec and Jeffrey, but Uncle Turron and Enam, too. They were playing "What's Going On." Hoping this would balance out Enam's dismay over the Enam and the E-Sharp Band shirts, Lydia hummed along, and let her feet dance out the rhythm.

Looking over the gardens, she saw the dogs, beyond the lily pond and heading toward Bobolink Meadow Two. Marty was still chasing them, with the gang of small Czech and American children trying to keep up, their mothers close behind, prepared to rescue those who couldn't. But where was Ben? There he was, having abandoned Marty to laze in the shade with Tommy and Dušek. (Lydia needed to have a serious talk with Marty about not getting exploited.) Over at the Greek pavilion, Dušek's brothers and Nick were helping Cagney set up benches, and in a different spot, the various parents of the grooms were deciding where Cagney's finished tables should go. And that accounted for everyone—Natalie and Alice were still out shopping, and Lydia's own parents hadn't yet arrived, although they were expected at any minute.

But I hope not too soon, thought Lydia. Her parents represented home, and home represented leaving Arundel. If only Jane and Skye (and Stephen Hawking) had worked out time travel, she'd stop the clocks from moving forward—now, this second!—and everything could stay exactly as it was, and she could be here for as long as she wanted. Except that she'd want Alice and Natalie to come back from shopping. And Jane would get itchy about the book she was writing. Ben wouldn't get to finish editing the alien movie. Batty would yearn for the music room, and Jeffrey and Alec. Rosalind and Skye would start wondering when they could ever get married. And it did seem unfair to leave her parents out of this family gathering, and Lydia did like them very much, and would probably miss them eventually. She sighed, then heard her mother's laugh.

They were here! They were here! Lydia leapt up to greet her parents.

It had been explained several times to Mr. Penderwick that there would be a thorough rehearsal that evening for the wedding ceremony. Lydia had also reassured him that he would not be doing any dance steps, that she'd worked it out so that he could simply walk down the aisle, left-right, left-right. Nevertheless, he asked her to give him a private pre-rehearsal rehearsal, to give him more confidence going into the real rehearsal.

She took him to the Greek pavilion—where the benches were now in place—and explained what would happen.

"I'll be first in the formation, doing this little dance as we cross the garden." She demonstrated the steps. "Jane and Batty will be behind me, and Skye and Rosalind behind them. You're standing here behind the last bench, waiting for Skye and Rosy. When we reach the last bench in the row, we stop dancing and begin to walk, first me, then— What, Daddy?"

"I can't picture it."

"Here is the last bench in the row. Stand behind it." She touched it, to make sure he knew what she meant, then backed up several yards. "And here I come, being me."

She danced to the bench, then switched to walking.

"Now I'll be Batty and Jane. You'll just have to pretend there are two of me." She went back and did the same again. "And now I'll be Rosy. Skye will be to my right. When we reach you, step in between us and walk us down the aisle. You ready?"

"*Videbimus*," he said. "We'll see."

This time Lydia started even farther back, to give her father more time to prepare, hummed the music—"Dance me to the end of love, dum de-dum dum dum"—and made encouraging faces to him as she approached.

"You're Rosy?" he called out.

"Yes, and Skye is to my *right*. Get ready, get ready—here we come!"

Smoothly, he stepped behind Lydia, gave her his arm, and together they walked down the aisle, Lydia proud, her father prouder.

"I didn't think I had it in me." He whirled her around. "Good job, my Lydia, my dancing elf. And I hope I don't have to walk you down the aisle again for another few decades."

Lydia took his arm again. She liked the way that felt, walking beside him. "Daddy, I'm still mulling over my motto."

"You've decided not to use *Minima optimus est?*"

"Oh, that one. I wasn't really serious." Earlier this summer, she'd asked her father to translate "The youngest is the best," a tool to have at the ready for whenever Ben was too pushy. "I want something more—I don't know . . ."

"Dignified?"

"I suppose so." She smiled up at him. "Lydia is dignified."

"*Lydia dignitatem habet.*"

She let go of his arm and danced as though she were dignified—shoulders back, chin held high but not too high—

*Ly-di-AH-AH-AH-AH. Ly-di-AH-AH-AH-AH.* An eastern towhee was calling.

"Dad, that's Alice, finally back from shopping! Can you be a black-capped chickadee?"

Birdcalls came more naturally to him than dancing, and a piercingly sweet *Aaa*-lice, *Aaa*-lice had the desired result: Alice, rushing toward Lydia, full of news she tried to tell all at once. About the *two* dresses her mother had made her pick out—but they both had pockets, a small victory—that Jack still hadn't sent any answer to the dying-alien scene, and that she'd met Enam and he'd given her a band shirt.

"I'm already wearing it, just like you, Lyds," she added unnecessarily. "And Marty shot me doing tae kwon do, and I met your mom, and she's nice and said I can call her Iantha. Is that your dad?"

"Yes," said Lydia. "He's nice, too."

"Glad to meet you, Alice," said Mr. Penderwick. "You may call me Martin, if you like."

"Martin," tried Alice. "Martin, Martin. Maybe."

Lydia's mother had been following Alice at a more leisurely pace, and now caught up.

"Martin, I've figured out why Lydia hasn't been homesick," she said.

"Why?" asked Alice.

"Because of you," said Mr. Penderwick.

Alice was stricken with solemnity. "Thank you, and Lydia is a good influence on me."

"We agreed that I'm not!" cried Lydia.

"Lydia's a good influence on me, too, Alice," said Mr. Penderwick.

"Mom, please, help."

"It's all right, honey. You're not a good influence on me," she said. "Now, let me see this procession of yours."

They ended up doing the procession several more times in various combinations. First Lydia and Alice were Rosalind and Skye, then they were Jane and Batty, both times with Iantha as Lydia, and then Lydia was Lydia, while Alice and Iantha were Rosalind and Skye. This went on until Alice as Skye added tae kwon do to the choreography, somehow managing to make herself look just like Skye, if Skye had happened to know tae kwon do. And then Lydia just had to show off her newfound skill at imitating Wesley. By that time, her dad was laughing so hard, he started messing up the procession, and it was decided to stop practicing before he forgot his part altogether.

# CHAPTER TWENTY-TWO
## *An Ending*

"GOOD MORNING, ZEUS." LYDIA placed a handful of raspberries at his feet. "This won't be the last time I see you, but it might be the last time we chat. My sisters are getting married today, and tomorrow I have to go home."

Zeus looked as confused as always—no, wait, maybe there was a bit of regret in his face, enough to encourage Lydia to continue.

"I'll miss you, you know. There's almost nothing about Arundel I won't miss, but I'm trying hard not to be sad. Would you like me to dance for you?"

He didn't have a choice and knew it, but watched without complaint as Lydia did a farewell dance just for him, different from the one she'd done for Hitch—in part because she didn't adore Zeus like she did Hitch. Realizing that, she tried to inject more sorrow into the dance, not wanting to hurt Zeus's feelings.

"My best to you, my dear god, and farewell, except for when I get a chance to wave in passing."

Lydia was on her way to the carriage house apartment, for a pre-wedding Meeting of Penderwick Siblings (MOPS) plus Jeffrey—or a MOPSPJ, to be precise. Rosalind had announced it last night without explaining what she wanted to discuss. MOPS topics were never announced ahead of time. As Skye said, if people knew, they might refuse to go.

"Lydia, Lydia!"

No, thought Lydia, No, no, no. Mrs. Tifton should not be looking for her, not today, the day of the wedding. Or any other day until forever. Lydia had already said her good-byes.

"Lydia? Are you over there?"

Mrs. Tifton was calling from the cottage side of the hedge. Since she probably didn't know about the hedge tunnel, she'd have to go the long way around to get here. Lydia had time to run away or, better, hide. What about that empty urn near Zeus? It looked large enough to hold an eleven-year-old girl. She tiptoed over to see if she could manage to get herself into it. Yes, she could, but unless someone helped her get out again, she'd be stuck in an urn for the rest of her life. And now it was too late—Mrs. Tifton was crashing through the hedge tunnel. Lydia sighed, and was glad Alice wasn't there to witness the trespass.

"There you are." Mrs. Tifton was in her hat and sunglasses again and was carrying a large silver shopping bag with CLOTHILDE's printed in gold letters. "Natalie told me you're on your way to see your sisters and that I might catch you if I went through the tunnel. Not my usual route, but better than risking the driveway and being spotted by you-know-who."

"I guess." The tunnel was low and, if people didn't know what they were doing, could scratch. Mrs. Tifton's hat seemed to have gotten the worst of it—a twig was now embedded in its crown. Lydia stifled a vision of Mrs. Tifton using plant life for camouflage. "Nice to see you this morning. Unfortunately, I don't have much time to chat."

"Don't be huffy. This won't take long." She showed Lydia the contents of the Clothilde's bag, two large boxes with gold and silver bows. "Mimi and I were shopping yesterday afternoon and came upon these. We thought they'd be just the thing for your sisters' wedding and bought them. That is, I bought and paid for them and want you to deliver them to your sisters."

"You bought presents for my sisters?" This was wilder than the idea of Mrs. Tifton in plant camouflage.

"I do buy gifts for people."

"But for my *sisters*?"

272

"Just the two getting married. Forget it." Mrs. Tifton closed the bag. "I told Mimi it was a bad idea."

Lydia desperately wished she could see beyond the hat and sunglasses. "Did I hurt your feelings?"

"You're kidding."

"Because I wouldn't want to. And, thank you—umm—thank you for—" Lydia didn't know how to finish the sentence. She'd been taught to thank people who gave gifts, but not what to say to people who changed their minds and decided not to.

"This isn't worth stuttering over, Lydia. Oh, here, take them." She handed Lydia the bag and let go, making sure she'd keep hold of it. "If your sisters like them, fine. If not, they can do whatever they want—use them for dust cloths—I don't care. I suppose this is the last time I'll see you."

"Yes." Lydia clutched the bag, not sure what to do if Mrs. Tifton wanted a hug—after the shock of presents, anything seemed possible. "Good-bye."

"Yes. Good-bye, and good luck in the future." Mrs. Tifton went back to the hedge tunnel and crashed through it to the other side.

"We have a special guest for our MOPS, Honorary Penderwick Jeffrey," said Rosalind. "He says this is his first one—"

"It *is* my first," said Jeffrey.

"It certainly isn't," said Skye. "You were part of our

273

emergency MOPS fifteen years ago—the night you wanted to run away. Remember, you shot arrows at my window to wake me up?"

"I know I shot arrows."

"There was definitely a meeting," said Jane. "You told us you were going to take a bus to Boston."

"Was that a formal MOPS?" asked Rosalind. "I do remember, Jane, that you wanted to go with him, to keep him company on the bus."

"And you said I couldn't."

"Was I there?" asked Batty.

The ones who had attended this long-ago meeting thought about it. The rest thought about other things. Ben thought about light and camera angles. Feldspar thought about Batty, food, and his red shoe, in that order. Sonata thought about taking a nap, and did.

Lydia thought about the Clothilde's bag, now hidden behind a bush right outside the carriage house. She'd taken a closer look at the boxes before stowing them away, and thought she knew what they contained. And how Rosalind and Skye would react when they opened them. Especially Skye.

She hadn't yet decided when to bring them out into the open. Too early, and she'd disrupt the meeting's cheerful tranquility. Too late, and someone—probably Batty—would notice how jumpy she was.

"Batty, I think you and Hound *were* at that meeting," said Jeffrey. "You wanted to go to Boston with me, too."

"Sounds right," she said. "I wasn't a practical child."

"Big heart, though."

"People," said Rosalind. "We're supposed to be having a meeting."

"And, Jeffrey," said Ben, "a few years ago, you and I had a Meeting of Penderwick Boys."

"That was a secret, wasn't it?" said Jeffrey. "Shh."

"What did you talk about?" asked Skye.

"We talked about girls," said Ben. "Jeffrey gave me tips."

"What tips did he give you?" This was Skye again.

"It was a *secret* meeting," said Jeffrey. "Therefore, he can't tell you. Ben, I mean it."

"Quiet, everybody, and please pay attention," said Rosalind. "We haven't even started and we're way off course. MOPS come to order."

"Second it," said Skye.

"All swear to keep secret what is said here," said Rosalind, "unless you think someone might do something truly bad. Which certainly won't happen today, and now that I think of it, nothing I want to talk about has to be a secret anyway. Still, we should swear for the sake of tradition, if nothing else."

Rosalind made a fist and stuck it into the middle of the circle. Skye did the same, putting her fist on top of Rosalind's, and so on. As the youngest, Lydia was supposed to go last, but she hesitated. Maybe Mrs. Tifton's gifts weren't appropriate for a MOPS. Maybe she should get them out now before the MOPS officially began.

"Lydia, your fist," said Batty.

Lydia's fist was still hovering when the screen door burst open, and here came Blakey and Dyson, rushing inside to give slobbery kisses to the people so conveniently sitting on the floor, then urging Feldspar and Sonata to join them in a race around the apartment. It took the combined efforts of Batty, Ben, Jeffrey, and Lydia to catch the dogs and organize them into some kind of order and quiet. At the end, Blakey joined Sonata on the couch, Dyson settled into Jeffrey's lap, and Feldspar crouched behind Batty so that he could periodically poke her with his red shoe.

"Skye, stop laughing, please," said Rosalind. "Let's start over. MOPS come to order."

Lydia chided herself for her earlier hesitation. Of course the gifts should be part of the MOPS. There would be no better place or time to discuss such a highly sensitive topic. This time she would dive right in after the oath.

"Second it," said Skye, sitting up.

"All swear to keep secret what is said here, unless you think someone might do—"

Jane's phone started making its typewriter sound.

"Sorry," said Jane, pulling it out.

"I thought phones weren't allowed in MOPS," said Ben. "Because remember that time I was waiting for Rafael to—"

"Shush, it's Aunt Claire," said Jane. "Good morning, most beloved aunt. . . . Sure, that sounds easy. . . . We're in the middle of something right now, but I'll be over soon to take care of it. Bye."

"Trouble?" asked Rosalind.

"She's found a rip in the dress she's wearing for the wedding—she thinks it has something to do with Blakey." Jane shook her finger at Blakey, who put his chin down in shame. He had torn the dress, but just a tiny bit, and he hadn't meant to. "I'll stitch it up for her when we're through here."

"Good," said Rosalind. "Third time's the charm. MOPS come to order."

Lydia made a fist, ready to get it onto the top of the pile no matter what happened.

"Second it," said Skye.

"All swear—"

"Hey, guys?" someone called through the door. "Do you have Blakey and Dyson?"

Rosalind groaned and covered her face with her hands.

"It's Enam," said Lydia.

"Come in!" called Skye.

It turned out to be both Enam and Marty. A bright spot for Lydia—the first since her encounter with Mrs.

Tifton—was that Enam was finally wearing an Enam and the E-Sharp Band shirt. She waved and pointed to hers, and he grinned sheepishly. Meanwhile, Marty had brought along his camera and was already using it.

"Stop shooting, Marty," said Ben. "This is a secret meeting."

"It doesn't look very secret," said Marty, lowering his camera.

"We are indeed having trouble with the secrecy aspect," said Rosalind. "If you two take the runaway dogs with you, that would help."

While Marty untwined Blakey from Sonata, Enam picked up Dyson.

"Jeffrey, when's our next band practice?" he asked.

"We'll have a quick one midmorning, before the guests start arriving."

"Excellent." Enam succumbed to passionate face-licking from Dyson and, temporarily blinded by dog tongue, had to be led out of the cottage by his brother.

"*Fourth* time's the charm?" asked Jane. "What do you think, Rosy?"

Rosalind thought that she was determined to have a MOPS whatever it took, and began once more. Lydia decided that if they were interrupted again, maybe it was destiny's way of telling her not to produce the gifts, to instead take them to her parents and let them figure out what to do.

This time they went so far as to complete the fist

278

pile, with Lydia's victoriously on the top, and were be-ginning the swearing-in.

"This I swear—" said everyone.

"Rosy, love, wife-to-be, are you in there?" It was Tommy, calling through the screen door.

"Yes." Rosalind looked sternly around the circle, forbidding anyone to break apart the fist pile now, not after they'd worked so hard to build it. "But I'm still in that secret meeting I told you about."

"How secret could it be? We just saw Marty and Enam leave with the dogs. Can we come in?"

"The twins and the dogs were a mistake. Please, Tommy."

"Rosy, ask him who 'we' are," said Jane. "Just in case it's Mrs. Tifton out there, looking for Jeffrey."

Lydia could have reassured her about Mrs. Tifton, but it wasn't necessary, as the other half of "we" was now speaking in Czech.

"*Pojď k mně, ty moje malá mořská hvězdice.*"

Whatever Dušek was saying out there, it had an extraordinary effect on Skye. She blushed—Lydia could see it start at her neck and spread upward until her face was aflame—and she smiled, thinking secret thoughts, and answered him.

"*Chvíli na mě počkej, Dušku.*"

"*Honem. Stýská se mi.*"

Skye let her fist drop out of the pile, which then fell apart completely. "*Ano.* I do, too."

"Care to translate?" murmured Jeffrey.

Skye shook her head—and Rosalind took hold of her sister's arm, as if to keep her from floating away.

"Maybe we should just skip the swearing-in," she said. "I want to thank all of you for putting together this perfect wedding for us, and I love you very much and always will. Anything else? No? Oh, one more thing—Skye, stop!—remember, we're gathering our own bouquets this morning. All right? Skye, did you hear me? Yes? Now go to him."

Lydia had waited for everyone to leave—Jane went last, with her sewing kit for Aunt Claire's dress—then waited more before retrieving the Clothilde's bag, which by now she loathed with a passion, from its hiding place. Even then, she looked and listened carefully and only dared to take it from behind the bush when she was certain she was alone.

"There you are, you dumb bag," she said. "How am I going to get you to Mom and Dad without anyone noticing?"

It wouldn't fit under the Enam and the E-Sharp Band shirt, not even close. But she could make the bag less obvious by turning it inside out. When that was done, she'd changed a look-at-me bag into a simple white one that could have had any old thing in it. A spare outfit or a snack, in case she got hungry.

Lydia had barely set out for the mansion when she was suddenly trapped, hedged in. Batty had a firm hold on her left arm, Jeffrey her right, and Feldspar and Sonata were blocking her path.

"Spill, Lydia," said Batty.

"You mean about what's in the bag? Just a snack, in case I get hungry."

"I'm not asking about your bag. I want to know why you were so jumpy during the meeting."

"You came in jumpy," said Jeffrey. "You kept tugging your right earlobe. That's what you do when you're nervous."

"I do not!" Lydia had never heard of such a thing, but found herself wanting to tug her right earlobe.

"Honey, we're not trying to harass you. But you seem worried." Batty stared into Lydia's face, making one of her inspections. "You're definitely worried."

"Lyds, do you want me to leave?" asked Jeffrey. "Can you tell Batty without me here?"

"No! If I'm going to explain, I want you here, too. You can help."

"Help with what?" asked Batty. "That's what we're trying to figure out."

"I can show you," said Lydia, "but you have to let go of me, and tell the dogs to back up, please."

"Feldspar and Sonata, stand down," said Batty.

When Lydia could move again, she put the bag on the ground and pulled out the two boxes with their bows. "These are presents for Skye and Rosalind from Jeffrey's mother. She gave them to me this morning and told me to deliver them."

281

Batty and Jeffrey were shocked, stricken into silence, which seemed to ripple out from them, spreading utter quiet as it went. Lydia would have sworn that even the birds had stopped singing. "I think they might be veils. The boxes are the right size, and she definitely thinks brides should wear veils."

Jeffrey recovered first. "She asked me if she should get gifts for Rosy and Skye. I thought she was being sarcastic."

"A natural assumption," said Batty. "Because why would your mother even think about giving them presents? It makes no sense."

"She did say something about being grateful to them for marrying men who aren't me." Jeffrey groaned. "I'm sorry. I'm sorry. I never know what she'll do next."

Now that others were sharing Lydia's burden, she was cheering up. "Let's see what's in the boxes. If it's veils, we'll just hide them until later. Skye and Rosy won't wear them, so it's not like we'd be keeping special gifts away from them."

"I agree," said Batty.

"Not out here in the open, though," said Jeffrey. "Anyone could see us."

They decided on the greenhouse, which thrilled the dogs—they'd loved their stay there way back on the day that Mrs. Tifton had first accused Jane of wanting to marry Jeffrey. The same day Lydia had first heard Mrs. Tifton discuss veils. Already it seemed so long ago.

It wasn't the cleanest spot for fancy gifts, but they ripped the bag open and spread it out on a table, then set the boxes down on that. Batty undid one bow, and Lydia the other.

"Open them together?" asked Batty. "One, two, three, reveal!"

Lydia had been right. Inside each box was an exquisite bridal veil, as superior to Skye's joke thrift-shop veil as a Bach concerto was to "Jingle Bells." That was Batty's first reaction, anyway, and the others couldn't disagree. The veils were identical, with thin headpieces covered in ivory linen—the same color as the gowns—and topped with small roses, crafted from the palest of pink chiffon. In addition, dozens of these roses had been sewn to the tulle, a tulle so delicate, it could have been spun by Batty's spider friends.

"I guess my mother has good taste in clothes, anyway," said Jeffrey.

Lydia and Batty were still lost in the beauty of the veils, the last thing either of their sisters would ever want to wear but, nonetheless, the stuff fairy tales are made of.

"But what should we do with them?" Lydia shuddered, remembering Mrs. Tifton's suggestion that the veils could be used as dust rags.

"We'll find someone to give them to," said Batty, "someone who would love them."

"Do you think we could"—Lydia touched the tulle; it truly was as light as cobwebs—"try them on, if we're really, really, really careful?"

"Why not?" asked Jeffrey.

They did, and they were really, really, really careful until Jeffrey started to sing "Chapel of Love," which is about getting married. It was peppy and impossible not to dance to, and so Lydia did, and Batty did, too, and Batty also sang harmony with Jeffrey, and the dogs got excited—Sonata wagging her tail in time with the music, and Feldspar losing his red shoe under a burlap sack, then barking until Sonata found it for him—and altogether it turned out to be one of Lydia's favorite times at Arundel.

"You two looked lovely in the veils, by the way," said Jeffrey when the delicate creations were back in their boxes, miraculously still in pristine condition.

"Maybe we can keep them until *we* get married." Lydia took one last look before the lids went back on.

"I doubt I'll wear a veil, let alone one Jeffrey's mother picked out," said Batty. "If I even get married."

"That's a long way off for both of you," said Jeffrey. "We can talk about veils when the time comes."

# CHAPTER TWENTY-THREE
### *Another Beginning*

Tʜᴇ ʟᴀsᴛ ᴏғ ᴛʜᴇ wedding guests was gone, and only a few Penderwicks remained—Lydia's parents and Jane—and her parents were in their car and ready to go. Lydia, to her enormous delight, wasn't going with them. Instead, she was staying on at Arundel until the summer was over and school about to begin.

"You're certain you don't want to come home, Lyds?"

"Mom." She'd already answered this question five times this morning.

"Iantha," said Lydia's father. "Wouldn't you stay here if you were eleven?"

"You know I would." Iantha hugged Lydia again— for the fifth time—and got into the car. "We'll be back in a week and a half to get you. Have fun with Alice."

Now it was her father's turn for a hug.

"Thank you for translating my motto," she whispered.

"You're welcome. It's a good one. We love you—be safe and well."

Lydia had chosen her motto near the end of the wedding procession while she was doing her final turn. "I dance to my destiny." *Ad fatum meum salto*. It covered everything important, and Lydia loved how it felt to say, the syllables rolling off her tongue. She waved good-bye to her parents, still scarcely believing she'd been given a reprieve. It had come at almost the last minute, after the wedding cakes and before the speeches, and it had been Jane's idea. She'd said that if she didn't have to go back to work, she'd want to stay at Arundel forever, and Lydia said that she *did* want to stay forever, and Jane said, so then, why didn't she, at least until school started? Jane then asked Natalie and Cagney, who discussed it with Lydia's parents, and before long, Alice and Lydia were celebrating to the band's raucous version of "Never Gonna Give You Up."

When her parents' car had disappeared down the lane, Lydia danced her way to the carriage house, chanting *Ad fatum meum salto, Ad fatum meum salto*. She needed to see Jane before she, too, was gone,

286

to ask her a question—intriguing, startling, and important. It had come to Lydia that morning as she was drifting awake. Not all at once, but in pieces, as memories popped, scenes flashed, and hints untangled. Veils and wings, Mrs. Tifton and Jane, Wesley and . . . Wesley, songs, and jitterbugs, until they were fitting together like jigsaw pieces, into a picture that was either nonsense or excitingly possible. Lydia was going to find out from Jane which of those was true.

When she got to the carriage house, Jane was loading a box of books into her clunky old car. The sewing machine, ironing board, and dress dummies had gone home in Flashvan with Batty and Ben, but Jane always kept her books near.

"Nothing yet from Alice?" Jane asked. "Still no idea about the secret?"

Lydia had been banished from the cottage since after breakfast and told not to come back until she was summoned. Alice had a surprise brewing, which she'd said Lydia would probably like, but if she didn't, they could just ignore it. Lydia had tried to guess, but Alice wouldn't even listen, telling Lydia she would never get it right and had to be patient. But she couldn't be stopped from thinking about it and, after dismissing a few wild ideas—like a pony come to live at the cottage—had decided on something more prosaic, and thus possible.

"I think it might be another chicken, to give Hatshepsut a new interest, now that Hitch is gone."

"Another chicken would be fun. Maybe I'll find a way to fit a chicken into my book."

"The chicken wouldn't time-travel, would it? Because I'm not sure they'd like it."

"Good point. The chicken can be in one of the pasts my detective visits, maybe the one in which Philippa meets Pieter de Hooch, the painter. What do you think?"

Lydia thought she'd need more information about Pieter de Hooch before deciding. She also still thought that Lydia Nel would be a better name than Philippa Nel for Jane's heroine, but she had more important matters to discuss. "Jane, I have a question."

"Pieter de Hooch would have to be a side story. I don't want to write a mere time-traveling romance. I want to make some solid points about the validity of art as done by the individual."

"Jane—"

"I thought of Rembrandt instead of De Hooch, but that's too obvious."

"Jane!"

"What?"

"I have a question." Lydia took a deep breath. "Remember when I asked why you wouldn't promise Mrs. Tifton that none of us would marry Jeffrey, and you said it was a matter of principle?"

"Yes, I remember." Jane began to fuss with her books, rearranging the ones at the top of the box. "Was that your question?"

"Just the first part." Lydia waited until Jane was looking at her instead of the books. "I think it was more than a matter of principle. I think you didn't want to promise because Batty might marry Jeffrey someday, and you didn't want your promise to be a lie. Even to make Mrs. Tifton stop being angry, you didn't want to lie."

"And you want to know whether or not that's true?"

"Yes, please."

"Yes, that's true."

"Oh! I didn't, I mean—" Lydia was trying to figure out how she felt, and wished she'd done it before asking the question. "Batty's only eight years older than I am, and I haven't even had a real crush yet!"

"Don't panic, Lyds," said Jane. "You said 'someday,' remember? If Batty and Jeffrey do get married, it won't happen until she's older, when they're both older. Like in seven or eight years."

"And you think they will."

"I think they *might*. This could be a phantasm. I have no idea what Batty thinks or if she's even considered it. And I won't ever ask her unless she brings it up. Skye and Rosy are both more certain than I am— Skye swears they're perfect for each other."

"Then Batty is Jeffrey's destiny."

"That's what Wesley said, actually, when he called me the night before he left. He also said that you and Alice helped him figure it out."

"We did?" But she hadn't known herself.

"That's what he said," said Jane. "It seems that Wesley noticed more than we'd given him credit for. On the other hand, he also said my first big success will be with a series of novels, maybe five of them."

"That could happen."

"I don't want to write a series."

Here came Lydia's signal, the call of the eastern towhee. *Ly-di-AH-AH-AH-AH.*

"That's Alice. She's ready for me. But, Jane—"

"Everything's going to be okay, Lyds, honest, whatever happens. And look at it this way. Mrs. Tifton is so certain one of us is after Jeffrey—she can't be wrong about *everything,* can she?"

"Poor old Mrs. Tifton." Now that Lydia was certain Mrs. Tifton wouldn't suddenly reappear—Jeffrey had said she planned to go back to New York City any minute—Lydia could afford to feel a little sorry for her.

Jane didn't agree with Lydia's sympathy. "Poor Mrs. Tifton! Poor *us,* if she becomes Batty's mother-in-law!"

*Ly-di-AH-AH-AH-AH.*

"I should go," said Lydia.

Jane hugged her fiercely. "Yes, go, and don't think

too much about Batty and Jeffrey. Just have a wonderful time being eleven at Arundel. I'm jealous, sort of. No, I'm not really. I've had another idea for Philippa—"

"Who should be called Lydia."

"No, she shouldn't! Go! Go, before Alice runs out of whistles."

*Ly-di-AH-AH-AH-AH. Ly-di-AH-AH-AH-AH. Ly-di-AH-AH-AH-AH.*

Three times! The eastern towhee was getting impatient. Lydia hugged Jane, one last time, before sprinting off to the hedge tunnel. A quick wave to the lily pond—she'd already told the frogs she was staying for another week and a half—and onward. Another wave to Zeus, and an extra spurt of speed to get her through the tunnel, and—

CRASH! Lydia slammed her head into something surprisingly solid. She fell, stunned. She didn't think she was badly damaged, but for now it felt best to keep her eyes closed.

"Are you unconscious?" asked someone in a panic, and Lydia felt a breeze on her face. "Please tell me, are you dying?"

Her eyes fluttered open, then shut again. In that brief moment, she'd seen a Canadiens hat being waved over her—that had been the breeze—and, beyond the hat, a boy with a cast on his arm. She must have bumped into the cast.

"Some chicken," she murmured.

"What did you say?" he asked. "Are you babbling?"

The hedge tunnel got more crowded—Alice had joined them.

"Jack!" she said. "What did you do to Lydia? Why does she look dead?"

"She kind of ran into my cast."

"Kind of! It looks like you slugged her with it. I wanted you to surprise her, not murder her. Lydia, Lydia, can you hear me? It's Alice and my stupid brother."

"She's not dead," said Jack.

"Not yet, anyway. She could be on her way out."

Lydia smiled, trying to reassure the Pelletiers that she wasn't dying.

"Now she's smiling at you, Jack, so she's probably brain-dead." Alice held up two fingers. "Lydia, how many fingers?"

Lydia opened her eyes. "Two."

Jack held up four. "How many now?"

"Four. Hello, Jack. I didn't know you were coming home."

"Alice wanted to keep it a secret."

"And, Lyds, aren't you amazed I did, for twenty-seven entire hours?" asked Alice. "I found out yesterday while you were at your MOPS. Get this: Jack came home because he broke his arm falling out of a tree he was climbing in his *hockey skates*—because he's the dumbest person on the planet—for a film he and

292

Marcel were making that never would have been as good as our alien film."

"You don't know that, Alice," he protested. "Our film was going to be really good."

Lydia tried to sit up, but there wasn't room.

"Don't move," said Alice. "It could be dangerous."

"I'm okay, Alice, honest."

"No thanks to my brother."

"Shh," said Jack. "Listen—is that who I think it is?"

The call had come from across the gardens. "Lydia!"

"I can't believe it," said Lydia. "She's supposed to be on her way back to New York City."

"Not until this afternoon," said Alice. "That's what she told Mom."

"Lydia. *Lydia!*"

"She's getting closer," Jack whispered. "Do you want to see her?"

Someday Lydia might have to see Mrs. Tifton again, but that wouldn't be for another seven or eight years. Until then, Mrs. Tifton was on her own.

"No, thank you."

"Good, because I don't, either. Alice, back up and give us room."

Jack took Lydia's hand to help her crawl out of the tunnel, then stand up, slowly and carefully, in case she had any effects from the bonking. But she felt fine— oh my goodness, she felt wonderful.

"Hurry," said Alice.

"Ready, Lydia?" Jack asked. "Can you run?"

Could she? A bobolink warbled the answer.

"Yes," said Lydia, all hope and exhilaration. "Yes, I can."

And away they went, the three together, prancing, leaping, gamboling into the future.